TALONSPOTTING

By Andrew Harman

THE SORCERER'S APPENDIX
THE FROGS OF WAR
THE TOME TUNNEL
101 DAMNATIONS
FAHRENHEIT 666
THE SCRYING GAME
THE DEITY DOZEN
A MIDSUMMER NIGHT'S GENE
IT CAME FROM ON HIGH
THE SUBURBAN SALAMANDER INCIDENT
TALONSPOTTING

TALONSPOTTING

ANDREW HARMAN

An *Orbit* Book

First published in Great Britain by Orbit 2000

Copyright © Andrew Harman 2000

The moral right of the author has been asserted.

A CIP catalogue record for this book
is available from the British Library.

ISBN 1 84149 013 X

Typeset by Hewer Text Ltd, Edinburgh
Printed and bound in Great Britain by
Mackays of Chatham plc, Chatham, Kent

Orbit
A Division of
Little, Brown and Company (UK)
Brettenham House
Lancaster Place
London WC2E 7EN

To Jenny, for everything

Acknowledgements

Thanks to Janet and Colin Bord for their book, *Mysterious Britain: Ancient Secrets of Britain and Ireland* (Harper-Collins, 1995), which provided essential realism in Bertrand Matlock's 'sightings'. Cheers.

Also, thanks must go to a totally disparate bunch of folks whose work has provided an essential background to this latest book. In no particular order, the CDs most on the hi-fi this time were: Marillion, *Marillion.com*; Faith Hill, *Breathe*; XTC, *Apple Venus Volume 1*; Queensryche, *Q2k*; Trisha Yearwood, *Real Live Woman*; Martina McBride, *Emotion*; Def Leppard, *Euphoria*; Kirsty MacColl, *Tropical Brainstorm*; Imani Coppola, *Chupacabra*; Meredith Brooks, *Deconstruction*; Tori Amos, *To Venus and Back*; Ultra Nate, *Situation Critical* . . . and many, many more.

And a special mention to Kate Rusby, whose beautiful *Hourglass* and *Sleepless* albums provided the, ahem, 'inspiration' behind some of Bernstein the elder's outbursts. Can't wait for the new one, Kate!

And a final musical thanks to Cliff and Dave. Cheers guys, drumming with you is such therapy!

Contents

Skitter   1

An Underdone Alaska   36

Faith, Hope and Security   57

The Best Laid Plans of Morris Men   96

Death by Advertising   126

Talonspotting   172

Doing Delilah   211

Crossfire   247

Skitter

February 12th. Tintagel, Cornwall.

Dear Logbook,

Back out on our travels again, this time heading S.S.W. Party feeling v. happy as last night's runes promised good hunting. Ray believes we're in for an undersprite third class for sure. But then he is wont to err towards flights of optimism especially after he's just finished one of those cigarettes he rolls.

Maybe the suggestion we adopt pre-Gregorian Calendar for predictive purposes was a bad move. Rest of party is convinced tonight is a secondary inter-solstice subjunction. Still, morale good. Even let me use b-roads.

Crossed Devon-Cornwall border 16.32. Although Bernstein was certain it had happened ten minutes previous. Once again I am disappointed at the shoddy bordermarking which continues to plague our land. Was told to shut up. Again.

Arr. Tintagel 20.03. Wouldn't have made it that quickly in summer. Disappointed to find no cream teas available at pub. Had to settle for choc ice. Did get blob of squirty cream after complaining though. Nice of them.

Second roll of runes confirmed three ankhs, a circumvolent and pair of stridulars. Morale rose. Bernstein even bought me a martini. Shame I don't like martinis. He was kind enough to drink it for me.

Decanted from hostelry 22.47. Donned boots and cold

weather gear. Wind blowing N.N.W. Drizzle. Force 6 rising. New Goretex jacket and Tog 24 fleece working a treat. Bernstein the younger complained of forgetting his boots. Moaned at getting mud on his trainers. Said they cost over a hundred quid. Just goes to show the mentality of people who spend fortunes on fashion footwear. Was told to shut up after reminding him my boots were three fifty from a junk shop.

Proceeded towards castle and found gates locked. Yet again am disappointed at the attitude of Heritage Bodies at refusing us specified nocturnal access. Or maybe my letter got lost in the post again. Had to use the bolt cutters on the chain. Left a fiver taped to gatepost in a plastic bag, of course.

Gathered in central courtyard, sat in circle. Wind veered three points to north. Midnight passed. 02.36 activity at S.E. Proved to be a territorial tussle between neighbouring kitti-wakes. Amazing how like undersprites third class they can look in certain lights.

Restlessness set in 04.24. Ray sure he felt residual spirit-type shivers in his left leg. Everyone else sure it was pins and needles again. Why he sits in lotus position will never know. Rumours abound to which I hold no ear.

Dep. Tintagel 06.12. Van started first time.

No sightings confirmed.

Avge 18.3 mpg. Good.

1

It was a normal morning. Typical Tuesday. You know the sort. Drizzle on a light easterly. Gridlocked traffic through grimy bus windows. And a throbbing behind my eyes. Same every day. Even the same throbbing.

I really ought to sort out my sleeping patterns. Come to

think of it, I really ought to get more than just that sorted, but earlier to bed would be a start. Then could come the life. I really ought to get one of those. I hear they're popular. But then so's adultery and you wouldn't catch me doing that. Oh no. Burn in hell for that you would.

The bus I was on shuddered to a halt with a blast of horn and shouting. The driver was already half-way out of the window and swearing.

'Can't you read?' he yelled at the motionless car in front. 'Bus lane, asshole. Bus lane. That means lane for buses.' His accent stank of yellow cabs and New York. Too much late-night TV. Had to be. Nobody really spoke like that around here. It wasn't the Bronx.

'Cut the sarcasm,' came back the feeble answer, as a particularly hairy man leant out of the front window.

'Shift that car, if it can be called that. Or else . . .' I winced as he let the threat hang. I didn't like violence. Well, certainly not at this time of the morning anyway.

'Or else what?' snapped back the driver of the car.

The bus driver stared and continued to chew on cheap gum whilst he tried to think of a suitable threat. He was having trouble. The car was distracting him. He was sure it had once been a Volkswagen Beetle. Once. Now it had a gaudy mess of goldfish and seashells glued to the bodywork. Inside it looked unnervingly like a dining room aquarium. Even down to the plastic shipwreck on the rear parcel shelf.

'Or else what?' repeated the driver of the carnival Beetle currently constipating the entire Camford bus network. As replies went that was a mistake. It forced the bus driver to act.

I held my breath. I was certain this wasn't going to be pleasant. I began looking for the emergency exits, trying to convince myself it wasn't time for prayer just yet.

'Or else . . . er . . . this.' The bus shuddered forward two feet as the driver slipped his foot off the clutch. There was a nasty sound of shearing metal and shattering razor shells.

'Shithead! Look what you've done to my bumper.'

It was strange, I was almost relieved. He hadn't said fender. At least there was some part of English that was still ours.

'Oh yeah. Just watch what I can do to your trunk,' yelled the driver, metamorphosing into Danny deVito.

I cringed. Bet he called the police cops, loved bagels and drank Bud, too.

The clutch ground again, and a four-litre diesel engine powered the bus half-way up the back of the parked car. Metal buckled rapidly towards write-off and a pack of leopard cowries exploded.

And I started to enjoy the situation. I shouldn't have, I know. Tantamount to being accessory to sin that was. I was enjoying the prickle of tension in the air, the static charge of temper. The bishop would have been annoyed with me. Had to confess that one later if I could just figure out what sin it actually was.

Time to get out of here before I had a crisis of faith.

'The doors, please,' I asked, standing.

The driver ignored me, revelling in the victory of a destroyed four-door. For a brief moment I wondered if the bus man had ever heard the word 'pyrrhic'. Somehow I doubted it.

'My car!' screamed the Beetle owner, gesturing wildly. 'And my unleaded,' he added as the petrol tank ruptured. 'And I just filled up! You wouldn't believe what that cost. How am I going to recoup that? How am I supposed to take part in the carnival driving a written-off car?'

'Er, the door?' I repeated hopefully, sensing that it really was time to leave. The hairs on the back of my neck prickled.

The driver was lost on a wave of insults. 'Exactly. It's your car. Not a bus. Not allowed in the bus lane. Rules, see.'

I eyed up the small panel which offered some escape. In Emergency Press Here.

'And I suppose it's the rules that allow you to destroy my car?'

'Timetables, mate. More than my job's worth to be late. Shouldn't have been there.'

I winced. He was beginning to sound too much like something out of *EastEnders* now.

I grew even more worried as the car owner began to laugh uncontrollably as a small tank ruptured and the Volkswagen appeared to begin filling with water. It was an old fairground trick I know, but I almost stayed to watch. If the situation hadn't been rapidly approaching an emergency I might have. I pressed the panel. Nothing happened. I pressed again. 'Shit,' I cursed, quickly absolved myself and began to wonder if maybe they should supply detailed maps of escape procedures on the back of bus tickets.

Outside, the man in the carnival car was creasing himself toward hysteria.

And I was getting claustrophobic. A waft of Sainway's unleaded tickled my nostril hairs.

I'd pressed the panel. Nothing. Done it by the rules. This was different now. I grabbed hard at the centre of the doors, forced my hands between the rubber seals and pulled. It was a struggle, but somehow the doors concertinaed back against the wall.

'What you laughin' at, asshole? You shouldn't be . . . Hey, you, you can't get off here. This isn't a designated stop,' shouted the bus driver.

'Looks like you're not going much further,' I shouted back as I fought past the springy doors and squeezed myself towards the relative safety of the pavement. 'By the way, tardiness is still a sin, you know?' I added before I jumped.

I nearly lost my knees on the handlebars of a passing bicycle.

'Watch it, idiot!' yelled the student as Alanis Morissette blasted from his headphones.

'Get a puncture!' I screamed in a manner unfitting of a man of my position.

I wasn't sure if he had actually heard, but something made him stick two fingers up at me.

'Get two, then.' It was pathetic, I know. But I was finding it hard to think. What with the growing cacophony of car horns filling the air, the intoxicating stench of petrol fumes, and the absurd sight of a shiny red double-decker balanced on the back of a flooding Beetle like some precariously rutting animals, well . . . suddenly work seemed almost refreshing.

But it would have to wait. Other business first.

I ran away, turned left and headed up Camford High Street.

A bell on the door of the pet shop pinged as I took a nervous breath and entered.

'Hello, welcome to Noel's Ark Pet Emporium,' called a voice from the back. 'I'm Noel, how can I . . . oh, it's you.' He appeared from between rows of fish tanks, wiping his hands on a dirty towel. 'What d'you want, Father? And don't ask for charity,' he spat with just a little too much sarcasm. I forgave myself for wishing him a swift kneeing in the groin. Then I forgave him. I suppose it was odd to have to call me Father. I guess I was about half his age.

'Fin rot, again?' I asked, changing the subject as he dropped a small goldfish into the bin.

He gave me a dirty look. As if it was my fault his fish were

6

infected. As if it was my fault he'd forgotten that cleanliness was next to profit margins in the world of pet shops.

'What d'you want?' he sniffed.

'I've come about the . . . you know.'

'The what?' He knew damn well what. He just liked to watch me squirm. Bastard. Ahem. Three Hail Marys for that one.

'Just give it to me.'

'Give you what? The hamster? Is that what you want, eh? Come to collect your hamster.'

'Yes. Of course I have.' I shivered as he emphasised the 'H' word.

I was sure a grin twitched on his lips. 'Hamster. Ahh yes, here's the little chap,' he announced, reaching under the desk and placing a small cardboard container next to the cash register. Thin scratching sounds floated out of the shoe box through the rough-edged air holes. I felt cold inside. It was irrational I know. But for some people it was spiders, or the number thirteen. For me it was small golden rodents with a desire to run around in wheels.

'That'll be . . . er, twenty-five quid.'

I was shocked. 'How much? I could've bought a whole new herd for that.' Briefly I wondered what the collective noun for hamsters actually was. A colony? A murder . . . no, that was crows.

'But you didn't buy new, did you?' I heard him say. I could tell he was feeling pleased with himself. 'You wanted that one checking over. Expensive that is. Time. Swabs. Sending off for the tests. Vets aren't cheap. Even at St . . . er . . . Tinky-Winky's.'

'Where?'

'Tinky-Winky's,' he repeated and something didn't sound right. I knew there was a pet hospital with a daft name somewhere. But I was certain it wasn't named after a Teletubby. He was lying, I was sure. My nose twitched with the smell of sin.

'Fifteen quid for this, it was.' He waved a sheet of test results at me. 'And then there's admin costs.'

I looked at the animal health report. 'Allergy? But you said it was pneumonia when I brought him in last week.' I was beginning to smell more than sin. The distinct aroma of rat. And it wasn't caged.

'Pneumonia? I said that? Er . . . Hey. What do I know?' He shrugged. 'I just sell the things. I'm no vet. Twenty-five quid. And I'll even throw in some free advice. Don't use Mr Sheen anywhere near him again. Hamsters have sensitive lungs. Now, is that cash or Visa?'

'Beatrix Potter,' I answered. He looked confused.

'That some new kind of debit card?'

'St Tiggywinkle's.'

'You've been at the gin again, haven't you? Now, come on, twenty-five quid.'

'After the hedgehog.' I frowned. 'The hospital's called St Tiggywinkle's.'

I saw his jaw clench. He'd been discovered. 'Tell you what. As a valued customer . . . how about twenty quid?'

I spied the computer in his office and the printer next to it. 'Let me guess. Word?' I began tearing the forged report into rodent bedding. 'You never sent any tests anywhere, did you? I bet you never even fed him all weekend.' I stiffened my spine and gave him one of my patented holier-than-thou looks. The one that somehow makes my dog-collar light up. 'If he's even slightly malnutritional . . .'

I told myself quickly that it was all perfectly safe and snatched at the shoe box. The lid flipped open and I caught a glimpse of cold, black, ball-bearing eyes and shimmering

8

whiskers. I closed my eyes, shoved the lid shut. Breathe, breathe.

'He's not coughing any more. C'mon, that's got to be worth fifteen quid?'

'You're not a vet. Bye.'

I heard him kick the wastebin as I closed the door with Skitter the hamster in a box at arm's length.

As I headed off towards work, a thought suddenly occurred to me. The collective noun for hamsters. The way they look at you through those caviar-ball eyes. The way they chew incessantly. Those little stubby tails. A loathing of hamsters. Had to be. And if it wasn't, it damn well should be.

2

As usual, it was flashing down. Streaks of flame crackled into the streets in showers of sparks. They danced off roofs, backed up in woefully inadequate gutters and spilled over in curtains of brimstone.

'Oh dear.' In the shelter of a lounge, a butler shook his head. He flicked a phoenix-feather duster absently around a lava lamp. 'Oh dear, oh dear.'

Another peal of seismic thunder echoed overhead.

'He won't be pleased with that. Not pleased at all.' A heap of Nognite Parchments were shuffled by expert talons and placed back on to the marble desk. Dead centre.

And then he spied the folded cinderella in the rack. 'Oh dear, he'll be soaked to his scales. Soaked.' The butler shook his head and resigned himself to the fact that it was going to be something of a difficult evening.

And it was about to begin.

He heard the clatter of hooves almost too late. They hit the front door and kicked it open at full gallop. With expert flair, the butler hurled a mat on to the floor in the fraction of a second before his master's hoofs hit marble. In a blur of black he was across the room, an armful of fresh towelling at the ready.

'Shocking weather, sir.' He knew the placatory tone would cut no mustard. But he knew his place. Subservient.

'Shocking?' hissed Seirizzim angrily. 'You haven't been out in it. It's bloody awful!'

'Yes, sir. Let's get you dry, sir.'

'Why didn't you remind me to take my cinderella? You knew it would be like this, didn't you?'

'Prescience is not one of my many talents, sir.' He held out a towel.

'No, but sarcasm is. Gimme that.' Scowling, Seirizzim wiped his dripping horns. The butler headed for the door. 'And bring me a—'

'Drink, sir?' He held out a tray bedecked with a steaming brimstone and tonic.

'Of course. Bring me a lava,' he called from underneath a fluffy towel.

With only the slightest curl of his lip, the butler waved a talon and the drink metamorphosed into a nice cold half of lava. In moments, condensation formed on the outside of the crystal glass.

'Make it a large one,' added Seirizzim, waggling the corner of the towel in his leathery ear.

The drink on the tray doubled in volume with another flick of expert talons. Seven centuries in service had taught him a few labour-saving tricks. Amazing the amount of unnecessary to-ing and fro-ing that could be avoided by the careful application of a simple metamorphic incantation. If he'd only been able to get the hang of seeing into the future . . . ahh, life would be so much easier. But then this was the Underworld. Easy wasn't the norm.

Seirizzim snatched the drink and strode off towards his favourite armchair, dripping drops of lava on the way.

The butler rolled his eyes. He knew the sticky patches lava could leave on marble. Time for action before it was too late. And he knew the very thing for such a situation. One of his own inventions, he was quietly proud to admit.

Under his breath, he intoned a swift rippling metamorphic incantation and sent it off in the direction of the clump of towels. In moments, waves of stiffness and relaxation flowed through the material. Five towels crawled through the splash zone.

'Clear that mess up will you?' ordered Seirizzim through a lip of froth.

'Yes, sir,' muttered the butler, almost insubordinately. There were times when he hated working in service. Some folk just wanted to interfere all the time. If they would just let him take care of his job. He collected the towels and headed off towards the back room.

'Where are you going?' hissed Seirizzim.

The butler turned and waited; he knew a rhetorical question when he heard it. He'd stopped answering that particular one a good three hundred years ago. And he knew what was next.

'Come here, I haven't finished with you yet.'

Rolling his eyes only very slightly, the butler dropped the towels, flicked another incantation their way and dutifully returned to his master's side. The towels squirmed off stage left.

'Your urge is my desire, sir?' The question almost caught in the butler's throat. It had worn a little thin over the past seven centuries.

'I know,' coughed Seirizzim. 'So I want you to go and

collect a little something for me. The instructions are on this.'

The butler turned up his lip in distaste as he accepted the folded sheet. It was obviously cheap parchment. The edges were blackened, and as every demon worth his sulphur knew, Nognite was guaranteed 'Scorch-Free at ambient temperatures. Will not wrinkle, char or calcine. Honest.' It simply had to be a cheap fake. Probably from one of the dodgier sweat shops down by the Phlegethon.

'And here's the cash.' Seirizzim pulled an extremely large envelope from the depths of his favourite armchair and held it out. 'Are you still here?'

'No sir. What you are seeing is merely an afterimage burned upon your retina. Already, I am three blocks away.'

'What have I told you about sarcasm?' hissed Seirizzim. 'You know how much I loathe sarc–'

The sound of the front door closing cut him off in mid-rant.

And out in the street the butler grinned to himself as a glass hit the back of the door. He licked a talon and chalked up an imaginary point to him.

It was only when he opened the instructions that his heart fell. He shrugged and headed off towards the River Phlegethon, just as he had expected.

3

It took ten minutes for me to get to work.

It should've been more like five but I had to stop and gawk as I passed the bus lane again.

An innocent traffic warden was having a bad morning trying to stop a punch-up between a bus driver and the owner of a write-off shell Beetle. Hopefully, she was trying to radio for help and at least attempt to keep the traffic flowing. Truth was, she was doomed to failure. No one wanted to move while there was just a chance of a real scrap. Something that transport companies just haven't got the hang of yet is the idea that commuters don't really mind being late. As long as they get to see at least a bloodied nose before ten o'clock. And if that's a management nose, so much the better.

I shook my head and hurried on, and in moments I was through the doors of St Cedric's with a lean half minute to spare. As I headed for the cleaning cupboard, I began to wonder about the currency of sins. If tardiness was wrong then what about being perfectly on time? Was that extra good? You know, one on time equals two lates? Somehow I doubted it. Religion was never that black and white.

It was strange, but it was only as I slipped on my overall and picked up the bucket of aerosols and sponges that I actually noticed just how quiet it was in here. No sound from the streets. Must have good double-glazing or something. But then, they needed it. Loud noises were bad for the recovery of the 'clients', as I had been told to call them.

Clients. That was a joke. Like they had more than one at a time in here.

Didn't make any odds to me though. Polishing a windowsill is still polishing a windowsill, whether there's anyone there to see it or not. Still tough on the elbows. Still the risk of RSI.

Wondering briefly if a polished windowsill still gleams so brightly if there's no one there to see it, I started on the hardest room. Number six.

It was hardest for two reasons. One, it was actually occupied. And two, it had a colour scheme.

I cringed as I opened the door and stepped in on to the

purple carpet whilst trying to ignore the yellow skirting board. It almost worked. Until I pulled back the curtains and the full glory of Camford's drizzly light flooded in and reminded me of the wallpaper. How anyone could put tangerine and lime stripes against cherry curtains I'd never know. The throbbing behind my eyes tried to return. I massaged my temples and reminded myself not to look up. I'd done that once. Bad mistake. It had taken a full week in a darkened room to get over the sight of the 'kaleidoscope sky' ceiling tiles.

'Colour therapy,' I muttered to myself and longed for the safety of BUPA internal decor. 'Like it'll make a difference to you,' I added to the woman in the bed. 'A coma is a coma and no amount of wallpaper is going to change that.'

As usual she said nothing. She just carried on breathing in that way she had. Long, shallow. Comatose.

The sun glinted off the bridge of her nose. And that was when I spotted it. The spider's web. What had possessed the creature to spin a web across her left nostril I hadn't a clue, but there it was, in all its finery. I was on the case in seconds. A swift waggle of cotton bud dealt with it. Although where the spider had gone I hadn't the foggiest. I checked her other nostril, just in case. Nothing. And a good job too. It would be a shame if she was to choke to death minutes after coming round. If she ever did come round, that is. Sometimes they didn't. Or so I'd heard.

'You're best off out of it, dear,' I said, polishing her forehead with a quick dab of Mr Sheen. 'There's nothing decent on telly these days. And the videos aren't much better.'

I don't really know why I talked to her the way I did. To keep her company I suppose.

'Fancy coming round for a video one night? Get some pizza in, bottle of wine?'

14

Get a life, man, I told myself. You're in a bad way if you're asking comatose patients out for a date. But then, she was kind of cute.

I stepped back and looked at Miss Williams and realised she had quite a lot going for her. All right, so conversation wasn't high on the agenda, but hey, that could change. Just look at what she did have going for her. Doesn't answer back. She doesn't smoke. And, the clincher, she doesn't snore.

It was weird. I almost felt sort of affectionate as I finished polishing her brow. Well, eight weeks seeing her in bed, you know . . .

Suddenly I leapt away from her, realising I was surfing uncontrollably on a wave of very improper thoughts. I conjured up images of cold showers, dead dogs and long lonely hours in the Confessional.

And then it happened.

I almost missed it.

For the first time in eight weeks, she moved.

It wasn't much. Just the twitch of an eyelid.

I leaned over. Had to look closer to check.

Then she curled her lip. Just like Elvis.

'Jeezusmaryjosephandallthearchangelsupinheaven!' I screamed as I ran out of the room, my heart pounding.

4

'Jeezusmaryjosephandallthearchangelsupinheaven!' was the first word she heard as she woke up.

She twitched, coughed and sat bolt upright.

Moments later, she was back under the bedclothes, shivering. 'Shit, it's cold in here.'

How long she stayed there hugging herself in a tiny ball

she hadn't a clue. It didn't feel long. Not long enough to actually get warm anyway.

'Er, Miss Williams? Hellooooo?' The greeting was muffled by two pillows and a duvet. 'Lovely to see you're awake at last, Miss Williams. Er, now could you just be a dear and come out from under there? You know, be a sweetie and show yourself, like.'

'No way. It's freezing!' She shivered, convinced she'd see her breath against the sheets. She was almost disappointed when she didn't. Maybe it wasn't that cold. Perhaps it was all in her mind. Her body disagreed and thought about turning blue at the edges.

'Ohh, you big softie,' mothered the man's voice from the other side of the duvet. 'It's not cold. The sun's out, the sky's blue, well, okay, there's a slight drizzle from the east but all the little birdies are up in the trees fluffing out their little feathers and—'

Another voice interrupted. Darker, harder. 'I'll handle this if you don't mind.' A throat cleared. Businesslike. 'Miss Williams, you've been in that bed for eight weeks. It's high time you got up.'

'Turn up the heating and I will.'

'Now, I know you're feeling a little chill—'

'*Chill?* It's bloody subzero!'

She was sure she heard sharp intakes of breath from the outside world. And questions started to form. Were they shocked at what she had said? Or had it been the way she'd said it? 'I'm getting frostbite in my bloody toes,' she added, testing the water.

'Oooh, language, Miss Williams, you know we don't like the "B" word here,' answered the first voice. Half jokily, half deadly serious. Then quieter, as if to a superior. 'Yes, yes, I'm sure she's fine. Everything worked just dandy-pandy. She'll be just fine. Right as rain. They're always a little tetchy when they first come round.'

The businesslike voice spoke again. This time in the tone used by police officers talking jumpers down off tall buildings. 'Miss Williams, I understand how you are feeling. Come out of there and we can deal with it. Talk about it.'

'Let's talk about hot water bottles. Can you stretch to a few of them?'

'They won't do you any good.'

Under the duvet, she cursed. *Inflexible bastard won't bend a degree.* She shivered again as she thought about that word. Degree. One hundred and eighty of them in the shade would be good right now. Mmmmmmmm, nice.

'I can assure you, Miss Williams, what you are feeling is completely normal.'

She almost coughed. Almost screamed about freezing to death. But no. That wasn't the way to deal with these people, whoever they were. Something else was needed. Time for a different tack. Attack. Yes. She took a breath. '*Normal?*' she blurted from beneath the covers. 'You call it normal that as soon as I wake up my room is invaded by strangers?' With a tingle of satisfaction she felt a little cosier round the toes. Outburst therapy. Hmmm, could be a winner. She found himself warming to the idea.

'We're not strangers—'

'You sure? Hanging about in other people's bedrooms seems a bit strange to me. Bloody strange!' Her buttocks warmed a good half a degree enjoying a good point well made.

But the voice wouldn't give up. 'How can we be strangers? We of all people. We've been looking after you.' The tone was far too reasonable. And in a second they had her.

Muffled silence. Cooling buttocks.

You? Looking after me? Really . . . Curiosity woke up in

17

her mind. Why were they looking after her? What had happened? It wouldn't hurt to have a little look, would it?

You'll be sorry. Curiosity and cats and all.

'At least cats have warm fur coats,' she muttered and pulled the duvet down.

Two faces beamed honest, helpful smiles at her. At least, one looked honest. The other looked a little forced, uncomfortably businesslike. 'Ahhh, Miss Williams, there you are,' said the taller of the two white-coated men, in a tone sailing dangerously close to condescension. 'I'm Bishop Hutch—'

'Tut, tut, tut, you're doing it again. Introduce yourself properly,' interjected the other shriller voice just a little too quickly. Secretively. 'Thinks he's still at public school he does. Surname first and that. Habits. Once they get a grip . . . Miss Williams, meet Hutch Bishop. But you can call him Mister Bishop. He likes that. Me, I'm just called Lyndsey.'

Already she was bored with the pleasantries. Temperature going down. 'Uh-huh. Now about this heating—?'

But her demand was cut off in mid-stream as Lyndsey leapt suddenly across the room. There was a flash of white-coated sleeve. Her nose was pinched and a thermometer was jammed expertly under her tongue. 'And don't you go biting that now. Mercury's bad for you, if you didn't know. And as for the glass bits you'd swallow . . .' He shuddered in cartoon horror. 'Well, just promise me you won't call me when you next have to do number twos. Messy . . .'

Mr Bishop was peering closely at her. Scrutinising. Being Doctor. 'Hmmm, well she certainly looks good enough. It all seems to have taken.' He took out a small magnifying glass and focused on the patient's left ear. 'Slight discoloration around the lobe and the hairline isn't quite straight, but apart from that . . . Satisfactory. Yes. Very satisfactory. A good eight out of ten. Well done.'

Miss Williams shrugged against the bedclothes. Well done for what? Having satisfactory lobes? Since when was that a thing to be congratulated about? Well, except for life on the catwalk.

'Now let's see about the other thing,' grinned Bishop scientifically. 'Tell me, what do you think about that over there?' Bishop stepped sideways and pointed to a small occasional table.

The brunette in the bed shrugged again. This time she was really lost. This was a riddle, right? Had to be. What was she supposed to think about a small semi-transparent box with a scatter of fluff in the bottom? Or was it the plastic bag of black and white seeds on the shelf below that should have her reacting?

'Nothing but apparent mild curiosity,' grinned Bishop, making notes. 'Excellent. You don't feel anything else?'

She nodded her head. The thermometer waggled under her tongue.

'Er . . . You do? Lyndsey, take it out. She wants to speak. What else do you feel?'

'Freezing.'

'That's not what I meant and you know it.' Bishop flicked his wrist and Lyndsey shoved the thermometer back under her tongue.

Bishop drew a large tick on Miss Williams's chart. 'Fantastic. Trauma quotient zero. A full recovery. Well done.' And, frowning only slightly, he reached out, shook the patient's shoulder and left the room.

After a few minutes Lyndsey pulled the thermometer out, squinted hard and smiled. 'Ahh, you're still running a few degrees on the high side, but I bet you a squirrel to a carthorse you'll be right as rain by morning.'

'What? You saying I don't get the hot water bottles?'

'Sorry, no can do. Rules.' He snatched the pillows from the bed and began enthusiastically fluffing them.

'*Rules?* But I'm blood—'

'Ah, language,' admonished Lyndsey from behind a barrage of pillows and an exclamation mark of a finger.

'Rules? But I'm freezing,' she corrected herself. As if to prove the point, she shivered. Somehow, for the first time she knew she had actually got through. It had worked.

Lyndsey pursed his lips as he shoved the pillows back under the patient's head. He glanced quickly over his shoulder and scuttled across the purple carpet. 'Now, don't you whisper a word. Not a syllable. Not even a . . . what's smaller than a syllable? Oh, who cares?' He tweaked the thermostat on the wall and slipped out of the room.

Miss Williams shook her head, balancing a mild victory with . . . well, what? She stared at the garish ceiling. After a moment she closed her eyes. It was safer that way. Easier on the retina.

In the privacy of her mind she tried to make sense of the last few minutes. What had any of it been about? They seemed happy enough about something. Whoever 'they' were. They seemed almost joyous that her ear was only slightly discoloured, whatever that was supposed to mean. And what *was* that about the stuff on the occasional table? Fluff. How was she supposed to have reacted to a cage of fluff?

As she tossed scattered fragments of nonsense around in her head, she heard someone bustling down the corridor outside.

5

It wasn't the most direct route the butler could have taken. Strictly speaking, if he had been really keen on getting whatever it was that Seirizzim wanted quickly, he would have cut through Downtown Angst, crossed Oedema and Thirteenth and he could have been at the banks of the Phlegethon in minutes.

There were two reasons for taking his detour. One, he was early and he really didn't fancy hanging about in the seedier parts of Mortropolis with a bag of cash. And, more importantly, he could visit Reception.

How long it had been since he'd last popped in he couldn't quite tell. Well, one decade was pretty much like the last down in the Underworld. It was a strange thing, but eternal torment doesn't change that much.

He trotted up to the observation gallery and stepped close to the railing, his heart pounding with excitement.

Reception. Just the mention of the word made him quiver with envy. This was a place you could be proud to work. Not like being a butler. That was for wimps. No self-respecting demon would actually want to work for eternity making other demons happy.

With the thrill of the voyeur, he looked down upon a freshly killed entrant into the Underworld Kingdom of Helian.

'Name?' grunted a huge scaly demon barely fitting inside a booth.

'Er . . . Peterson. Albert Peterson,' answered the man, showing the distinct signs of road kill.

'Occupation?'

'It . . . I'm in IT. Er, what's that got to do with . . . ?'

'Married?'

'Look, I've already answered these questions. What kind of a hospital do you call this?'

'Kids?'

'Aren't you going to get on and treat me? I'm in agony here. Look, that's blood there. And there. And, if you

21

wouldn't mind, I'd like this sewing back on again.' He held out his ear.

'I'm sure you would. Ain't going to happen though.'

'What? Look, I've got BUPA. I've paid. Get me a surgeon!'

'Or else?'

'I'm dying here. I've already lost a good armful of blood.'

'More than that, mate. You look more like you're a good seven and a half pints down. Bit of septicaemia setting in. And, oh yeah, did you know I can see your brain through the back of your head?'

'Don't talk nonsense. If all that had happened I'd be dead.'

'Yes. Two minutes twelve,' squealed the demon, leaning out of his window and tapping on another booth. 'Two minutes twelve. Told you he didn't know. Pay up.'

'How do you pick them?' tutted the other demon, reluctantly handing over a few obuls.

'Just a knack. I can spot them a mile off. That bewildered look. Holding on to a bit of themselves. That's the killer. You can always tell they think they're in hospital if they've got a spare bit of themselves in their pocket.' He turned to Mr Peterson and grabbed his earlobe. 'You won't be needing that here.' The few ounces of skin was tossed into a small puddle of brimstone. It sizzled for a second then vanished.

'Oh my God . . .' coughed Peterson.

The demon made a noise in the back of his throat. It sounded nothing like the gameshow buzzer he was aiming for. 'Wrong. This is the other place.'

'But . . . I . . . my church . . .'

'Your wandering hands.'

'I confessed to that.'

'Don't count if you don't mean it. Was she worth it? You know, did she really make you feel like a man, eh?'

'That's none of your business.'

22

'She did. Ooooh, tiger.'

'This is some kind of joke, isn't it? I'm . . . I'm hallucinating. Yes, that's it. Hallucinating.'

'Does this feel like an hallucination to you?' asked the demon, waggling a nine-inch talon in the space where Mr Peterson's ear once hung.

He screamed. But to the irritation of the demon, he started to grin. 'At last. I'm in surgery. I can feel the scalpel. I'm going to be all right.'

'Shit. Full denial. Ahh well, he'll come round soon enough.' The demon scribbled on a piece of parchment and pinned it to Mr Peterson's lapel. It read 'CessPool No 9'.

In seconds three smaller demons had grabbed him and were carrying him off to the pool, which had been newly refurbished after extensive riots. There he would spend his first twenty or so years hanging around head down blowing bubbles. Maybe then he'd come around to just where he was.

'Excuse me,' called Mr Peterson over the clattering of hooves. 'Could I have a little more anaesthetic, this is really starting to hurt now. Fifty cc's. Hundred. Please?'

'Next!' snorted the demon in the booth.

In the observation gallery, the butler shook his head in admiration. That was what being a demon was all about. The casual tossing of utter misery at unwitting people. You could be proud of that. You could stand tall and know that you were responsible for an eternity of suffering. And what was he responsible for? Making sure Seirizzim had a nice cold lava waiting when he came in. And fetching and carrying a host of other trivial items.

He snorted miserably as he remembered the latest little errand thrust upon him.

Shrugging, he turned and headed off to a covert meeting in Darkest Tumor.

6

I ran down the corridor as fast as I could.

It wasn't that fast.

Well, having a cardboard box tucked up my overall didn't help. I couldn't believe I'd left it in the store room. Any handy psychologist would probably have had some kind of field day with that one. Writing papers about repressed subconcious desires to avoid confrontational rodent experiences. There were probably a dozen papers to be had from me. I hurried around the corner, hating the fact that the damned rodent had been ill. Last week would have been loads better if it hadn't rolled its eyes, coughed and . . .

'Ahh now, Brother MacFadden, just what are you in such a rush for? Where's the fire?'

I nearly dropped the shoe box when I heard him. He'd been waiting, I'm sure. Checking up on me, you know, the way he does.

'Brother Lyndsey, ahh . . . fire? There's no fire. Just my customary devotion to duty. Work, work, busy, busy.'

It sounded good to me.

Water off a duck's back to him. 'And the truth, now?' He tried for that look of authority. I barely checked a nervous laugh.

'I just love my work. As I always say, a perfect table is a polished table.' I think I would've got away with it if a certain rodent hadn't decided to start excavating a new nest in the corner of the shoe box. I cringed. I had almost managed to wipe the thought of that thing so close to my spleen from my mind.

'You're scuffling,' he said, sharp as ever. 'D'you often do that?'

'Only on Tuesdays.' It was almost true. Well, not a complete lie anyway. It was Tuesday after all.

He frowned, calculating penance potential. 'There's something in your overalls, isn't there? Something alive?'

'Me?' Pathetic for the second time that morning. I was way off form.

'Come now. Open the box.'

I had no choice. It was a fair cop as they say. He'd got me.

Reluctantly, I hitched up my overall and pulled out the ageing shoe box. 'It's not what you think,' I began. Of course, I didn't know what he was thinking. But it had always seemed like a good place to start. 'It's not my fault.' Maybe I was over-egging my defence, but people had been sacked for less. Rodent rustling was not policy in St Cedric's, I was sure.

'Open it.'

I shut my eyes and peeled off the lid.

A small golden hamster peered up at Lyndsey. Whiskers shimmering, eager to get out and be played with.

'An explanation, please?'

It took me a moment to realise that Lyndsey wasn't actually talking to me. He beamed as his finger stroked the back of the creature's head. Encouraged, it scrabbled up the side of the box towards him and then, with the blind faith that only hamsters possess, it leapt out.

Lyndsey caught it and in seconds was giggling as Skitter started to sprint across a moving walkway of hands.

'Look, it's not my fault,' I said again. 'I didn't know the daft thing would be allergic to Mr Sheen, did I? Anyway, the vet's given it the all clear now, so I'm fine. I'm putting it back in its proper place. You won't tell?'

'Er, get him off.' Somehow the hamster had outsmarted him; changed direction in mid palm probably. Skitter was good at that. He was currently perched on Lyndsey's shoulder. 'Oooh, stop it. He's tickling my ear. Get him off.'

I stared in alarm. 'You want me to . . .'

'Get him off!'

The hamster peered at me inscrutably.

'You won't tell?' I blackmailed.

'No, no, no.'

'You're sure?'

'Would I lie?'

I knew there was no getting out of this. Good job I had my favourite feather duster with me. I swept Skitter back into his temporary shoe-box home and headed for the door of room number six.

'Just go quietly in there,' warned Lyndsey. 'She's still a bit . . . you know?' He rolled his eyes and pulled a face that looked like he was under the influence of strong drugs. I was worried. He did that far too well.

Shaking my head, I pressed the door shut behind me.

On the bed, Miss Williams lay motionless, eyes closed. Asleep again. Perfect. She wouldn't even have missed her animal companion.

It seemed a strange thing to do at first, place animals in with patients in recovery. Well, it did to me at least. I mean, animals carry disease, don't they? Chameleons and salmonella. Dogs and rabies. Chickens and er . . . pox. But after the management consultants had been, everything had changed. They said that 'recovery was substantially quicker and more stable if suitable non-human company was present' - Paragraph 23, section 111, I think. And so the animals had been drafted in. How they figured out who got what I hadn't the foggiest. Once they said a patient had to have a bear. Would you believe it? A brown bear, here? Health and Safety had a fit. He had to settle for a constant loop of as many edited wildlife documentaries as they could find. I don't think he actually recovered properly. But then, I never actually get to find out if any of them recover properly. Still, that's not part of the job.

I pulled myself back to the task in hand and headed off towards the wire hamster cage.

7

Miss Williams's thoughts were disturbed by the conversation in the corridor. She groaned, lay back in the bed and tried thinking about warm things instead. Coal fires burning. Logs spitting flames in a crimson bonfire glow. Lava flows streaming through tunnels of black basalt . . .

These warming thoughts shattered as the door squeaked open and a man in overalls and dog-collar crept in.

Damn, why won't they leave me alone? I wake up, they're there. I try to rest, they're there. Ignore it all. Pretend to be asleep. Yes. Then they'll go away.

Across the room, the man fiddled with something in a cardboard box. With a struggle, he eased open the wire caging and tipped whatever it was in. He dropped a couple of black and white seeds in between the bars in the lid, wiped his hands obsessively and headed for the door.

Where am I? What is going on?

Brother MacFadden made a swift exit with the shoe box. He knew what would happen next. The creature would do what it had to do. What generations of its forefathers had done before it. What the entire species did best. With a satisfaction known only to itself, it hopped up the half inch on to the familiar red tread of plastic. And started to run.

As the wheel accelerated on the metal spindle, icy fingers of fear began clawing at the soul of the woman in the bed.

That sound. It was familiar. Hauntingly familiar.

Suddenly, the extra few degrees of heating just weren't

enough. Cold shards of fear froze in her spine. Terror crashed in waves through her body. Her breath caught in mid scream as she opened her eyes wide and stared transfixed at the cage.

Blissfully unaware of the catatonia he was inducing, Skitter the hamster sprinted pointlessly around his plastic wheel.

8

A blackened ferry struggled sluggishly through the sticky currents of the River Phlegethon, belching out plumes of smoke.

A hundred yards away, in the darkest of shadows which lurked in Downtown Tumor, two demons were talking in hushed tones. Secret tones.

'What'll it be this time?' asked the one wearing a cloak with large pockets.

'Whatcha got?' sniffed a wasted-looking silhouette.

'Depends how much cash you got, don't it.'

'Look, mate, it ain't been a good week . . .'

'Never is down here. How much you got?'

'What can you give me for twenty?'

'Twenty? Hmm, let me see. That could give you ten "e"s. Or a dozen "o"s. Or, fresh in today, a packet of "m"s.'

The wasted one licked his lips. 'You got "m"s? Show me, show me.'

'What is this, you don't trust me? After all you've bought from me?'

'Show me.'

There was a rummaging in pockets and, in a matter of seconds, the triumphant dealer held out a small and very brightly coloured packet. It rustled enticingly, catching what light there was on its shiny surface.

'Oh, look at that,' whispered the other demon in awe. 'That's beautiful, that is.' He stared longingly at the packet of "m & m"s. Salivary glands oozed overactively.

'Twenty obuls and they're all yours.'

'Shit, shit. Will you take twelve?'

'What?' He snatched the illegal sweeties away. 'Twenty or you don't get them.'

'I can get the rest by next Firesday.'

'Do I look like I do credit?' sneered the dealer, fastening up his cloak.

'Aww, come on. I ain't never had an "m & m".'

'You never will if you keep wasting my time. So what'll it be? "E"s or "o"?s' In a flash of talons the dealer produced a small packet of Everton Mints and a half used roll of Polos. He already knew the answer.

'Gimme them.' Desperately, the wasted one reached for the green and black roll of mints with holes.

'Cash. Now.'

The smaller demon made a snarling sound in the back of his throat and reluctantly handed over a small clump of coins.

The supplier flicked the sweets into the air.

They didn't get far.

A set of talons snatched at them and had peeled three out with barely a rustle of foil. In moments a satisfied sucking sound was coming out of the shadows.

'Same time next week?' called the supplier.

The only reply he got was a rude gesture and more sucking noises.

'That's gratitude,' he tutted to himself and backed into his favourite pool of shadow.

He didn't have to wait long for his next customer.

As if on cue, a surprisingly well-groomed nine-footer

walked warily into the alley. The supplier's expert eye locked on to the bulge in his pocket in a fraction of a second. A smile licked at the corner of his mouth as he calculated just how much a bulge that size could be worth. It would buy many 'm & m's. Even at his prices.

'Can I help?' he asked, stepping to the edge of his pool of shadow. Much to his satisfaction, the well-groomed one jumped. A bit of apprehension in the customer was always helpful in the inflation of prices. 'Anything you want I can get. So, what'll be your pleasure?'

'Er . . . I don't know,' began the butler with a shrug.

'You look like a demon with a sweet fang. I've just got some "m"s in.'

'It's not for me.'

'Yeah, right,' grinned the supplier. It was a common excuse with all but the lowest of underworld life. Swiftly, he recalculated all his prices, adding in an extra ten per cent discomfort premium.

'It's not. I've just come to collect.' He handed over a sheet of parchment.

The supplier frowned and angled the message to catch any available light. 'Oh, it's this. You wouldn't believe the trouble I had getting this—'

'If this is some kind of preamble to hike up your prices then forget it. This is all I have.' He pulled the bag of obuls out of his pocket. 'The agreed fee, I believe.'

'Aren't you going to haggle?'

'Would it do any good?'

'No.'

'Thought not. Now, the merchandise.' He handed over the bag.

The supplier reached into the dark, pulled out a surprisingly small sack and tossed it to the butler.

'That's it?'

The question hung in the air of Downtown Tumor, the only answer being the clatter of hooves in the dark.

'Guess a receipt's out of the question,' shrugged the butler.

Curiosity burning in the back of his mind, he ran off to deliver the goods.

9

A pair of black ball-bearing eyes peered out across the room. Glinting. Shining with rodent delight as the hamster chewed at the tip of its water bottle.

'Shut up,' growled Miss Williams, scuffling in bed, grinding her molars. The incessant gnawing was really starting to get to her. Had been for the last two hours. 'Just shut up. I know you're doing this on purpose.'

The hamster ignored her, changed its grip and carried on. And much to its satisfaction, the noise was almost twice as loud. Some subtle shift of weight meant that the sound of teeth on aluminium was joined by the collision of water bottle against wire. In seconds the entire cage was amplifying the sound. Gnashing and rattling filled the room.

'Shut up!' spat the patient in the bed. 'Shut up!' She jammed her head under the pillow. It didn't help. The noise still got through to her. Scraping at her mood. Irritating her.

And suddenly it was too much for her to stand. Something had to be done. Now.

She was out of bed in a flurry of bedclothes and half-way across the room before she stopped. The hamster was looking at her, fixing her with a fathomless stare.

Anger rose inside her. Her mind spun ahead, ignited with white-hot fury. She saw herself ripping open the cage, plunging her hands deep inside, grabbing at the damned creature, crushing hard until . . . She winced as her mind filled with images of incisors clamping around her thumb. Hmmm, bad idea. Maybe there was a safer way. She imagined herself tearing at the cage, hurling the damned beast on to the floor and bringing her heel down hard across its vulnerable head and . . . uh-oh, bare feet. Teeth and big toes. Not a good idea.

So it would just have to be the old cage-out-of-the-window scenario. Not quite as satisfying as going *womano-a-rodent* and inflicting actual bodily harm, but it would do the job.

Blissfully unaware of the waves of malevolence racking at Miss Williams's body, the hamster continued chewing. But not for much longer.

Growling, she leapt forward, grabbed at the bottle and tore it off the side of the cage. Water gurgled and splashed across the highly polished surface of the occasional table.

It was at that instant that the door burst open and Brother MacFadden bustled in, his plastic box rattling with a dozen different cleaning products.

'Ah, Miss Williams, you're . . . you're up and about I see.'

10

'Ah, Miss Williams, you're . . . you're up and about I see.' I heard myself say it and winced. It wasn't inspired, but then, inspiration hadn't exactly been strong in my star sign that morning. And besides, I hadn't expected her to be up and about quite so soon. Or quite so naked for that matter. I tried to avert my eyes. They didn't want to move.

I stared at her. All of her.

A sigh whistled between my lips.

It wasn't as if I hadn't seen her naked before. I mean, that was part of the job. Well, you try getting sheets off a bed without catching a glimpse of a buttock or two. But all that had been different. She'd been in the way. Just so much meat to work around. And besides, bodies are different shapes when they're flat on their back. Far less interesting than if they're up and on the hoof. They're hung together far differently in the vertical.

Whoops, shouldn't have thought that.

'I . . . I came in to do your room,' I offered, suddenly not knowing where to look. Oh God, had she heard the stutter? She was bound to think I was lying if she heard that. Bound to think I was some kind of voyeur.

'Bloody creature won't shut up.' She gestured towards the cage, agitated. 'Wouldn't stop chewing.'

'I . . . I can come back later if you . . .' And then I saw the state of the table. Skitter's bottle lying there, a puddle of water growing by the moment. And the professional side of me just took over, calculating seepage rate versus frequency of polishing and cross-referencing that to what it said on the can of Mr Sheen. In short, was it waterproof? How long did I have before limescale discoloration would set in? I wasn't going to take a chance.

I don't remember actually crossing the room. I was just suddenly there next to her, pulling a large yellow sponge out of my box of bits and wrestling with thoughts of using it on her. In a Hollywood shower, all marble and gold fittings and soap . . .

Stop it!

'Ohh, look at this mess,' I babbled, sounding unnervingly like my mother. Get a grip, man! A couple of hours ago she was in a coma. Calm yourself, do the job and get out, or you'll spend the rest of your life in a cold confessional.

Skitter hopped on to his wheel again and began running. Plastic grated on metal. I clenched my teeth.

33

'It's doing it again. It's doing it on purpose,' she said. 'It just wouldn't stop chewing . . .'

I stopped myself from looking up. She sounded genuinely upset. Right now I couldn't cope with that. I might just have to comfort her. To hug her. And God knows where that would lead. It would be more than my vows could stand.

I stared at the table and buffed for all I was worth while trying to ignore the dynamo hamster. Hating it. 'It's . . . it's all right, really. No real harm done. I'm sure we . . . they can afford a new bottle for it.' I reached for my chamois leather, casting an expert eye over the walnut. Slightly dulled, but nothing unexpected. Quick squirt of Mr Sheen and it would be perfect. I'd be able to see my face in it. And anything else that was near.

Concentrate, man!

I grabbed at the aerosol can and began to shake it.

'You do believe me, don't you?' I heard her say and my heart leapt. Something in the way she spoke resonated inside my head. 'It wouldn't stop. Wouldn't shut up. I had to do something. I had to stop it.' She reached out and grabbed my spraying hand, squeezing, staring at me, imploring. I could feel my jaw dropping. And I guess I must have hit the plunger.

How long it hissed polish into the air I haven't a clue. Well, you don't keep track of time in a situation like that. I mean, her hands were so warm and smooth and, well, nobody normally held my hands. Make no mistake, hands can be so sensual. Skin on skin, finger to finger.

I was melting. I could feel it. I looked at her standing there, the curve of her shoulders, the plunge of her cleavage, her come-to-bed navel. Somebody had really known what they were doing when they put her together.

Then I realised I'd forgotten something. Breathing.

I gulped air and furniture polish in almost equal proportions. It stung the back of my throat, acid on my tonsils. Oh, and the taste. Don't try this at home. For external use only.

I pulled free and sprinted for the door, coughing. My head reeled with propellant and something unexpected. Something, well, frankly, carnal.

11

Miss Williams watched as the door pulled shut. She stood, confused. Was it something she'd said? Or something she'd done? She was only trying to explain about the . . .

And then she saw it.

In the cage, the hamster fell off its wheel, picked itself up and staggered forward three steps.

She sniggered and her face started to curl into a sneer. 'Not so happy now, are you, eh? Not quite so lively.' And feelings rose in boiling waves within her. Dark feelings. Wonderful. She didn't stop to ask why. Not yet. It didn't seem important. She just enjoyed it. Revelled in it.

The hamster coughed again as the cloud of Mr Sheen settled over it. Tiny lungs strained to breathe through an allergy-inflamed windpipe. Its tongue swelled.

And Miss Williams headed back for her bed, warm in the certain knowledge that she wouldn't be troubled by hamsters any more that day. She folded her arms behind her head and stared at the ceiling, a self-satisfied smile forming on her face.

The hamster coughed its last and fell over in a bowl of sunflower seeds. In minutes, its body began to stiffen as the polish dried on its fur.

An Underdone Alaska

April 19, Avebury, Wilts.

Dear Logbook,

Passed Woodhenge 23.56. No activity. Not surprised since they've replaced wood with concrete posts. Nice idea, albeit misguided. About as much use as a pickled herring – spiritually speaking. Made a note to buy a pickled herring when next in Sainway's.

Bernstein rolled runes in lay-by on dot of midnight. Two mattocks, ante-hex, stridular and a bord. Ray unsure whether to expect underharpy class four, or simple atmospheric floating torso-type apparition. Book opened almost immediately. Underharpy is six to four favourite. Was told to shut up after disapproving. Forced to place 50p on floating torso-type apparition. Sometimes they have no respect.

Arr. Avebury 00.53. Headed for S.W. tip of Avenue of the Solar Serpent. Settled into our trad. ring. Mourned the loss of many sarsens, now local pubs and farmhouses, as I began my vigil. Wind, light northerly. Mist rose 03.23, heading in from Hackpen Hill. Others failed to see significance of this. 'Hac' means snake and 'pen' means head. Underwhelmed by their response. Sometimes think I'm only one who cares.

Heavy excitement 04.25 (approx). Adrenaline rose. Flickering light round sarsen to S.W. Hovered. Flickered. Fired a twelve-bore at us. Plenty of swearing. We ran. Others convinced it was just torchlight from local poachers. I remain

*unsure. Certain I saw a definite torso and waving arms. Ray
says I'm just saying that to win the pot.*

    *Tonight will remain a mystery and raises hope in me that
at last we are doing something right. Maybe soon we'll have
contact with the other side.*

    Dep. Avebury 08.09.

    Caught in rush hour in Marlborough.

    Avge mpg 12.2. Never did like motorways.

    Made a note to raise petrol fees at next meeting.

12

'You stupid, selfish git.' It was one of those thoughts that just
leap into my head. They don't hatch, don't germinate. They're
just, bang, right there. First in the queue, capital letters.

    I was on my feet and out of the store room feeling guilty
as charged. Selfish. Stupid and a git. A prize one. How could
I have forgotten about the damned hamster? After all I'd
done for it that morning. It wasn't as if I liked the thing, but
emptying a full can of Mr Sheen its way . . . the RSPCA had
people up in court for less. All I'd thought about was myself.
Getting *me* out of that room. Finding *me* some fresh air.
Making sure *I* didn't cough *my* guts out. God, just think if
firemen thought that way . . .

    I skidded to a halt outside the door of room number six,
my fist tight around the handle. And I froze.

    I couldn't go in there and face her, could I? I was bound to
blush, bound to make some kind of fool of myself.

    There I was again. Self, self, self. Worse than Alanis Mor-
issette. Get a grip. Just turn the handle and get in there. Skitter
needs you. There might still be a chance. Yeah, in a pig's eye.
That much Mr Sheen. How could I have done it? How could I
have kept my thumb on the trigger for so damn long?

The only defence I could conjure up was that I had been distracted. I mean, she was beautiful. And whose fault was that, eh? His. After all, everyone was supposed to be made in His image. I shook my head. God looked like Miss Williams? No, that couldn't be right. Get a grip.

I took a deep breath and turned the handle, chamois across my face, firefighter style.

Nothing moved in there.

I didn't look across at the bed, just headed straight for the cage. Straight for Skitter.

As soon as I saw him face down in the bowl of sunflower seeds, I knew it didn't look good. Desperately, I thought he could just be asleep, just having a snooze. But I knew. Deep down, I knew.

I ripped off the cage lid, dropped my chamois and, fighting my fears, plunged in.

His fur was crispy. A toffee-apple cardigan.

I gasped, swallowed and turned him over. My heart sank. *Titanic* had nothing on this.

'No. No. No.' I heard my voice as I pushed on his chest, trying to get his little heart beating. With a twelve-volt battery and a couple of crocodile clips I might have stood a chance. Might have tried for cardiac stimulation. *'Fifty cc adrenaline, stat. Clear.' Zap. Body spasm of discharge. The wavering bleep of monitors.*

I had none of it. Not even the nurse to gently take the gelled paddles from my shaking hands and whisper, 'It's too late. Leave it. He's gone.' Not even a blanket to cover his furry face.

I really must stop watching hospital dramas. Or at least cut down a bit. They were bad for me.

Trembling only slightly, I slipped the cold, stiff rodent into the pocket of my overalls and headed for the door. I could

38

give it last rites – it was only a few minutes late. It was an innocent creature and its soul could still be saved. Maybe.

I tried desperately to tell myself that it had all been an accident. An industrial accident. That I hadn't been to blame, hadn't just exterminated a small, naive, innocent—

'You all right?' I heard the voice from the bed.

I froze.

'You all right?' asked Miss Williams again quietly and sat up. She didn't seem to notice that the sheets had slipped away from her. Or she didn't care.

'What? Me? Er . . . why d'you ask?' I spluttered and reached for my overall pocket. Doh, sure sign of guilt that one.

'Well, it's just . . . you know?' I wasn't sure if she pointed to her eyes. What was that supposed to mean? That she'd seen everything? Or that I was crying? Surely not. I wasn't that much of an emotional mess, was I?

I edged a little closer to the door, had to get out of there. No one was allowed to see me in tears. Priests don't cry, at least not before lunch anyhow. 'No, I don't know,' I snapped back. 'Don't know anything. Didn't do it.'

'What have you got in your pocket?'

'Who d'you think I am, Bilbo Baggins?' It was obvious from her blank expression that she'd never read Tolkien.

'Is it dead?'

She had me there, pinned and mounted. A direct question. 'Is it dead?'

'He has a name, you know. Skitter, he's called . . . was called.'

'So he's dead, then?'

'Yes! Dead! As a doornail, doorknob, dodo! Today's death was brought to you by the letter "D". All right?' I didn't realise I was shouting until I stopped. I was taking it bad.

'I only asked,' she said. 'Just making sure.'

'Yeah, well . . .' I didn't know what to say. She *had* only asked. It was true enough. And I bet she had a lot of other questions after being out of it for eight weeks. How Pierce Brosnan's love life was doing. If Tiger Woods was still over par in bed. You know, important woman things. 'I'll . . . I'll get you another one. There's a pet shop just around the corn—'

'NO! Another one? Oh, shit no!' It surprised me the way she said it. Well, squealed it, really. Weird tone of voice. Sort of terrified. Piglet, butcher's knife type thing. She pulled herself together quickly though, I'll give her that. Quicker than I normally manage.

'That won't be necessary,' she said, all calm and business-like. 'I'm fine on my own.'

'Huh, I can take a hint.' I shut the door as quickly as I could, without looking like I was in too much of a rush.

13

'Huh, I can take a hint,' hissed Brother MacFadden and slammed the door.

'That's not what I meant,' said Miss Williams to the empty room. 'I just don't like hamst . . .'

Her voice faded quickly. She couldn't even bring herself to say it. Hamster. The thought of it sent icy fingers of terror down her spine.

Terror, or was it anger?

'Neither. And both,' said Dr Freud from behind the leather couch. 'What you have here is terror manifesting itself as a channelled and focused anger. The classic mild-mannered fallow deer reaction to being cornered by the hunt. Fight and flight. Kick a few beagles' teeth out and make a run for it.

40

Come again next week and we'll discuss the sexual imagery of chimneys and tunnels in the civil engineering of your dream landscape.'

Anger she could understand. The damn thing *had* been making a lot of noise. The chewing, the running on the wheel. But surely that wasn't enough for her to want it dead? Not choked-to-death-by-furniture-polish dead. That was just vindictive. Devilish.

'Something brought on by a history of childhood hamster abuse, perhaps?'

Her mind spun back through her memory, rewinding through the teenage years, delving into her distant childhood, revealing . . . nothing. There was nothing there *to* reveal. Her memory was a complete blank.

Well, except for an overbearing hatred of hamsters. Live ones anyhow.

Truth be told, now it was actually gone, she felt terrible about it. She actually felt guilty. Guilty for wanting it dead.

She didn't have long to wallow, though.

'Din-dins!' announced Lyndsey, bustling through the door with a covered tray. Somehow, he managed to pull a wheeled table across the room and into position above the bed using nothing but his left leg. He took great delight in tucking a pink serviette up under Miss Williams's chin and tying it around her neck before laying out the plastic cutlery and pulling off the thermal cover. 'Tan-naahh. Now look at that, hey, isn't that something? An extra special waking-up dinner just for you on your first dinnertime awake. Go on then, tuck in. Don't mind me. I'll have mine later. Go on. Yum, yum.'

Miss Williams just stared at the plate. 'What is it?'

'Oh dear, your memory playing tricks, is it? Well, I'll help, shall I? They're carrots, those green things are peas and—'

'That. What is that?' She poked a large slice of flesh with a distinctly suspicious and curiously well-manicured finger.

'Don't you recognise it? That's steak. Nice fresh Sirloin. Yum, yum. Now are you going to eat it up?'

The woman in the bed shuddered. 'I can't eat that.'

'Ohhh, I think you can,' beamed Lyndsey with far too much enthusiasm. 'As soon as your tummy gets the taste of it your appetite will come rushing back and it'll all be gone in a flash. Shall I cut it up?' He didn't wait for an answer. He knew best. He grabbed at the knife. 'I know the thought of actually chewing something isn't really pleasant right now. What with having all your food dripped in through your nose for the last eight weeks, but I tell you—'

'I can't eat that.' She stared at the pink flesh on the fork.

'C'mon, aeroplanes. Neeeyhow!'

'No!'

'Oh dear,' sighed Lyndsey with a shrug. 'Don't tell me you've gone all . . .' He looked over both shoulders and lowered his voice. 'Vegetarian?'

'No, I'm not eating that because it's the wrong colour. And it's too soft. Steak should be black and hard. That's not cooked.'

'It is. Medium, that is. And very nice too. Now eat it up. It's baked Alaska for pudding.' As if to tempt his awkward client, Lyndsey flashed the lid off the dessert bowl. What met Miss Williams's eyes didn't impress.

'You call that baked? Where are the black bits? The charcoally sort of bits. What . . . why are you looking at me like that?'

Lyndsey packed the plate away quickly and hurried out of the room.

'What have I said? Tell me.'

For the first time in eight weeks, the door was locked.

14

Hutch Bishop, otherwise known to fellow clergy as Bishop Hutchinson, looked up from his desk as Lyndsey bustled in with a tray in his hands.

'Ahh, splendid, tea time already.' He pushed the papers to one side and licked his lips, failing to notice that it was only just gone half two.

'It's not yours,' whispered Lyndsey, dropping into a seat and looking tired and emotional. He pulled the lid off and pointed to the spread. 'Look at that and tell me what's wrong with it.'

'Oh, I get it. Another one of those patient-charter food-accreditation inspections again, is it? Well, at first glance I'd say there's no serviette and it looks like someone's been chopping up the Sirloin.'

'That was me. And the serviette's still in her room. And no, it's not accreditation time.' Lyndsey looked across the desk, his moon eyes round with concern. 'What's wrong with it? Does it look cooked to you?'

'Carrots are a bit hard—'

'The meat! The steak, how does that look?' gabbled Lyndsey.

'Quite delicious actually. Are you sure it's not tea time?'

'And that, the baked Alaska. How does that appear, hmmm? Does it look appetising? To your taste?'

'What is all this? What are you talking about?'

'Miss Williams. She wanted it black and hard.' Lyndsey almost sobbed as he pointed to the steak. 'And she wanted charcoally bits on the . . . the . . .' He waggled a hand towards the dessert. 'Charcoal, can you believe it? *They* have it with charcoal.'

'She actually used the "c" word?'

Lyndsey nodded. 'It hasn't taken. We'll have to put her under again. Increase the dosage this time.'

'Oh, come now,' said Bishop, pulling the Alaska towards him with a spoon. 'We can't be certain it hasn't taken. Some people like different things in different ways. Coffee, for instance. Me, black no sugar. You, cream and two sweeteners.'

'It's three now. Stress, you know?'

'Well, there you are.' The spoon slurped in the Alaska as if it was over. Case closed.

It wasn't. Far from it.

Lyndsey looked at his shoes. It was either a sudden interest in footwear, or confession time. 'I . . . I turned up the thermostat.'

'You did what?'

'She asked me to. She was cold.'

'Now, hold on here. Before you go off on a tangent, screaming for sanctuary and announcing the end of the world as we know it, look on the positive side. She had no reaction to external unexpected stimuli. Nothing. Clear. The other things are just, well, personal taste.'

'You're basing all this on her reaction to the hamster?'

'Yes. No reaction to it at all. And that's the crucial test. I don't have to remind you of that, do I? It proves she's fine. After the trauma she's been through, I tell you, she's almost ready to be released into society – under control of course. So maybe she looks a little strange in the ear department and her hairline's still a bit weird but, hey, we can sort that. I mean, it wouldn't actually take a full miracle. She'll be out of here before the end of the week, mark my words.'

'Er, about the hamster. There's something I should tell you. I think there was no reaction because . . . how do I put this? There was nothing to react to. No stimulus.'

'Nonsense,' tutted Bishop, taking another spoonful of baked Alaska.

'Sir, I regret to inform you that, ahem . . . there was no hamster in the cage.'

Bishop almost choked on his stolen dessert.

'Explain.'

15

It was just starting to flash down again as the butler trotted up to the door. But even before the brimstone hit his scaly forehead, something was already burning. Curiosity.

Just what was in the small sack he was carrying? And why hadn't Seirizzim taken delivery of it through more normal channels?

It didn't bode well. Not well at all. In fact, it smacked of something far into the realms of the extremely unwell. There wasn't much that went on in these parts that required any real degree of secrecy. And with the vast majority of things, if Seirizzim wanted it, he got it. Just like that. One of the perks of being Second-in-Command of Mortropolis. In the last five centuries there had been nothing that Seirizzim hadn't got just by flicking his talons. Well, except for full ruling command of Mortropolis, of course, but that was one of the problems of working in the eternal torment industry. Promotion was slow.

And being a butler in the eternal torment industry, one soon learned not to ask too many questions. Demotion was swift.

He pushed open the door, resigning himself uncomfortably to the fact that he'd just have to bide his time. Sooner or later he'd find out what was in the sack. If he just kept his eyes and ears open for the next couple of centuries, he'd crack it. After all, it was a well-known fact that it's almost impossible to keep a secret from your demonservant.

'Well, d'you get it?' barked Seirizzim, spinning around in his favourite armchair.

'Of course. Your urge is my desire.'

'Nobody saw you?'

'With the unique exception of the supplier, I was un-witnessed.'

'A simple "no" would have been fine.'

'Probably,' shrugged the butler and pulled the sack out of his pocket. 'Will that be all, sir?' he asked as he handed it over with enforced disinterest. Much to his satisfaction, he caught Seirizzim's look of irritation.

'Bring me a half of lava,' growled Seirizzim. 'Leave it on the desk.'

'Sir,' nodded the butler with a twinge of satisfaction. Whatever was in the sack was going to be used tonight. And not very far from Seirizzim's study. Probably in the secret ante-room that was accessed from behind the book-case and which he wasn't supposed to know about.

Straining his ears to the full, he listened carefully as he poured his master a cold lava.

What he heard chilled him to the bone.

16

It was the first time I'd come across a locked door in all the time I'd been working there. And it nearly gave me a nose bleed.

Well, after however long of elbowing the handles open and breezing through with a boxful of cleaning stuff, humming to myself, to suddenly come across a solid lump of wood in the way . . . I still don't know quite how I avoided a messy collision. It was close. The only door that was locked around here was the front door. But that was to stop people coming in by mistake. Wasn't it? You know, like a toilet cubicle.

For the first time, I began to wonder.

But not half as much as I was wondering why Miss Williams was behind closed doors.

Nervously I fumbled for my key and let myself in.

The first thing that hit me was the heat. Automatically, I turned towards the thermostat and checked its setting. Couple of degrees up but nothing that should make it this hot.

I started to sweat as I caught sight of the fire.

All four bars of it were heading towards electric melt-down.

And Miss Williams was loving it. Happy as a lizard in the Sahara.

'I found it in that cupboard,' she said, rolling over and fixing me with those eyes of hers. Ironic really, but they were what people called icy blue. It startled me. I was still used to her being out of it. Hearing her move and talk was going to take some getting used to. And as for the way she perspired . . .

'I . . . I didn't know they kept stuff up there—' I began, before she changed the subject.

'Why's the door locked?'

I felt as if the carpet had shifted two inches to the left. Direct questions from the recently comatose was unnerving.

'Why'd he lock it?'

'Er, I was hoping you could answer that,' I shrugged. Truth was, I hadn't a clue about St Cedric's locked door policy. It had probably been mentioned somewhere in the paperwork I'd been given on the first day. But I hadn't read it. Well, you don't, do you? Make sure take-home pay's what you expected, make sure the annual leave's up to standard and check you know where the fire exits are. Anything else is just details to be perused later. They were still waiting to be squinted at.

'Have I done something wrong? Have I?' she asked in a strange tone of voice. I'm sure it wasn't as confident as she would have liked it to sound.

My shoulders twitched upwards again, palms to the ceiling. Hopeless. 'Don't ask me. I know nothing.'

'Look, I only complained about the food,' she confessed, seeming keen to talk. As if she needed a sounding board. Someone to listen.

'That'll teach you to criticise. They hate complaints about the service.' It just came out. She didn't take it well.

'It wasn't cooked,' she snapped back, pulling the covers up around her shoulders like a stroppy ten-year-old. 'I hate raw steak. And how they could even have the nerve to call that a *baked* Alaska. It was my right to complain.'

My jaw dropped a quarter inch. Was that the normal menu? BUPA would have to keep an eye on these guys. 'And the claret?' I suggested frivolously. 'Hadn't been left to breathe, I suppose?'

'Claret?' she asked.

'Er, red wine? You know, like er . . .' My mind tried to think of other types. It came up blank. Serves me right for being a sherry man. 'Er . . . pinot . . . Bull's Blood.' I remembered it from my shady past.

'No, there wasn't any of that, either.'

She's probably still on some strong medication, I thought, remembering a recent conversation with Lyndsey in the corridor.

And I suddenly remembered why I was back in her room

for the third time that day. The hamster cage. It shouldn't have been left in her room this long.

I fiddled with a large hand towel and decided that I'd cover the cage before removing it. Should look a little more professional that way. Efficient. And besides, she might be upset if she saw hamstery things in there. Things that would remind her of this morning's unfortunate incident.

I looked into my box of stuff and surreptitiously hid a new can of Mr Sheen. I even made a mental note never to use it around her again. I'd heard somewhere that smells can really dig up long-buried memories. Maybe that was why I liked having colds. It was safer. No risk of unexpected trips down dodgy memory lanes. And there were a few of them just a sniff away I can tell you.

I made a move towards the cage.

'About this morning,' I heard her say. 'I'm sorry.' She sounded genuine but I didn't notice.

'You're sorry? It was my finger on the trigger.' I missed irony by a good ten feet. Got pathetic a full bullseye, though. Third time. This was turning out to be a record day.

'No, I'm sorry. I shouldn't have . . . It was annoying me. I so wanted to shut . . .'

I couldn't handle this. Maybe this was why the door was locked. She messed with people's heads. Harriet Lecter in room six. Keep your head down, do the job. Get out.

My mouth had other ideas. 'So you wanted a bit of peace. We all do. Don't stress. It was an accident. I'll get you a nice kitten, or parrot, or . . .' I was babbling again. I stepped forward, reached for the cage.

I didn't see the electric cable belonging to the fire. My ankle caught it and pulled.

I always thought it was some naff cinema trick when really dramatic moments go into slo-mo. I changed my mind right then. It happens. Fate's way of rubbing it in, I guess. When the shit hits the fan, you get to see it all. And all you can do is stare.

All I *could* do was stare as the four-bar inferno toppled forward off the bedside cabinet and rolled towards the purple carpet.

I tried to say something but it was too low to hear. Seismic.

Images in my head whirred away at triple speed. The fire landing face down. The ignition of carpet. Followed swiftly by skirting board, wallpaper, curtains, bed and Miss Williams. Suddenly one hamster seemed remarkably unimportant in the whole scheme of things. I was stripped of my dog-collar, after all the expenses of refurbishment were removed from my bank account. It seems that was another bit of St Cedric's policy that was still waiting to be read. No job, no rent money. My belongings were hurled unceremoniously into the street.

Geez, my mind could really shift when it wanted to.

Shame about my body.

I stood there, motionless, while the fire tumbled towards destruction. My destruction.

I screamed in the privacy of my head, yelling for a chance, for something, anything to stop the impending disaster. I knew the dull thud of red-hot element on shag pile was moments away. 'Oh God, no, please no!'

I was surprised when I heard a clang. Metal on metal.

And everything went back to normal speed. Okay, so the hamster cage was a total write-off and was starting to melt, but it had saved me. Somehow, it had ended up half-way across the room, directly underneath the fire. Don't ask me how.

I did a double take.

'Extinguisher,' I heard her say, as the bedding ignited with a crackle. I was on it in a second, cracking the release valve and squirting foam like a trooper.

It was out in moments. Thank God.

Thank God?

I couldn't help it. I looked up. No. He couldn't have . . . surely? He wouldn't interfere with anything as trivial as a falling electric fire? Well, unless there was something special about the consequences of it hitting carpet. My mind began to spin. It couldn't be anything to do with me, could it? I had to stay alive so I could affect the world in some special unique . . . Get a grip, man. Too much *Quantum Leap*.

My jaw hung limply open. The question haunting my brain. What had just happened?

I knew damned well it had been none of my doing. Even if I had been capable of hurling a hamster cage across the room faster than gravity could shift an electric fire, I was certain I would've missed. Just ask my basketball teacher at school. Accuracy, zero. Effort, zero.

So it must have been Him, right?

Or her? No way. She was still in bed. And besides, nobody could move that fast. Could they?

We scratched our chins and looked at each other, mystified.

'Er, I don't know how to say this . . . but,' I heard her say, 'I think you did that.' I was sure the jangly guitars from *The Twilight Zone* were only moments away.

I wasn't sure whether to laugh. Or scream. Or just carry on mopping up the foam from the floor.

The foam won. It was the safest option. And besides, it had to be done. I'd be jobless in minutes if I left the smouldering wreckage of a destroyed hamster cage on the carpet.

'I'm not kidding,' I heard her say. 'I think you did it.'

'Yeah, right. Whatever you say.' Well, what do you say to someone who's convinced they've seen you suddenly crack telekinesis? Humour her and get out. It was probably safest.

'I've never seen anything move that fast. Tell me how you did it.'

That was it, too much for me. I scooped the last of the charred wreckage and foam into my bucket and stood up. 'I don't know what you're trying to do here, but change the record.'

'Okay. Who am I?'

It wasn't a question I'd expected. I had no time for games. 'You know who you are. You're Miss Williams. Audrey Williams.'

'And my address?'

I scowled as I grabbed her chart from the end of her bed and for the first time I noticed just how little it said. Well, it wasn't my job to look at their charts. Nosiness was a sin, I think.

'What about my occupation? Or next of kin? Or treatment?'

'Don't ask me,' I shrugged. 'Try a qualified member of staff.'

'There isn't one in here.'

'I'll send you one.'

'No, wait. Just answer me two more questions.' She grabbed at my elbow. There was something in her eyes that made me stop in my tracks. Desperation verging on panic, I think. Although expressions aren't my strong suit.

'Okay, just two. Then I'm out of here.' I pulled my elbow free and folded my arms, bucket of debris at my feet. A picture of the stroppy cleaner.

'Look, is it normal to be scared of . . . of hamsters? Be honest.'

Personally, I couldn't believe I was hearing this. It was a wind-up. Had to be. The chances of two people in the same room being scared of those small, furry rodents with black, deep eyes were minuscule. Only someone who'd suffered trauma could be scared of them, surely? I mean, okay, if they'd caused serious damage to the odd finger or two, then maybe a bit of apprehension would be entirely understandable. But there were no scars on her fingers. No scars anywhere, in fact. She was perfection.

'Well?' she begged.

I wasn't going to give her the satisfaction. 'People are scared of different things. Me, it's unemployment. I've got to go.' I edged toward the door with the distinct feeling she wasn't over-impressed with the answer.

'One more, you said.'

I nodded, hand on the handle, key at the ready.

'How do you like your steak?'

'Get a life, you weirdo. There are ethical considerations about asking your cleaner out.'

I slammed the door and locked it.

'Answer me,' I heard her call.

'Well, if you must know,' I whispered through the keyhole. 'Well done. But don't tell anyone I said so.' And I cringed. There was definitely something wrong with me today if I was flirting with patients . . . sorry, 'clients'. So it had been a traumatic day, but that was no excuse for it.

No excuse at all.

I raised my eyes to Heaven as I hurried off down the corridor. 'Look, it's not every day you get to see a miracle, is it? Well, actually I suppose it is for you. Me, I'm just . . . look, when I've sorted my head out I'll get back to you, okay?'

17

There's feeling nervous, and then there's the throat-knotting terror of . . . well, being really nervous, I guess. I was stood in the corridor outside His Worship's office, and for the first time I reckon I understood how St Bernadette felt after clapping eyes on the Virgin Mary.

Okay, so in the grand scheme of all things miraculous a flying hamster cage wasn't exactly premier league, but I'd seen it. One minute it was on one side of the room, a quick prayer and *whoosh*, disaster is avoided. I didn't do it. Miss Williams didn't do it. So what's left?

I peered once more beyond the ceiling and felt strangely light-headed. For one thing it didn't make sense. I know He works in mysterious ways, but what in His name did He think He was going to achieve by stopping an explosion in a hospital room?

I kept coming back to ever more absurdist *Quantum Leap* theories. That the miracle of the cage had happened to save me for some amazing deed of immense importance to the human race. Or that somehow it was Miss Williams who had been saved. But why? For herself? Or her offspring? And just who was it that was going to provide the essentials necessary for that particular miracle? I shuddered. I shouldn't be thinking thoughts like that. Well, not so close to the bishop's office anyhow.

I hadn't a clue why I'd witnessed a miracle. I just knew I needed to talk it through with someone with a better grasp of His ways. The bishop would help.

If he didn't laugh me out of St Cedric's first. 'Er, Your Worship, I've just seen a miracle. Honest. See, there was this fire and a hamster cage and . . .'

How did Bernadette do it? Did she walk into the local police station, point to a photofit of one Mary, Virgin, aka Blessed Mother of God, and announce, 'Yup, that's her. She's up in them there hills.'

I felt like my head was going to explode. I simply had to tell him something.

I raised my hand to his door. And was nearly trampled by the pair of them. I was almost certain they didn't see me. They just dashed out of his office, talking wildly. And I didn't understand a word of it.

'But it's impossible,' hissed His Holiness. 'Never happened before.'

'That doesn't mean it's impossible,' countered Lyndsey, hurrying to keep up. 'We've never dealt with such deep cover before.'

'But you can't be certain.'

'And we can't afford to be uncertain. There's too much at stake here. Put her under again.'

'We need more tests.'

'But the baked Alaska should be all you need.'

They disappeared around a corner in a flurry of cassocks.

'Excuse me,' I called. 'Er, I think I've just seen a miracle.'

There was no reply.

'Oh well,' I muttered. 'There's bound to be another two along soon enough. They always come in threes, don't they?'

18

It wasn't a simple trick, walking quietly. Hooves and polished stone floors make a real racket. Unless one has been practising. In another fifty or so years the butler would be totally inaudible if he wanted to be.

Carrying a tray bearing a cold lava, he entered Seirizzim's study and headed for the desk. As he had expected, the distant bookcase was ajar, offering tantalising glimpses into the room beyond.

However, he hadn't expected the view to be quite so obscured. Curtains of cooling vapour flooded out on to the floor. Plumes of condensing gas rolled off a host of vast, humming refrigeration units in a flagrant abuse of every power law in Mortropolis.

The butler's jaw dropped as he caught sight of his master huddled inside the cold room, wrapped in a cocoon of blanketry.

Avoiding the torrents of icy air, the butler held his breath and listened to the whispers from his master's voice.

'Who's a good boy, eh? Look what daddy's got for you. Nice and fresh. Yum.'

The butler watched in mounting amazement as Seirizzim's heavily gloved talons rummaged about in the sack and pulled out a palmful of small black and white objects. Black and white seeds.

'C'mon, eat them up.'

Burning with curiosity, the butler placed the tray soundlessly on the desk and peered past the bookcase to get a better view. He squinted into the not-so-secret room.

Barely visible through the curtains of coolant, his master sat cross-legged on the floor, back to the door, staring devotedly at the something that was held in his left claw.

'You must be hungry. C'mon, eat up your seeds. Yes, that's it.'

And, as if on cue, it hopped into Seirizzim's open palm.

The butler forgot to breathe as he saw the tiny golden hamster peeling a sunflower seed with expert teeth.

It was the very last thing he saw for a long time. Without warning, a jet-black sack was pulled down over his head and what felt like a dozen arms bundled him noiselessly out of the room.

'That you?' called Seirizzim nervously, hiding his pet. All he saw was a slowly warming glass of lava on the desk, just as he had ordered.

56

Faith, Hope and Security

July 24, Maiden Castle, Dorsetshire.

Dear Logbook,

Must remind myself to look up what the abbreviation for Dorsetshire is. Ray is convinced it's just Dorset. But then how can I possibly trust someone who smokes the thin cigarettes he does? I feel sure he is less likely to know what day it is than any of us.

Our travels take us west today. Party in good spirit. Although Bernstein the younger is somewhat restless. Doesn't believe we're ever going to witness anything resembling otherworldly forces. How impatient are the youth of today? Certain he blames me for our recent misses.

Circumvolents and stridulars have dominated the runes lately. Good chance of something big.

Crossed into Dorsetshire 20.42. No sign again. Typical. Stopped for petrol and chunky Kit-Kat on outskirts of Dorchester.

Arr. Maiden Castle 22.08. Gates locked. Bernstein the elder forgot bolt cutters; had to scramble over fence. Still, cheaper that way. Wind N.N.W., Force 4 easing. Vigil established at west entrance 22.24. Drizzle started 22.26. Complaints started 22.27. Heavens opened 22.34. Mission abandoned 22.35 due to wet socks.

Party remain unconvinced of my belief that rain was summoned to drive us away. Why they cannot see signs I don't know.

Journey home subdued.

Avge mpg 16.8. Moderate.

P.S. Ray rolled six circumvolents. Sense something big is on its way. Bigger even than the Llanvihangel-nant-Melan vision of 1976. Fingers crossed.

19

The sound of running feet echoed down the corridor and pounded to a halt outside the door.

'Lock and load.'

Ammunition clips were thrust home with the heels of hands.

'Positions.'

The squad drew back, encircling the door. Knees bent, sprung for action.

'Fire!'

Hinges exploded in a hail of bullets. Shoulders hit the door and the squad were in, rolling for cover. Laser tracers shone through the smoke, looking for targets. Anything that moved.

Or was simply too terrified to move.

Automatic fire riddled into the large wooden desk, instant woodworm. Full metal jacket. Terminal.

It was more than the hiding secretary could stand. She freaked. Screamed and dashed for the door. She was mince in seconds.

'Yes! Five thousand points!' grinned Tony Keswick, waggling his joystick for all it was worth. 'Now to nix the President!'

'Nice move, Your Worship,' said Meekins, the Staff Improvement Liaison Officer, looking down over his shoulder. 'Is that level six?'

'Eleven, buffoon,' answered the Mayor of Camford. His eyes didn't leave the screen.

'Eleven? You are doing well.'

'The power of training, my boy.' For a split second his finger left the joystick and pointed to a certificate in the wastepaper basket. Meekins picked it up.

'Oh, I see you took up my suggestion for that course. "Computers: Usage, Abusage and Timewasting – Part Five." Nice. The council taxpayers will be pleased to see how you are embracing modern technology.' As he dropped the certificate in for recycling, his heart swelled with pride. It was good to be working for such an appreciative man. If only more mayors would put themselves out the way Tony Keswick did, the country would be a better place. Meekins smiled with admiration as he considered just what Keswick did for the community. It was amazing the way, at the drop of a hat, he'd sacrifice his whole social life to go off on a World Cruise, just to prove to himself and his voters that you *could* access the Camford County Council Website from New York, or Melbourne or Tahiti. Amazing. Such devotion. Such love for Camford.

'Hardest two damn weeks I've ever had in the Bahamas, that was. Lessons for half an hour every day. Slavedrivers.' Feverishly, the mayor ground away at the joystick, skipping a helicopter over a fence. Fast and low. Under the radar. A gun emplacement vanished under two sidewinder missiles.

'The Bahamas? Ahh yes, I thought I detected a tan.'

'Still, it wasn't all toil. They threw in a free copy of this.'

Meekins looked at the game box. It showed a white-haired middle-American political type lying in a pool of blood and debris on the White House lawn. ' "Die You Presidential Bastard!" Tasteful. Was the hotel up to scratch?'

'Only five star,' scowled Mayor Keswick, sending his troops into the President's private villa. Fourteen dobermans expired messily in a rain of gunfire. 'Geckos in the sauna. Still, what d'you expect for five grand a week?'

'Hmmm, makes this month's suggestions seem a mite penny-pinching. Still, there's one I'm sure you'd enjoy.'

A grenade took out the front door and a shiny sports car that just happened to have been left there. 'Yes! The lucky Ferrari. Spent all last week with my laptop on the beach looking for that. Extra thousand points. So, what you got for me?'

Meekins looked at the three glossy brochures in his hand. ' "Public Manipulation Skills Module Eight: Kissing Babies the Germ-Free Way." Bournemouth. November. But there is a mini-bar in the hotel.'

'Euch. No way. Mini-bar's tempting though. Next.'

' "Transcendental Accounting: Make Millions by Meditation." Loughborough. Twenty-seventh of—'

'Send Figgis.'

'He's dead. There's a good Chinese in town,' he offered, trying to make it all the more enticing.

'You like Chinese? Send yourself. Next.' Three state senators were decapitated by a stray Sam missile.

'Now, hear me out on this one. It's in Sweden in two weeks' time and it's a seminar on, well . . .'

'C'mon, man, spit it out. I've got things to do.' An armoured car ploughed across the front lawn. 'It's a seminar on what?'

'Ahem. Breast awareness.'

'What?' The armoured car crashed through a brick wall. 'What kind of a topic is that? That's a woman thing. I don't want anything to do with women's things—'

'That's what I thought. At first. But, er, may I introduce Doctor Ophelia Hawny. She's come all the way from Sweden.'

It could have been the way her white lab coat reflected off the computer screen. Or maybe it was the highlights in her

Abba-blonde hair that did it. But, for the first time in three and a half hours, Mayor Tony Keswick turned away from the computer screen.

Standing almost six foot in her stilettos, the good doctor stood gently teasing her stethoscope. Slowly, she winked over the top of her wire-framed spectacles.

Keswick's jaw dropped.

'I'll, er, leave you to it,' whispered Meekins, backing towards the door. He was ignored.

Doctor Hawny placed a CD player on the mayor's desk, slipped in 'Now That's What I Call Lap-Dancing Vol 1' and flicked play. The room filled with sultry saxophones and a long slow rhythm.

Keswick heard none of it. He was transfixed by the woman's hips as they rose and fell in time with the music, pulsing beneath freshly starched cotton labwear. He should have been looking higher up. Slowly, as she licked her lips, she began unpopping her press-studs with a perfectly manicured thumbnail.

'Breast Awareness . . . two weeks did you say?' whispered Keswick. The labcoat slid to the floor and she stepped forward wearing nothing but a smile, stilettos, spectacles and a very lucky stethoscope.

Behind him the President took full advantage of the distraction and barricaded himself into his bunker. Government troops surrounded the armoured car and opened fire.

Keswick heard none of it. For some reason his mind was elsewhere.

20

Bishop Hutchinson whirled around a corner in his customary flurry of cassock, pulled his keys out from a secret pocket and let himself in through the highly reinforced door.

'It's not as bad as it seems,' he insisted to Brother Lyndsey, as he tugged at the oddly gothic-looking light switch. Barely slowing, they hurried down the narrow stone steps with the expertise of those all too familiar with their surroundings. Anyone else would have hesitated on the badly chipped tread of the fourth step down and reached for the rusting chain which passed as a banister.

'But how can you be so sure?' pleaded Lyndsey, panting to keep up.

'Faith,' tutted the bishop, galloping into the cellar and flicking on another light. A cobwebbed expanse spread out before them, looking disturbingly like a strange cross between a champagne store and a long-disused James Bond set. It smelled of damp, mould and too many mice.

'I'll settle for hope and security,' muttered Lyndsey.

For the first time in half a mile, the bishop stopped and whirled around to face his colleague. 'Look, we haven't had any problems before, have we?'

Lyndsey only barely avoided the collision. 'Well, no, but–'

'There you go, then.' And he was off at full speed again.

'But Your Holiness, Miss Williams's Stimulus Reactivity Test showed categorically that–'

'There was no hamster in the cage.'

'Er, yes.'

'And since there was no stimulus, there would naturally be no reaction, would there?'

'Er, no . . . but . . .'

'Everything else she has said, her dislike of undercooked Sirloin and a preference for charcoally baked Alaska, all that's just personal taste. There is nothing wrong with her.'

'But they are remarkably peculiar tastes.'

The bishop fixed Brother Lyndsey with a surprisingly fatherly look. 'Sometimes,' he began, his voice heavy with implied wisdom, 'women can be peculiar. Fact of life. You know, it's not that unusual for some women to crave soil or tuna fish and cranberry pizzas.'

Lyndsey shook his head in confusion. He was sure that was something to do with the weirdness that was pregnancy. And a thought hit him. She wasn't pregnant, was she? No, she couldn't possibly be. Not after six weeks surrounded by men of the cloth. And she certainly hadn't started out pregnant. That was definite. For a moment he began to wonder if any of this had been a good idea.

'But what if it's the first signs?' pleaded Lyndsey. 'What if she's rejecting—'

'You are right to be concerned,' interrupted the bishop, pulling a cloth off a large cage. 'And whilst I am convinced that there is nothing wrong with the procedure, it would be a dereliction of my duty to ignore it. Er . . . bring me that one, would you?' He pointed to a somewhat overlarge piebald mouse spread casually on top of a clump of other panting rodents. 'I'll scrub up.'

Brother Lyndsey breathed a sigh of relief. He was being listened to after all. Faith was all well and good in their business, but a bit too much of it could be dangerous, especially in potentially volatile situations like these.

The sound of splashing holy water echoed around the cellar as the bishop anointed his forehead and dabbed a little oil behind his ears.

Lyndsey dropped the confused mouse into an old baptismal font and stood back. Much to the rodent's relief, it was empty and had been lined with shredded newspaper.

'Er, would you mind?' said the bishop, pointing to a pair of incense burners. 'The matches are in that cupboard.'

'Do you want the joss sticks today?'

'No, no. I think I overdid them last time.'

'Yes, it took a week for my eyes to stop itching,' observed Lyndsey, disappearing in a cloud of blue smoke as the incense caught.

'Now for the hard bit,' grumbled the bishop, smoothing out a large book on a lectern. 'Why do they insist this has to be done . . .', the sound of cracking bones echoed noisily for a few moments, '. . . kneeling. I tell you, if they tried to introduce this today the Health and Safety guys would have something to say.'

'Too right,' agreed Lyndsey as he peered through a growing cloud of smoke. 'Has anyone ever done a CoSSH risk assessment for incense? And what about myrrh?'

'Let's just get on with it before my knees give up. Ready?'

Lyndsey nodded and began swinging the pair of burners in slow figures of eight.

Almost immediately, Bishop Hutchinson launched into a barrage of machine-gun Latin. Rapid-fire, incessant and monotonous.

Brother Lyndsey was certain that to be a real success in all things ecclesiastical there had to be something seriously wrong with your airways. He was sure that there was some knack of breathing in through your nose whilst chanting. Or was it the other way round? Was that why high Latin always sounded so nasal?

He waggled the burners closer to the bishop. Maybe if he could just get some smoke in the right place he'd be able to determine air flows and figure it out.

As usual he was just too late. With a particularly Gregorian-sounding Amen, the chanting stopped and silence crept back into the cellar.

Well, it would have been silent if it hadn't been for the squeaks of confusion emanating from the baptismal font. There was a scuffling of claw on paper, a brief scratching at stone and then a peculiar sigh of rodent disappointment.

'Has it work . . . ?'

The bishop put a finger to his lips and struggled to his feet. His knees objected in their customary fashion.

Moments later, an overweight piebald fruitbat struggled its way on to the lip of the font and paused to catch its breath. The bishop smiled with satisfaction.

'Any moment now,' he whispered, admiring the shape of its ears. 'Got them just right.'

And, almost before he was ready for it, the fruitbat jumped. For a moment it seemed to hover in the air, lip curled, wings flapping desperately.

And then gravity had it.

Trying desperately to soar majestically on the leathern wings it could suddenly see and feel on its body, it fell a good three feet. Baffled by the way air seemed to pass straight through its airsurfaces as if they weren't there, it crash-landed in a safety net of cassock.

'There you go. Nothing wrong with that,' grinned His Holiness. The rodent disagreed. 'Amazing what a few thousand years of honing can do to the water-into-wine miracle. A perfect-looking fruitbat, functional in everything other than that ever-elusive thing called flight. Shame I can't get a bit of levitation in there, too. Might look into that.'

'All right, so I was wrong. Maybe Miss Williams will be fine.'

'Oh ye of little faith,' tutted the bishop and tossed what appeared to be a very confused fruitbat on to a nearby desk. A look of irritation crossed its forehead as it thrashed pathetically amongst the piles of research papers and wondered why aerodynamics were suddenly proving so difficult.

A golden hamster sat contentedly in the centre of a foot-wide gloved palm and stuffed yet another sunflower seed into its cheek pouch. It cheerfully ignored the special-effects-fest of vapour falling in cold curtains around it, cooling it from the current ambient of Fahrenheit 666 – the temperature at which devils are the happiest. It was probably better for its rodent mind that it didn't realise quite how quickly it would be toast if the fridges packed up.

'Now come on, Horatio, if you're not going to eat them I'm going to put you away. You're not as cute when you're not eating them.' Seirizzim grinned to himself as his mind filled with an image of his pet rodent up on its hind legs nibbling at a seed. 'Besides, I'm getting cold. One more.'

With surprising dexterity, the demon tugged another minute sunflower seed out of a sack and held it out. It was in the hamster's mouth in seconds.

'Right, that's it. Time's up.' With uncharacteristic genti-lity, Seirizzim placed his pet in the centre of its enclosure and refitted the lid. 'I'll see you later.' He shivered and blew the oblivious creature what passed as a kiss or thereabouts. It just avoided a ninety per cent scorching.

In moments he had shut the bookcase and was stripping off his layers of thermals, amazed that anything would actually choose to live in such a cold climate. But then it was an amazing world up there. Imagine a place where lead was actually frozen solid. He shivered, caught sight of the lava on the table and found himself aching for something hot. A decent half-fat magmacino would really go down a treat right now.

He took a breath, ready to call for his butler, and stopped in his tracks. A hot magmacino might raise suspicions. Might cause questions . . .

What the hell, just so long as nobody found out about his illegal pet there wouldn't be a problem. And he was good at keeping secrets now. After all, he'd used a dozen different refrigeration contractors. No one suspected a thing.

'Butler!' he called, clicking his talons. 'Bring me a . . . Butler? Where are you?'

Seirizzim found himself shivering. And this time it wasn't from the cold.

22

There are certain topics of conversation that you can come across in the normal course of an average day and you won't think anything of it. The weather's a good example, especially if you're British. Sport's often another.

But baked Alaska?

If I was nearing the end of a particularly comprehensive catering course, I might have expected it. Working as a dog-collared cleaner in the employ of St Cedric's Hostel for the Less Than Perfectly Well, I'd guess it would crop up with the regularity of moons of a blue-ish hue.

And yet today, in the space of less than an hour and a half, I'd heard mention of that very dessert from two totally independent mouths. I felt sure this wasn't normal. Statistically speaking, there was unlikely to be much in common between a Roman Catholic bishop and an up-until-recently comatosed brunette. Surely it was millions to one against that common ground being cooked ice-cream products.

Factor in a certain young woman's curiosity as to how I prefer my sirloin, sprinkle with an unhealthy fascination regarding Brother Lyndsey's urges to 'put her under again' and, frankly, I was beginning to wonder about what Miss Williams was in for. I was starting to sense that there was more to her than met the eye. Which was something of a surprise since she was quite an eyeful. Those curves . . . ahem.

I know that curiosity has allegedly been known to cause the death of many a feline and that murder is a definite no-no where the Commandments are concerned but, well, surely apathy's a sin, too? Just ask any passing good Samaritan if you're not convinced. I had to do something about the questions multiplying in my head.

Nervously, I turned the key and let myself into room six.

'Er, when I say well done, I mean *really* well done.' I suppose I should have started with something else, but my mind was a seething mass of query. You try mundane pleasantries when your brain's boiling. It's not easy.

Strangely enough, she knew exactly what I was talking about.

'Like leather?' she asked, sitting up in bed again.

'Grilled leather.'

'That's been barbecued already.'

I nodded.

'I knew it.'

'You . . . you did?' I took a step backwards. I never like it when people said that. Makes me feel sort of inferior. Like I haven't really been paying attention to who I am. Like I'm an amateur at being me.

'As soon as I saw you I knew it.'

'What? You're saying you can tell how I like my steak just by looking at me?' I looked myself up and down. What was the giveaway? Not the clothes for sure. Jeans, T-shirt, apron and dog-collar. Nothing unusual there.

'Well, not exactly, it's more . . . a feeling . . . like we've got something in common. Kindred spirits maybe. Oh, I don't know.' She shook her head.

'Look, it's just that coming-out-of-a-coma thing. You know, the first thing you see you sort of get attached to.'

'That's things coming out of eggs,' she tutted.

'Oh.'

'Don't tell me you can't feel it?'

I shrugged.

I could feel something, but that was to do with the fact that she was utterly naked. And I wasn't going to admit to that. Not being in my profession. That way lay eternal damnation. 'Feel what exactly?'

'That I can do things for you.' She looked up from under her fringe.

I took a step backwards as damnation beckoned. 'Things?' I stuttered. 'What sort of things?' It was one of those questions I was sure I shouldn't have asked. But it was out there before I realised I'd spoken.

'Well . . . anything.'

'Ahh.' Of all the things she could have said, I was hoping that wouldn't be it. That was a very leading thing. Damnation grinned.

'Anything at all,' she added.

'Look, I . . . I think I've got to be somewhere. I've got some, er . . . Bibles to wash or something. It's been really nice talking and . . .'

She was out of bed and across the room in seconds, standing palms against the door, chest heaving. 'No, don't leave, you can't. Not yet. You've got to go with me on this.'

'Miss Williams . . .' I missed stern by a good light-year. It came out as a squeak. God, what was I, mouse or man?

'Tell me what you want? I can give it to you.'

'I really must be . . .'

'C'mon. Tell me what it is you want. Anything you desire.'

'I'll scream.' It was a hollow threat and I knew it. The

trouble I'd be in if anyone saw us. The tabloids would think it was Christmas.

'We connect, you and I. We're kindred spirits. Whatever you want I can make it happen. Think of the cage.'

She just let the last sentence hang there. Floating in the air, nagging deep into my mind. I had to ask. 'What about the cage?' My finger tugged at the ringpull on a shiny new can of worms.

'That was me,' she grinned. 'I did it.'

'Ahh, now come on. How can you say that? You were nowhere near it.'

'I'm not saying I know how I did it, just that I did. It's a bit of a mystery to me. But I sensed you wanted something doing and . . . well, it happened, didn't it?'

Reluctantly, I nodded.

'You don't believe me, do you?'

I shrugged.

'Okay, I'll prove it. Tell me something you want, something you really, really want and I'll do it. I'll give it to you. Right here, right now.'

I felt myself blush. I'd heard of some chat-up lines but that was ridiculously forward.

'No, not that. Sorry, but I don't think you're my type.'

'What?' I was sure there was more than a whisker of disappointment in my voice. But then, I've never been good at rejection.

'Think of something else. Go on, you know you want to.'

She was right. Try as I might – and I was trying remarkably hard – I couldn't actually find anything she'd said I could really disagree with. Other than her choice of men, of course, but that was a man/pride/ego thing.

'C'mon. What'll it be?'

'Lottery ticket,' I said. It was the first thing that came into my head.

'That all? I can give you anything you want and you go for that. Not very imaginative, is it?'

'Look, it's been a hard day. Give me a lottery ticket.'

'Any particular one?'

Somehow I had the impression that she was teasing.

'A winning one.'

'Done,' she grinned and headed back to the bed.

I stood in the middle of the purple carpet, a sense of severe anticlimax growing between my shoulder blades. 'Er . . . and that's it?' Well, what had I expected? Pyrotechnics, as a gilded lottery ticket materialised Kirk-like in the palm of my hand?

'You didn't say you wanted fanfares as well. Give me a moment, I'm sure I can supply a small brass—'

'Forget it,' I tutted, marching toward the door. 'And cancel the TV crews, too.' I stormed out of the room feeling utterly foolish. Totally stupid. God, was I gullible.

I shook my head as I locked the door and trudged away down the corridor. It was odd, I suddenly found myself feeling sorry for Miss Williams. I mean, she was bound to still be a bit weird in the head. Comas aren't exactly normal for most people. There were probably bits of her brain that were still mush. Yeah, that'll be it. Or maybe it was an attempt at getting attention. Hmmm, bit psychological that one, but there was a nugget of truth in there, maybe.

'Face it,' I heard myself mutter in a far from cheerful voice. 'You're just pissed off this isn't an episode of *The X-Files*. Admit it, you're watching way too much TV. Get a life, man. Go bowling, read a book, do a watercolour. Anything.'

I shrugged. The thing with the cage was probably easily explained too. Guess I just tripped and knocked it across the room. Just a lucky trip, yeah, that'll be it. Simple. Nothing out of the ordinary at all.

Shame that, though.

Boring.

23

In his office, Mayor Keswick was panting hard. 'More! More! Make me more aware. I want to know everything!'

Docter Ophelia Hawny placed a perfectly manicured two-inch fingernail on his lips. 'Oh no. Not yet.'

'Now, now! Please!'

'I am thinking not. After all, there wouldn't be any point in you coming to Sweden.' She stepped backwards off his lap and reached for her lab coat.

'But . . . wait. No. You've raised a worthy issue here.'

'Not the only thing I've raised.' She smiled as she folded a very large cheque into her pocket. 'Very generous.'

'Well, it was the least I could do.'

Slowly, she squeezed her final press-stud shut and turned the CD-player off. 'See you in a fortnight. I'll be waiting at the airport.'

'I'll be counting the hours,' whispered Keswick, wiping his brow. He knew his time was up. But hey, there would another two weeks of that personal, hands-on tuition to come.

With a final blown kiss, she slid out through the door and headed straight for the bank.

Keswick settled back in his leather office chair and sighed. Already he knew the next fourteen days would seem interminable. Stretching out for ever, endless lonely afternoons in the council chambers—

Suddenly there was a knock on the door. The handle

flicked and Keswick sat up as Dr Hawny strode back in on a clatter of stilettos. She marched purposefully across the room.

'So, you just couldn't stay away,' grinned Keswick, failing to pout attractively.

She placed a delicately turned knee on his chair and, leaning forward, snatched a long black item from the back of the chair. 'Forgot my stethoscope.' And in a flash of calf and white linen she was out of the door.

He wasn't alone for long.

'Ready for your five o'clock?' called a voice from the door.

'What?' Keswick's gaze flicked to the clock on the far wall. 'But it's nearly half six.'

'You were, er, otherwise detained,' winked Haskins, the Deputy-In-Charge of Funding Outsourcing and Minion-In-Charge of Creative Unemployment Opportunities. 'A successful meeting?'

Keswick's eyes rolled.

'I take that as a yes. I have a strange feeling this meeting won't be quite as exciting. However, the council coffers will benefit if you agree to the suggestions which I–'

Stop,' hissed Keswick. 'Which hat are you wearing? Scum or funds?'

'Mmmm, bit of both.'

Keswick's face fell. Dealing with the unemployed was so boring. So namby-pamby, he thought. The good short sharp shock that was the workplace was what was needed for those wasters, not the chance to plant flowers in the middle of roundabouts for forty quid a week. Still, on the bright side, it saved on the gardening budget. 'Just get on with it,' groaned Keswick. 'Funding first and give it to me straight. No speeches. What's up for grabs this week?'

'Well, the Committee for the Advancement of Feng-Shui

in Local Government are offering a grant of up to fifteen grand to raise the profile of this ancient art.'

Keswick looked interested. 'Oh really? They'll give us cash to rearrange our furniture?'

'Got it in one.'

He looked around him. 'I was getting a bit bored with this office. Let's do it. Next.'

'The Genetic Modification Steering Group are offering twenty-seven thousand pounds to the first unitary council to start using non-genetically modified printer paper.'

Keswick scratched his chin. 'Hmmm, get on to Monsanto and see how much they'll offer us to be their GM printer paper flagship. I'm sure they'll be generous enough when we remind them their field licences are up for renewal soon.'

'Oh, that is clever, Your Worship.'

'Guess why I'm Mayor. Next?'

'Er, lace,' said Haskins.

'And what's that supposed to mean? Three weeks' tutorial on the intricacies of Bruges Lace in Soft Furnishings? Or Cotswold Cushion Covers Throughout the Victorian Era?'

'I didn't know you were so knowledgeable, Your Worship.'

'Er, well, I . . . my aunt used to . . .'

'Your secret's safe with me,' grinned Haskins. 'But the lace I mentioned is somewhat different. The kind that invades children's areas in schools, seeps across every computer network and appears in a host of inappropriate and offensive places.'

'You mean Tenerifan lace. Pah, that's not proper lace at all, that's just bits of stuff sewn together into vague—'

'Your Worship, this is the "lace problem" I'm talking about.' He placed a laptop on to the mayoral desk and brightened the screen.

'Oh my . . . Er, yes. Gosh, what a problem.' The pixels of

the screen positively vibrated with the image of buxom femininity clad in nothing but a few strands of cotton.

'I thought you would be interested in this scourge of our publicly accessed Internet space,' chuckled Haskins as Keswick's eyes widened. 'After all, the government is dishing out three quarters of a million pounds to investigate further. I do hope that you will be able to free up time to head a committee to stamp it out.'

'What? Stamp it out? But this is artistic and tasteful and—'

'That's not.' Haskins stabbed at the keyboard and the screen changed. Two women were doing a little more than holding hands with the minimal amount of lace present.

'Oooh, that's rude.' Keswick tilted his head. 'Whose hand is that? Hers or—'

'I believe that is something else. Something requiring batteries.'

'Oh. And you want me to stamp this out?' His eyes didn't move from the screen.

'Before one can make such sweeping alterations to your voters' personal liberties, one must determine if there is a problem. And if one is to claim there is a problem, one must have a complete understanding of the situation. I have taken the liberty of signing this terminal up to seven hundred and sixty-nine similar sites for your perusal. Shall I get the paperwork moving?'

'You mean I can get cash for looking at this?'

'Doesn't one love Her Majesty's Government?'

'Indeed.' Keswick rubbed his palms together as he flipped to another web-site. 'Is that all? God, are they real?'

'Just one more thing. You remember a few months ago we secured a grant from the Inner City Identity Creation Board?'

Keswick looked blank. His mind was already lost to Internet sex.

'You remember? The quarter of a million to put on a festival-type celebration which reflected the diversity and vibrancy of local culture,' prompted Haskins to deaf ears. 'That was the reason you went to Rio for Mardi Gras and Munich for the Oktoberfest. Research.'

'You've found another one?' asked Keswick absently. 'Another week's festival research?'

'Er, no, sir. It's about the Camford Festival of Arts and Stuff. The good news is that the artists' fees have been kept to the barest minimum and that we still pocket a good eighty-five per cent.'

'And the bad news?'

'Curtain up tomorrow. And you have an opening speech to deliver.'

'What?'

'The CCTV division of the police have informed me that clowns and morris men have been seen arriving,' answered Haskins proudly.

Keswick was underwhelmed. 'Oh, tell them I've got a sore throat or something. I hate speeches. Leave me to peruse this valuable piece of, er . . . evidence you have left.' His finger flicked across the keyboard and another screenful of fleshy curves appeared. Waving a dismissive hand, he turned his attention to the screen. Already feeling his pulse beginning to quicken, he opened another site. Acres of tender young women lay draped in a variety of exotic poses. He knew some would dismiss it instantly as nothing but gratuitous pornography. But he knew that was a mistake. A short-sighted approach, he convinced himself, as he made himself all the more breast-aware.

24

Looking very small and insignificant beneath the curve of the thirteenth-century vaulted ceiling, a small piebald fruit-bat rustled amongst research papers. It flapped what it thought was its leathery wings and yet again failed to produce anything remotely resembling lift. Rodent curiosity fizzed in the forefront of its mind. It was sure it had experienced the joys of flight, the rush of wind through its whiskers, the sheer euphoria of being one with the air.

Okay, so the confused mouse couldn't tell the difference between soaring and falling, but it knew deep in its scampering heart that somehow it was no longer merely a beast of the earth. Baring incisors with the effort, it shuffled up to the horizon that was the desk edge and pushed off.

'I mean, there must be a way to do it,' muttered Bishop Hutchinson, his eyes buried deep in a vast illustrated manuscript. 'Angels do it all the time so there's got to be something . . .' His train of thought was interrupted by the dull thud of piebald rodent hitting peripheral computer hardware. 'What the . . . ?' He scowled at the mouse spread-eagled on the flatbed scanner. 'Idiot creature. Now where was I?'

'Well, that would be looking into the many and varied aspects of the phenomenon known as levitation,' offered Brother Lyndsey, his face creasing in concern as the mouse struggled to its paws and shook its head.

'Ahhh, yes. Birds do it, bees do it, maybe educated priests could do it.' He returned his gaze to the gold-encrusted pages dealing with all aspects of angels. 'Feather maintenance and grooming, nope. Magnetism and navigational skills, nope. Oh, I wish this thing was in alphabetical order. Let's see, what's this? Calcium: lack of, effect on eggshell integrity. What? I didn't know angels—'

'It knows, you know,' said Lyndsey, in a voice full of meaning. Donald Pleasance would have been proud. 'It can tell.' He pointed to the mouse on the scanner as it angled its head and peered at its reflection on the glass plate. 'It suspects.'

'Nonsense,' tutted the bishop. 'It's merely . . .'

As if on cue the rodent picked up a forepaw and started flapping. Its brow furrowed suspiciously.

'But, that can't be. It should be convinced it's a bat. It looks like a bat, behaves like a bat . . .'

'It can't fly like a bat,' pointed out Lyndsey. 'I'm telling you, it knows something's wrong. And it's going to figure it out.'

'Rubbish.'

The mouse started struggling over towards a handy table lamp, shinned eight inches up the stand and attempted to hang there from its back paws. A dull thud later and it had a nosebleed.

'Still don't believe me?'

'Yes, but that's just a mouse . . .'

'On the verge of a breakthrough.' He flicked his eyes towards the upper floors. 'We've got to put her back under. Just to make sure. If she starts remembering—'

'Look, in over two thousand years of this sort of thing, nobody's ever reported a failed miracle. They don't happen. Right from the start they've been spot on. Water into wine—'

'I know, perfect in every detail. People still had stinking hangovers a week later. But you can't tell me that mouse looks convinced. You ever seen a rodent that good at mime?'

The piebald creature grabbed at thin air behind it, took a breath and bit. It squeaked plaintively, the squeak of a mouse with a chewed tail.

'All right, all right. Let's give her a checkover,' agreed the bishop, heading out of the cellar.

'Put her back under,' insisted Lyndsey. 'Another week. Fifty cc Lourdes spring water i.v. Stat.'

'That might not be necessary. Just have a bit of faith, will you.'

25

There are definitely occasions when I really wonder if my brain is wired up the right way. You know, at times it feels like I've got all the right neurones, but just not necessarily in the right order. I suppose that could explain why logic and I are on different planets most of the time. I mean, who in their right mind would actually choose to walk past a pet shop after the day I'd just had?

Okay, so I was restless. Confused. In need of fresh air. Fine. But of all the streets in the whole of Camford I could have chosen to walk down, my subconscious chose this one.

How long I'd been there, staring at the hamsters in the window, I hadn't a clue. But it was going dark. And there was a damp trail on the ground where one of those street-sweeper things had detoured around me.

To anyone passing by it was as if I was just staring at them. A man transfixed by a ball of five golden hamsters piled in the corner of a cage, their chests rising and falling unnaturally fast. Probably have me down as being mad. Or homeless. Or both.

They couldn't see what was going on in the darkness inside my head. Good job I wasn't anywhere near a hospital. The radiation of firing synapses would have really stuffed up any CAT scans in a quarter-mile radius.

God, it was vivid. I was a microscopic droplet of Mr Sheen orbiting in for a crash landing on planet furball. Flash. Pull focus. Gaping nostrils loomed. Naked black holes disappearing into infinity. Flash. Hyper zoom. Walls of crimson tubes flashed past around me, curling, twisting red worm-holes. Branches careered off left, right. Deeper. Constricting. Flash. A red wall dead ahead. No warning, no time to pull out. Screaming collision. I powered into the back of a lung full-tilt. I was through the membrane and into the surging bloodstream. Doughnuts of red cells jostled me. Pounding. Flash. Zoom. The back of an eyeball headed towards me. I hit at max. Tearing sound, cavitation as I broke through the retina. Flash. I'm staring up at a man, manic grin, thumb turning pale as he squeezes the plunger of an aerosol. Flash. Cut to full widescreen spasms of dying rodent. Seismic rumbling as it collapses into a million acres of sunflower seeds. Eruptions of dust. Black-out.

I only snapped out of it when my cheek hit the shop window. In a split second, ten rodent eyes blinked open and stared up at me, accusingly. Reflecting me in tiny distorted ways. Terror and nausea fought with embarrassment.

'Mummy, that man doesn't look very well.' The young girl pointed up at me with the innocence of a five-year-old. 'Aren't you very well? Would you like a jelly baby?'

'Come away,' hissed her mother, glaring at me suspiciously. 'I've told you about people like that, haven't I?'

The girl thought for barely a moment. 'I got a Barbie for my birthday, would you like the cardboard box to live in? It's nice and red.'

'Sophie!' Her mother almost dislocated her shoulder in the haste to pull her away. 'People like you give Camford a bad name. Bad name.' She frog-marched her daughter off around the corner.

'But . . .'

'I don't want a *Big Issue*!'

What was it about today? It wasn't Friday the 13th. I

hadn't walked under any casually placed ladders and I was very certain that no stray black pussies had strolled across my path. I shook my head. It was just one of those day. File under 'Shitty'. Go home to bed. At least I'd be safe there.

I turned away from the shop window, pulled my coat up around my ears and shoved my hands deep into the pockets. A second later my thumb was in my mouth. Blood oozed from a paper cut. Damn, this was too much. Can't even put my hands in my pockets without coming out the worse for it.

Miserably, I put my hand back in my pocket and pulled out the offending piece of paper.

And I did a double-take. There, between bloodied thumb and forefinger, was a crisp new lottery ticket.

'Oh my God,' I whispered in shock.

26

Away across Camford, in room six of St Cedric's Hostel for the Less Than Perfectly Well, Audrey Williams was pacing about restlessly.

'Ungrateful git,' she grumbled to herself. 'Last time I give out any freebies.'

She pulled a single lemon-yellow sheet around herself and stared out of the window. Outside, the thoroughfare that was Jeroboam Hill was approaching its customary evening impasse. Cyclists struggled up the one in four, coughing out clouds of heavy diesel. Hosts of Transits tested their handbrakes to destruction. And many a clutch headed towards the scrap heap. It was a normal day. Audrey stared at it, bored.

It was the only thing left to her to do. After trying the door, jemmying the door, attempting to pick the lock and then just sulking, she was beginning to think that the only way out was using the correct key. They had her where they wanted her. Whoever they were. Right now, she wasn't actually sure she wanted to find out. She sighed as she thought about what she did know.

She was alive.

She was fussy about her food.

She hated hamsters.

But she was in one piece. And not too bad a piece at that if a certain cleaner's expression was anything to go by. He thought she hadn't seen him, but she had and she could tell what he thought. The way he'd tried to look away . . .

Still, those were the facts. The ones they had let her find out. It was obvious that things like who she was and what had happened to her and similar important stuff would have to wait. If they felt they had to keep such things from her then maybe, just maybe, it was best for her. Maybe it wouldn't do her any good to find out the truth.

Or maybe it could just be a simple admin error. Right now they could be digging her file out and heading off towards this very room, apologies at the ready. Yeah, right.

Her jaw settled on to the palms of her hands as she gawped out of the window.

Out beyond the walls of St Cedric's, waves of vehicles surged on to the streets and dribbled off, rapidly congealing towards a traffic jam. A strange smile crossed her face as a vast customised pantechnicon threaded itself gingerly on to Jeroboam Hill amid a crescendo of horns. This was more like it, she thought, a bit of conflict. A bit of entertainment.

The pantechnicon was decked out in a host of crimson and orange flames. Tacky, fourth-rate fairground realism, but there was something appealing about it. Maybe it was the row of cackling demons painted around the edges of the wheel arches. It shuddered three yards up the road on a plume of diesel and then slammed on its brakes. A BMW missed destroying its gleaming paintwork by millimetres as it squeezed in behind.

The driver of the BMW was out of the sunroof in a second. 'Watch where you're taking that thing. This is limited-edition "Chechnya" gun-metal grey. Five hundred quid a can.'

'Good job you didn't hit me then, ain't it,' shouted back the driver of 'The Infern-O-Rator-Twister – A Real Devil of a Ride'.

'That a threat?'

'Get a life. You'd've known if that was a threat.' The man in the cab peered for a moment into his rear-view mirror, sizing up his putative opponent. He wasn't impressed. Could take him out in seconds. He shrugged and reached for a packet of sweets perched on the passenger seat. It scrunched in a way that suggested the contents were more wrapper than boiled sweeties.

The traffic sloughed forward on its peristaltic squirm up the hill.

With childish delight, Mr Infern-O-Rator-Twister revved his ageing diesel and, exhaust blazing, made a great show of moving forward a full eighteen inches. The BMW was in behind him like a shot, just as he had suspected. Now he'd show him who was king of the road. He dropped his handbrake off and, in the same way that glaciers start to fall, the forty-ton fairground attraction began to roll backwards.

The BMW's was the first horn to be heard.

'. . . three . . . two . . . and . . .' A handbrake ratched on, sending shudders down the entire length of the truck. It stopped with a credit-card gap between rear bumper and prize gun-metal Beamer.

It amused all but one of the surrounding drivers no end.

'You got a licence for that thing?' squealed the BMW

driver. 'You got a licence for your face? Offensive weapon that is. Arsehole!'

The guy in the truck continued rummaging for any remaining sweeties. He didn't need hassle like this. He'd been with this truck of his since 1972 and he knew he could drive it anywhere. In fact he had. That carnival in '84 when he'd taken it up a one-thirtieth scale model of Sugar Loaf Mountain. That had been fun. Especially reversing down. He was good at reversing. Not backing down. That was different.

'I said, have you got a licence for it, eh? Arsehole!'

'Get a life, dick. Better still, go and get yourself laid. I hear that does wonders for stress.'

In her eagle's nest, Audrey settled down to watch further developments. This was feeling comfortably full of friction. Full of interest. It never occurred to her to ask why her pulse was quickening with the mounting tension. Or just why the hairs on the back of her neck were starting to prickle.

27

I stood across the street from the place, quivering, close to hysteria. Normally I wouldn't have even entertained the idea of actually going in. But today was far from normal. And the state I was in, I'd do almost anything to find out a certain few fragments of information. A certain few numbers.

I don't know how long it had been since I had discovered a particular lottery ticket in my pocket. It probably felt far longer than it really was. After all, I'd been through a few wild phases of emotion since then.

After the shock and the irritation of a stinging paper cut came the despair. Having miraculously found the thing was one matter, but surprising, even amazing as it was, the way my luck had been for the rest of the day I felt it was somewhat premature to get my hopes up. Not yet. Not until I knew what it was worth. Face it; today, if someone gave me the goose that laid the golden egg, it'd probably have salmonella.

But then had come the hope. It was born from the loins of logic, fertilised by the seed of possibility. After all, if I never played the lottery, what was a current ticket doing in my pocket? I had wished for a winning one. And nobody would go to the hassle of performing a miracle to give me a duff one, would they? Despair had tried its best to get back into the party but was somehow wrestled to the ground by Blind Optimism and Wild Desperation.

So there I was, standing opposite 'Il Diablo's Nightclub', my brain spinning. There'd be people in there. Surely one of them was bound to know what the numbers were. Bound to. It wouldn't hurt to just pop in and ask.

I took a breath, launched myself off the poster-strewn wall and ran down the stairs. It was almost a tragic mistake. It was darker in there than I thought. I hit the bottom faster than I would have liked.

The bouncer was nice enough though, very kind of him to drag me up to the bar and insist I had a drink.

'Hey, big boy, I haven't seen you in here before,' shouted a woman into my ear above the noise of music. She smelled of leather and something else. A bit like burnt camomile tea.

'Er, yes. You don't happen to know this week's numbers, do you?'

'Eh?'

'Lottery?'

'Eh?' she coughed. It was a surprisingly passable imitation of someone who'd been in the desert for far too long without a drink. I got the message. A pint of something very expensive-looking appeared almost immediately, complete with sparklers and umbrellas.

'The numbers?'

'Oh yeah.' She leaned over the bar. White thigh grinned at me between the laces that held her trousers together. It didn't take me long to realise that underwear was conspicuous by its absence. It seemed to be a day for that sort of thing.

She dropped the paper on to the bar, flicked through it and shoved it under my nose. 'Feeling lucky?'

'I . . . I'm not sure.'

'God, there's optimism.'

I fumbled the ticket out and stared at the list of numbers. 'Er, this paper, it is this week's?' I spluttered a few moments later.

'Yeah, sure. What d'you take me for?'

'Just tell me two things. What does roll-over mean? And this phrase here, "initial indications point to there being only one winner", er . . . is that good?'

She was ordering a round of celebratory drinks before I could say a word.

28

Outside Audrey's window, no further up the bottleneck of Jeroboam Hill, the man in the BMW was still yelling insults. He was poking out of his sunroof and looking more the irate Mr Punch by the moment. 'At least I can get laid,' he shouted, seemingly obsessed with matters carnal. 'At least I know what to do.'

'Yeah, right,' tutted the man behind the wheel of the largest vehicle on the Hill. He was bored with this conversation already. He just wanted another boiled sweet. It had been a long drive from Barmouth.

It was then that he spotted the small sweetshop across the road. In seconds he had calculated traffic flow rates, sugar deprivation co-efficients and the taste of boiled sweets in his mouth. Ahh, he'd be back in a few minutes. And if he wasn't . . . ? He could guess who would be the most pissed.

'Where d'you think you're off to?' squealed BMW-man, working himself up into a lather of road rage as his mortal enemy skipped down out of his cab.

'Duh. Guess.' He pointed to the only shop in sight and squirmed between a host of bumpers. In seconds he was staring at the jars along the shelves. Jars of boiled sweets. He hadn't seen that in . . . forever. 'Just give me a few minutes here,' he said to the shop assistant. 'This is going to take some thought.' His gaze ran along the tempting array of sugar confectioneries.

In her room, Audrey was actually smiling for the first time in eight weeks. The scene on Jeroboam Hill was shaping up quite nicely. Just the right amount of injustice, a pleasant degree of irritation and, ahh yes, the gentle frisson of a thousand hurled insults. Another peal of horns blasted across the Camford evening sky as the driver of the 'Chechnya' gun-metal-grey BMW tried to reverse out from behind the forty-ton fairground attraction and squeeze his way into the crawl of traffic.

A woman was yelling at him. So was her five-month-old. 'He's already late for his feed,' she snarled through the red-rimmed eyes of those short of sleep, the sort modelled by first-time parents the world over. 'You make him any later than he needs to be and I will find you. I will hunt you down. You will be sorry.'

'Don't blame me. I'm not the one parking scrap metal in the street whilst I go off and buy sweeties! Not like some arseho—!'

A heavily compacted and expertly thrown disposable caught him a bullseye. The crowd went wild. 'Don't you *dare* even *think* of using such language around my child!'

From her balcony perch, Audrey cheered. And then she started to scowl. She was the first to sense it. The change in the air. The dangerous part when someone goes quiet.

You can never tell what it's going to be until it's too late. That one defining factor that turns a good-natured rough-and-tumble pub brawl into something mean. Something deadly. Something devilish.

Often it's the almost subliminal click of a switchblade, or the cocking of a handgun. In this case it was Sainway's Pork Satay and Spare Ribs Kung Po. For toddlers. Several hours old and only one careful owner. Everyone looked at it leaking from the disposable on the car roof.

And something inside the owner of the BMW snapped.

For some reason, he decided the impact splatters didn't really go with 'Chechnya' grey. An artery began to pulse at his temple and his fists ground together. And, in that moment, all the hate and loathing that he had built up over a serious day's repping was focused on one vast object. The Infern-O-Rator-Twister. His molars ground together as he saw that forty-ton road block for what it really was. The van that was always in front of him going thirty miles an hour too slow. The so-called friends with no social status that were dragging him down. That damned boss of his who just milked all the profits of his hard work and would never, ever get out of his way and give him the run of the clear road of promotion. It was all of it. And more. That ex-wife's blood-sucking alimony claims. The goverment high-rate taxes for earning far too much money.

And he wanted rid of it all. Every ounce of his being fumed as he stared at the back of that machine. Immobile. Offensive.

And, up in her room, Audrey felt it too. Cold hard waves of extreme loathing. Guilt-edged, razor-honed. And something inside of her started to beat to the same throbbing pulse of anger. Sensing a need requiring filling.

'Anyone who wants something that bad deserves a bit of a helping hand,' she smiled and closed her eyes. She imagined herself floating in through the cab window, felt the turning of the ignition key, the letting off of the handbrake.

Suddenly, the truck was on the move. Metal ground hard on metal, sparks flew in every direction as it heaved itself out of the morass of traffic and accelerated on a cloud of uncontrollable diesel. People screamed and dived for cover as it mounted the kerb, flattening a bicycle.

And then it shifted gear, powering forward. It hit the outer wall of St Cedric's. Flints and stones showered everywhere as it ploughed into the garden and uprooted Lyndsey's prize lupins. And still it wouldn't stop. It ran on, plunged into the reception and, with a final shearing of metal and medieval architecture, six tons of rubble buried it.

Audrey blinked, rubbed her eyes and stared out of the window. It was then that she realised it wasn't there any more. The window had gone. In fact, none of the front wall was there.

Through the settling dust she caught a glimpse of the man behind the wheel of the BMW. His face creased into a grin and, over the stunned silence, he began to laugh. Hysterically.

'That's more like it,' smiled Miss Williams. 'That's far more appreciative.'

29

There were two things that amazed me about the mobile phones that suddenly appeared after the news of my lottery win broke. One was the number of them and the other was where they came from. I know that technology had somehow made them smaller than ever but, well, some of the women in there were dressed in things that would show knicker elastic at a hundred yards and yet, in a flash of polished pvc, the phones appeared.

'So what's the secret?' oozed Kirstee, the lap-dancer, pushing another dry martini, shaken, in front of me. It was the third one in about ten minutes and I was beginning to wonder if it had been a good idea to let Kirstee choose my beverage. She had insisted I looked like a martini kind of guy and, well, who was I to disagree? She was the expert.

'Secret?'

'The numbers? They your usual ones? You know, birthday of your cat kind of thing?'

'Is that what people normally do?'

'That or bingo generators. How d'you choose?'

'Ahh, well, it wasn't actually me. In fact . . . Oh God.' And the floodgates of memory burst open.

Tell me something you want, something you really, really want and I'll do it. I'll give it to you. Right here, right now.

'Give me a lottery ticket.'

'Any particular one?'

'A winning one.'

'Done.'

'You feeling okay?' asked Kirstee. 'You look a bit green.'

'M . . . m . . .'

She looked at the glass in front of me. 'Not used to them, are you? Toilet's back there.'

I stared at my thumb and the paper cut, barely visible now.

'Look, I'm not clearing up after you. I'll still be here. Go.'

I felt her push me off my stool. 'The excitement I guess,' she apologised to the others at the bar. And I headed for the gents, my head reeling.

It had been a miracle after all. It had been everything I'd asked for and more. And the thing with the hamster cage, that had to have been a miracle too.

I lurched into the gents and headed for the sink. Water. I needed to splash my face. Why, I wasn't entirely sure, but people always splashed their faces at times like this. Who was I to buck a trend?

And then the *Quantum Leap* theory raised its ugly head again. The hamster cage miracle had been there to save me from the fire that would undoubtedly have occurred. But . . . save me for what? To tell everyone about the miracles?

'I don't know how I did it. It's a bit of a mystery to me . . . mystery to me . . . mystery . . .'

And then it hit me.

I'd been talking to someone who worked in mysterious ways.

I was to be the messenger. The herald. All my training as a priest had been for this. I was to tell the world that miracles were back, big time. I was to bring the word that Jesus Christ was back in town.

And that he was a woman.

And that I'd seen her naked.

And fancied her and . . . Ohh God. No amount of splashed faces was going to make this feel any better.

I shook my head. The first two miracles for God knows how long and what had I done with them?

'Look, I've had a hard day. Give me a lottery ticket.'

What a thing to say to the son, er, daughter of God.

I had to get back there now. Explain it all. That it wasn't what it looked like. I wasn't the money-grabbing self-centred . . . That I . . . I wanted the cash for, er . . . charity. Yeah . . . the homeless in, er . . . Nicuador. Or Afghana-ragua, or somewhere else foreign.

I turned to the door, dripping. And somehow I thought that an entire barful of folks might not be overly chuffed if their new-found wealthy chum was to suddenly run out on them. People supplying free booze were always popular. I suddenly found myself wondering just what time Jesus had escaped from the wedding feast at Cana.

'Aww, go on, mate, just another twenty jugs into claret. It won't take long.'

I had the feeling I might be buying rounds for a very long time . . . Unless.

I spotted a tiny window high above the cistern. It would be a tight squeeze but . . . hey, I had no choice. And, after all, the path to salvation is never supposed to be easy.

30

A rotund man dashed out of the sweet shop on Jeroboam Hill, his jaw dropping to reveal a barely sucked jelly baby. His eyes blinked impotently at the wreckage across the street, pools of Munchian horror. 'Bessie! My truck . . . Oh shit, there goes my no claims.'

In her room, Audrey began to chuckle.

'Another satisfied customer,' she grinned in a surprisingly devilish manner.

Suddenly she heard a key in the door.

'Miss Williams? Is that you making all that noise? Do stop bouncing on the bed, you'll damage the springs. Miss Williams, I know you have some complaints regarding the catering but there is no need to take your irritation out on St Cedric's property. Miss Williams, have you put something behind this door? Miss Williams?'

She looked from the large girder which was jammed behind the door to freedom and back again. It was no contest. She knew where she was needed. She knew where the fun was.

Out there.

With only the barest nod towards decency, she wrapped a lemon sheet around her shoulders and skipped off down the convenient bank of rubble. And so, with only the briefest flash of almost perfect thigh, she disappeared into the Camford evening.

It was odd; nobody on Jeroboam Hill actually saw her go. They were all staring at the forty-ton truck wedged into the building and as one they were all thinking the same thing.

How had that actually crashed? And where had that building come from? Strange, but none of them had actually noticed it before and the vast majority of folk travelled that way every day. It was as if it had just appeared. But then, nobody could remember there being anything there before. Just . . . well, that bit of the street that was always there.

31

In the depths of St Cedric's, Brother Lyndsey was facing the door of room number six and attempting delicate negotiations at the top of his voice.

'Miss Williams? Er, would you mind removing whatever it is you've shoved behind the door? Please? It's not making our entry very easy, and that's not really very polite, now, is it? We just want to come in and have a nice little chat. And maybe a cup of tea and a bun?'

For some reason his pleas seemed to be falling on deaf ears.

'Now, I don't really want to have to get a crowbar out, it might damage the paintwork on the door, but I'll do it if I have to. Now are you going to help? Hmmm?'

He turned to the bishop and lowered his voice. 'Now do you think this behaviour is normal? Hmmm? Any self-respecting person would've taken whatever it is away from the door and welcomed us in, open-armed.'

'And you're sure of that, are you? It's the offer of tea and buns, I suppose?' frowned the bishop.

'Well, yes. But it's also the non-threatening tone in my voice, you see. I learned that on a negotiation and manipulative techniques course.'

'Non-threatening? You're shouting.'

'Ahh, volume can so easily be confused with aggression. That was lesson three.'

'I don't suppose there were any lessons on how to manipulate immobile doors?'

'Other than by persuasion . . . er . . .'

'Right, this needs more than persuasion.'

'You're going to forcibly open it? But that's tantamount to an invasion of privacy. It could lead to deep psychological trauma and . . .'

'She's barricaded the door. Somehow I suspect this is not the action of a normal woman ready to be reintegrated into society.'

'Well, I suppose if you put it that way. Just here with my shoulder, you think?'

Bishop Hutchinson shook his head and pointed down the corridor to a red case on the wall. 'That fire axe, there, I think.'

32

As timing went it couldn't have been much better. Or worse, depending on your point of view.

I dashed in through the back entrance having sprinted

half-way across Camford. I struggled up the stairs, dashed down a couple of corridors and skidded to a halt outside room six, just as Brother Lyndsey settled his feet firmly and swung a shiny new fire axe.

'What the . . . ?' I began.

'It seems Miss Williams is having a bit of a tantrum,' tutted Lyndsey, levering the handle free and lining up again.

'What? What's she doing?'

'Damaging St Cedric's property,' he answered, burying the axe deeper in the door.

'Er . . . Look, about Miss Williams . . .'

'Strange way to protest about the standard of catering,' moaned Lyndsey. 'I mean, what's wrong with a simple verbal comment? I can change the menu.' He pulled the axe free and brought half the door with it.

'Hello?' he called, peering through the gap. A few days' more stubble and a manic grin and he could have been Jack Nicholson. 'Oh, my . . .'

'What is it?' demanded Bishop Hutchinson. 'Is it bad?'

'Not if you like open plan,' coughed Lyndsey.

'Miss Williams? What is she doing?' pressed the bishop.

'Miss Williams?' I asked. Somehow I got the distinct impression I wasn't going to enjoy the answer.

Brother Lyndsey shrugged at me.

'What's that supposed to mean?'

'Haven't a clue about her. No sign of her.'

Suddenly I had to sit down. 'No sign of her? She's gone?' I whispered nervously. 'Gone!'

Oh God, I thought. *Now I've done it. I've lost the Daughter of God. Two thousand years between saviours and I lose her.*

This, I feared, was going to take some explaining.

The Best Laid Plans of Morris Men

August 5th, Camford.

Dear Logbook,

Heading south-east today. Definite amount of dissatisfaction amongst party. Bernstein the younger is adamant that my plan will not work. Remains unconvinced that pretending to be morris men is perfect disguise for this mission. After all, what could be more natural than to find morrisers at sites of special supernatural interest? That boy has no imagination.

Wasn't easy convincing them that Camford is the place. Only the detailed gematric analysis of the town plan was sufficient to persuade them of my claims. Even the most ardent sceptic would have difficulty refuting my findings.

Ray rolled three consecutive six circumvolents.

E.T.A. Camford 18.47.

33

Somewhere on the outer edges of the Camford one-way system, a voice called from the back of an ageing Volkswagen camper van. It wasn't a happy voice.

'Are we there yet?'

'In a manner, aye,' mumbled a white-haired man from the passenger seat.

'And what's that supposed to mean?' tutted the six-footer curled uncomfortably amongst a heap of cardboard boxes.

'We have happened upon the outer petticoats of fair

Camford,' muttered Bernstein the elder, who was attempting to make sure he was holding the map the right way up.

'We're on the outskirts,' translated Bernstein the younger with a rolling of his eyes. His father was off again. Ever since the decision had been taken to go undercover he'd been talking in this way, convinced it made him sound all the more morrisey. He was wrong.

'Well, how much longer is it going to be? My leg's gone dead. Any longer and they'll have to amputate,' complained Rawlings, fidgeting amongst the suitcases piled around him.

'Good,' giggled the sixteen-year-old Bernstein the younger. 'Might improve your dancing.'

'Right, that's it. Stop the van, I'm having him. There's nothing wrong with my dancing.'

'Well, nothing that electro-therapy won't cure,' chuckled Bernstein the younger.

'Are you going to stop this van so I can smash his face in?'

'Absolutely not,' insisted Bertrand T. Matlock, self-elected leader of the newly invented Matlock Morris Dancing Team. 'For one thing I will not condone so-called road rage within the confines of my Volkswagen. Secondly, I shall not allow personal aggression to force our late arrival.'

'And thirdly? I sense a thirdly. C'mon, spill it.'

'And thirdly, unnecessary deceleration will have damaging effects upon the miles-per-gallon average.'

'Just you wait till the sword dance,' threatened Rawlings, staring hungrily at Bernstein the younger. 'Your finger's coming off.'

Whilst he still had the use of all his digits, Bernstein waggled them rudely towards the back of the van, middle one raised offensively.

'Gentlemen, please,' hissed Matlock importantly. 'We are morris men. We don't fight amongst ourselves.' Five pairs of eyes drilled into the back of his neck, fuming. Each hating their self-elected leader for their own private reasons.

'The sword dance,' muttered the goateed one who was known as Ranzo Ray. He rolled a very thin cigarette. 'We doin' the sword dance tomorrow?'

'On the morrow shall our broadsword blades clash proudly,' announced Bernstein the elder with the wistfulness of a Klingon on heat.

'Of course the sword dance,' answered Matlock confidently, thinking back over the last few rehearsals. 'Our cover would be far from complete without it as the finale. People expect sword dances.'

'And the music?' asked the goateed one, licking the edge of the cigarette paper. 'What music we doin' it to?'

'The one we have rehearsed. "The Ballad of Sir Eglamore", trad. arr.'

'Oh man, you promised,' grumbled Ranzo Ray, lighting up with a frown of disappointment. 'You said we could do it my way.'

'Ohh no, the British public aren't ready for that just yet.'

'But it works, man. You said so yourself. "Performin' the sword dance to Marillion's 'Hooks in You' lifts morris dancing into the next century." That's what you said.'

'It was a moment of weakness,' tutted Matlock. 'Besides, we aren't here for that.'

'Thank God Talvin Singh didn't have that way of thinkin'. He never would've fused tight drum'n'bass mentality with ancient Indian melodies and tonal construction thus bringin' a new relevance to traditional—'

'Yeah, right.'

'What about the other dances?' asked Rawlings. 'We doing "Sowing Seeds with the Fairest of All Virgin Maidens of Buxom Proportions", eh? Are we?'

'No,' hissed Matlock, narrowly avoiding topping thirty-five miles an hour.

'Why not?'

'That's all you ever think about, isn't it?' challenged Matlock. 'That's all that goes on in that sordid, sticky little mind of yours, isn't it?'

'Well, we doing it then?'

'Firstly, tomorrow's performance is a matinee, therefore young children and those of a fragile disposition may be present. And since the subject matter of said dance veers more towards the sordid, it is unsuitable.'

'Bugger,' spat Rawlings.

'Secondly, look around you. This van of mine is lacking women of the female persuasion and essential buxom proportions for the necessary role.'

'Bugger,' chorused Rawlings and Ranzo Ray.

'And thirdly—'

'Knew there'd be a thirdly,' muttered Bernstein the younger.

'And thirdly, at this late hour it would be impossible to teach said buxom maiden the steps.'

For the first time Ranzo Ray saw a chance. 'So you sayin' that if no kids come and I can find a suitable scantily clad girly with requisite anatomy, we can slot that dance in?'

There was a thoughtful pause as Matlock calculated degrees of likelihood and measured the impending feeling of mutiny. 'All right . . .'

'Way-hey!'

'*Providing* that she is familiar with the steps.'

'Well, that won't be hard,' grinned Ranzo Ray, 'it's all pelvic thrusts anyway.' He pulled a face of excruciating lechery.

Bernstein the younger shook his head in wonder. 'God, and I thought it was about farming.'

'In twice thirty ells and twenty a veering to the east will be called for,' offered his father.

'What?' squeaked Matlock, looking reflexively into his mirror. 'What's that meant to mean?'

'Hundred yards on the left,' muttered Bernstein the younger.

'Remind me never to let him navigate again. You're never navigating again, clear?'

'Fah-la-la lanky down dilly,' growled Bernstein the elder.

'What? What's that supposed to mean?'

'Believe me, you're better off not knowing,' answered the navigator's son. 'Word of warning though, just check the toilet seat for disembowelling equipment.'

The rest of the journey was driven in a baffled silence, broken only by more terse and somewhat obscure directions from Bernstein the elder.

And as they approached the centre of Camford, Bertrand Matlock's mind filled with images of the map he had created. It had all started simply enough. A 1:25000 OS of the town. But when viewed with the unique ancient sacred science of gematria . . . oh, what treasures it revealed. Many had been the long nights he had stayed awake assigning definite numbers to specific letters, forging links between the written and the calculable, revealing the hidden message spelt out by the ancient geomancers who had laid the foundation of Camford.

He smiled as he recalled the night a week ago when he had completed tracing around certain streets. He had rubbed his eyes and looked. And, suddenly, the red biro lines on the map coalesced before his eyes. 'Here be beestees' the message had read. And a vast red arrow pointed to the centre of town.

'Here be beestees,' he muttered to himself and drove through the red lights of a pelican crossing.

34

Brother Lyndsey swung heavily on the axe and, with a final cracking of ancient woodwork, the doorframe gave up its hold on the wall. Dust, horsehair plaster and a host of confused spiders tumbled on to the carpet and Lyndsey waded in.

'Miss Williams?' It was a forlorn hope. He was almost certain that she'd fled. Almost certain that it had all gone wrong. But maybe, just maybe, there was good news. She could be trapped by the leg under a suitable slab of wall.

Moving through the rubble in a way he'd seen International Rescue do on TV, he stepped over a creaking wooden beam and headed for the bed. It didn't take him long to figure out that she was either thoroughly absent, or wafer thin.

'Any sign?' called Bishop Hutchinson, picking his way over the debris.

'She must have headed out over . . . Oh my God!' coughed Brother Lyndsey, staring out into Jeroboam Hill.

'Have you found her? Is she all right?'

'The people,' whispered Lyndsey, with a hint of the agoraphobic. 'Out there in the street. They're looking at us.'

'N . . . No . . . Nonsense, that's impossible.' He peered over the pile of Somme destruction.

'They can see me.'

'Calm . . . calm . . . calm,' breathed the bishop like an escaping prisoner pinned and mounted by a million-candle-power spotlight. 'It's the truck, yes, that's it. The truck. That's what they're staring at.'

Lyndsey shrugged and waved.

A dozen motorists waved back hesitantly before hiding their hands quickly.

'Uh-oh. This is bad. Very bad,' swallowed Lyndsey. 'Our Vision of Immaculate Camouflage has failed.'

'But . . .'

'No buts. It gets worse.'

Normally there would have been a screaming of sirens, a screech of burning rubber and the forces of Camford Constabulary would have arrived on the scene. Today on Jeroboam Hill it was all just a little different.

Three uniformed officers struggled up the incline, each suffering from differing degrees of exhaustion.

'Soon as I get back to the station I'm going to put in a demand that all Camford pavements are widened,' grumbled PC Plain, missing his favourite Rover.

'And get them to remove litter bins,' chipped in PC Skitting.

'And lamp-posts,' offered PC Sim, not to be outdone. 'They don't half get in the way. If they mounted all the lamps off the front of buildings then we could drive—'

'Shut up,' hissed Plain, feeling a blister growing on his big toe.

They rounded a final corner and came face to face with the whole scene. A vast fairground attraction was jammed under the heap of rubble which had once been the front of an ancient building.

'I don't remember that being there,' said Sim, scratching his head.

'That's why we're here,' tutted Plain. 'Contrary to popular belief, it's against the law to park vehicles in just any building you choose.'

'It's the building I'm talking about. I don't remember it being there.'

'That's irrelevant,' muttered Plain. 'Empirical observation of the current situation with particular attention to positional factors indicates that the building was here first. The question we have to answer is, was the collision deliberate or accidental? Now, does anything strike you as interesting about this scene?'

Sim shrugged. 'Simple case of a dodgy handbrake. Open and shut case.'

'And what leads you to that conclusion?' asked Plain, missing only the deerstalker, pipe and Stradivarius of the literary detective.

'Duh. Parked on a hill. Not parked on a hill,' explained Sim.

'Ahh, but observe the pattern of traffic,' pointed out Plain in one of his more irritating moments. 'Notice just where a forty-foot-long vehicle may have been parked.' He gestured towards a forty-foot-long space.

'Well, it didn't fall out of the sky, did it?' complained Sim, obviously missing the point.

'Notice also that said vacant space is downhill of the impact area.'

Plain and Sim looked from the road to the scene of destruction and back again.

'So . . . er, it was deliberate then?' hedged Plain.

'No way,' insisted a large man clutching a bag of mixed sweeties. 'I was nowhere near it. I was in that shop. See?' He rustled the bag for effect.

'Oh, so you're saying it's me now, are you?' challenged a man who looked like he should be driving a gun-metal-grey BMW.

'You wanted me out of your way,' growled the driver.

'I didn't touch your bloody truck.'

'And I suppose it just let its own handbrake off, fired itself into first gear and shot off on a suicide dash all on its own? Eh? That it?'

'Well, as a matter of fact . . .'

The three police officers shook their heads. It was always

the same with road traffic accidents. It was never anybody's fault. Never.

35

I couldn't believe what I had just heard. Now don't get me wrong, it wasn't like I wasn't used to hearing things I couldn't believe. Try talking to people who've just come out of a coma, they can be very surreal at times. Neurones getting used to thinking again, or something. And I'm not so innocent of the odd flights of total insanity myself, but this . . . this was . . . well, I don't know. Weird. With capitals.

Call me naive, but if a forty-ton truck ploughs into your average fourteenth-century Hostel for the Less Than Perfectly Well, one of the last things you expect to get uptight about is people looking. People do that when there's been an accident. It's true. If you're bored waiting in the queue at the Post Office, just feign a nose bleed and you'll be dealt with immediately. Fact of life. People love other people's suffering.

I stood in the corridor, my head spinning. Well, not literally of course, which was a good thing. I could have been in a neck brace for months if that had been the case, and then I would have had to put up with all the stares and the tea and sympathy. It just felt like it was spinning. All right, so I was confused. Who wouldn't be?

I mean, what *was* a Vision of Immaculate Camouflage anyway?

I was sure that was what Lyndsey had said.

'Uh-oh. This is bad. Very bad. Our Vision of Immaculate Camouflage has failed.'

Yup. That's what he had said. I'd heard it.

I tried that out from a few different angles and none of them seemed particularly wholesome.

immaculate camouflage [*imak*ewlit *kam*ooflaazh] *n (theol mil)* sinless concealment from the wicked enemy of troops, artillery, refugees, stores *etc* by means of paint, branches of trees, miracles, smoke-screens *etc*; pure subterfuge of making something without original sin appear different to those of unholy intent ~ **immaculately camouflage** *vb* camouflage by spiritual means: disguise beautifully.

immanence [*ima*nens] *n (theol)* pervasive presence of God . . .

Stop!

Nothing was making sense any more. Miracles. Lottery tickets. Dead hamsters. Hidden fourteenth-century hostels.

I needed some time to think.

I ran.

I was out the back door and half-way down the street before I even stopped to think where I was going. Right now, home was a bad idea. It had a telephone and Brother Lyndsey knew it. Go back there and I could guarantee I'd be called in for overtime in the next ten minutes. After all, there was a lot of clearing up to do.

I needed to be somewhere where nobody knew me. Where I was just one of the crowd . . .

'There he is!' cried a woman, pointing straight at me. I recognised her leather trousers in the instant before the rest of the clientele of Il Diablo's swarmed thirstily around the corner.

For once that day my brain actually worked. A life-saving excuse appeared. 'Ahh, Kirstee, there you are. I needed some air and what with all the excitement, well, I hadn't a clue where I was and . . .'

I was led back to the bar in a rather forceful manner.

Still, I thought, as they helped me down the stairs, *at least Bishop Hutchinson won't find me down here.*

36

'Well, here we are,' announced Matlock, pulling his ageing Volkswagen van around a sharp left-hand corner and entering a strangely deserted square. 'And no thanks to you,' he added, glaring at Bernstein the elder.

'Sheen tirie fearsum dilly,' muttered the eldest member of the Matlock Morris Dancing Team.

Matlock shuffled uncomfortably as the squad peered out of the steamed windows, frowning. 'You sure this is the place, man?' asked Ranzo Ray. 'It looks plain deserted.'

'It's always questions with you, isn't it,' huffed Matlock, staring at Ray and pulling a piece of paper out of his inside pocket. 'Look, Keswick Square. There in black and white. We're early, that's why there's nobody here.'

'I don't care. Just open the bloody door before my foot drops off,' pleaded Rawlings from his prison of cardboard boxes at the back of the van. 'Open the door!'

'Early? I should've thought someone would be here the night before we're supposed to go on.'

'And that observation is based on what exactly?' asked Matlock.

Ranzo Ray rolled another of his trademark thin cigarettes. 'This is supposed to be a carnival, right? Carnivals are for people, right? Conclusion, there should be people here.'

'Can't see any posters or anything. You didn't forget to actually book us in, did you?' asked Bernstein the younger, clearing a circle in the steamed window.

'Don't do that, it'll leave marks,' scowled Matlock.

'We in a parallel Camford, you think?'

'We could be in a divergent Camford for all I care. Just as long as we get paid for our gig. And I don't care how long we've been learning the dances, we're good,' said Ray.

Bernstein the elder fixed Matlock with an icy stare. 'Shall we find our purses filled with wondrous coins this night?'

'It's always down to money with you lot, isn't it? Five pounds for a new chain here, seven pounds sixty-three pence for petrol there.'

'He thinks morris dancing is a profession,' observed the younger Bernstein.

'Shall we sleep in silken beds, with golden sheets and wondrous ale flowing in heady fountains . . .'

'Uh-oh, he's having another senior moment.'

'. . . and bonny maidens finer than sow's ears willest cavort and tryst in bowers of dafferdowndilly and lark feathers . . .'

'Too much aluminium in his diet.'

'. . . and come white-stocking day our garters willest entwine till the sun gildeth fields of lily.'

'Enough of this,' shouted Matlock, thumping the steering wheel dictatorially. 'Let's at least look like we're here for a reason. Get ready for a dress rehearsal. Get the P.A. set up and get changed.'

'What?' coughed Rawlings. 'Without a dressing room? I ain't getting my kit off in the street.'

'You have to,' ordered Matlock. 'There's no way you can call yourself a morris man without wearing the correct attire.'

'I can do the moves in civvies.'

'Civvies?' coughed Matlock, turning pink. 'You can't possibly . . .'

'Nah, man, I like it,' suggested Ranzo Ray, pulling thoughtfully on his cigarette. 'Kind of urban, innit? Sorta, y'know, streetwise.'

Matlock shook his head and threw his hands up in despair. 'How many times do I have to tell you, morris dancing is not about being streetwise.'

'That's its fundamental root problem, man,' countered Ray with a strange hand gesture. 'Relevance, innit?'

'What?'

'Morris dancing to the average man in the street, what's it all about, eh? Sticks an' bells an' shit. What's its *relevance*, man?'

'It's traditional. It's not supposed to be relevant.'

Bernstein the elder growled.

'Besides,' continued Matlock warily, 'ninety per cent of the people watching won't have a clue anyway.'

'Pitiful attitude, man,' shrugged Ranzo Ray as if in mourning. 'Pitiful.'

'Just shut up and get ready,' hissed Matlock.

With far less enthusiasm than should have been present, the Matlock Morris Dancing Team began preparing for this evening's dress rehearsal.

And, throughout it all, their self-elected leader studied a map scrawled with red biro.

37

The sound of truncheon on oaken door rattled around the entrance hall of St Cedric's. It had replaced the dull collision of knuckles, showing at least some intelligence on the part of the caller.

'Well, open it,' whispered Bishop Hutchinson.

'Do we have to?' trembled Brother Lyndsey, his eyes wide. 'I mean, they might find things out.'

'We don't open it and they'll send in the fire brigade and sniffer dogs and . . .'

'All right, all right. God knows what the sniffer dogs would make of what we've got in the cellar.' Lyndsey reluctantly stepped up to the door. 'Hello? Hello? Who is it?'

'Police,' came the muffled reply.

'Police! Oh Jeezusmaryandjosephandallthesaintsintestines. Didn't do it, wasn't there,' answered Lyndsey.

'Sorry? Didn't do what?'

'Anything,' jabbered Lyndsey. 'Everything. Ooooh no. Didn't do any of it. Not at all. Never.'

Bishop Hutchinson stared at him. 'What are you doing?' he whispered. 'Open the door.'

'Trust me,' mouthed Lyndsey.

'Er, could you open up, please? I'd like to ask you a few questions.' The letter box flicked and an eye peered in.

'Ooooh no, no questions. Can't do questions. They're so personal. Personal and probing.'

Outside the door, PC Plain scratched his head. 'I could ask non-personal questions. Would that be all right?'

'Is that a question. Are you asking my opinion?' called Lyndsey. 'I don't think I can give you my opinion. Dangerous that is. Risky, yes, very risky. You might hurt it.'

'Er, are you feeling all right? You sound a little . . . er, edgy.'

'All right? Yes, yes. Fine I am. Fine. We're all like this in here. Comes from taking our vow.'

'What are you on about?' mouthed Hutchinson. 'Just open the door.'

'And what vow would that be?' asked the letter box.

'Ohh, he asked. I knew he'd ask. They always do,' spluttered Lyndsey, chewing at his fingernails for effect. 'Always the same it is. Can't help themselves. That's why we keep the door shut, isn't it? Ohh yes. Can't let them in. Can't have them coming in here. Looking at us. Looking at everything.'

'About this vow, sir . . . ? If you can give us a clue then maybe I can ask questions that . . .'

'Questions again. Always questions. We take a vow of paranoia and they come with their questions. Poking, probing . . .'

Bishop Hutchinson bit his lip. It was the only way he could stop himself from laughing.

'I wouldn't worry too much about paranoia, sir. We get that a lot in our profession,' reassured the letter box.

'It's the uniform,' added PC Sim.

'Argggh, how many of you are there out there?' squealed Lyndsey, hopping about on one foot.

'Us? Er, just three.'

'Just three, just three, they say as if it's not many. Out-numbered we are. Swarms of police out there. Swarms.'

'Look, sir. I need to ask you a few questions then we'll go away, okay?'

Brother Lyndsey feigned thinking for a moment. 'Three questions, just three. One each. That's fair, yes. Can cope with that.'

'That's good. Right, sir, if you could just give me your name?'

'My name? Ohh no, not at all. You might not give it back. Then I'd be in trouble. Wouldn't know what I was called any more. No, no. Next question.'

'Well, can you give me your address? This place doesn't appear to be on any street maps.'

'You want my address? What are you going to do with it? You'll write it down and take it away, won't you? Take it away and never come back. Ohh no. That can't happen. Can't risk being homeless. Never. I live here. Next question.'

Lyndsey could hear PC Plain scratching his head, thinking hard. 'Did you see anything to do with the accident out here?'

'Accident? You sure it was an accident? You can never be sure anything is an accident. There's always somebody behind it. Always. They should take out the word accident from every dictionary. There's no such thing.'

'Look, did you see anything?'

'That's four questions. Four. You see how they take advantage. Always pressing for more. Demanding.'

'Did you?'

'No. Didn't see anything. Never look out of the window. All too scary out there. Nasty. Not like in here. Safe in here. Warm. Safer in bed. Yes. Back to bed now. Hide under the pillow. Yes. That's what I'll do. Then it'll all go away. Yes.'

Outside the door, PC Plain pocketed his notebook and replaced his pencil behind his ear.

'Well, that went well,' grinned PC Sim. 'Got lots of relevant detail there. I sense an arrest imminently.'

'Shut up. Just go and measure some tyre tracks or something.'

Inside St Cedric's, Bishop Hutchinson was looking at Brother Lyndsey in a new light. 'Vow of paranoia, excellent. How did you think of that?'

'Wasn't hard,' came the answer, suddenly serious. 'For the first time in almost five hundred years, the outside world knows we're here. If that doesn't give your bowels something to think about I don't know what will.'

He pulled a mobile phone out of his habit. 'Pay as you go,' he said. 'No traceable bills, don't worry.' He pounded nervously at the keys.

'You're not calling them . . . ?' began the bishop, his heart sinking.

'They've got to know,' he answered, as the dialling tone rang in his ear. 'Five . . . six . . . Ahhh no. Don't tell me . . . Answerphone!'

'Hi there, you've a-reached the number of . . . well, actually I not say. It's a secret, capice?' The italianate answering machine rattled in Lyndsey's ear. 'Just a-let me tell you that if you've rung by a-mistake then don't do it again. An' believe me we'll a-know if you do it again, see? But if you are a-calling for a

111

reason then leave a message. Just make a-damn sure it's a-worth it. I hate a-time wasters. Ciao.'

Lyndsey heard the tone.

'Oh, the shame of it all. I hate you not being in when I call,' he tutted into his mobile. 'It's so degrading having to talk to a machine, you wouldn't believe. Just try it. Anyhow, if it wasn't important I wouldn't be telling you 'cause I hate answerphones. Now, just a call to inform you that the safe house here in Camford . . . well, it's not so safe any more. By the way, change that message. It's not friendly at all. Ciao.'

And, deep in a secret room two hundred feet below the banks of the Tiber, the answerphone clicked off.

38

A group of five men stood looking at each other in the centre of Keswick Square. They were dressed in white from head to foot and festooned with red and green ribbons. It had taken a great deal of practice for them not to feel as foolish as they looked. But then that was lesson number one of morrising. Never let anyone know how stupid you feel. Of course that was normally why it involved large quantities of real ale.

Sadly, the newly recobbled acreage of Keswick Square was a real-ale desert. And it was beginning to show.

'You sure this is the right day, man?' asked Ranzo Ray, shuffling uncomfortably. His ankle-bells rang with irritating cheeriness. 'See, I'm sensin' a whole stack of negative vibe potential.'

'For the fifteenth time, it's the right day,' snarled Matlock. To prove the point he snatched a paper flier off the munici-pally correct cobble footway and waggled it in his face.

'No need to invade my personal space, man. I believe you.'

'Oh yeah, and why the sudden change of heart, eh?'

Ray shrugged and pointed across the square. Two very embarrassed parents walked sheepishly into the square, each holding the hand of a brightly coloured five-year-old. One was dressed as a sea-horse, the other was swamped by a red sequinned octopus costume. It sounded like the sea-horse was crying.

'Here comes the dress-rehearsal for the carnival,' chuckled Rawlings.

'So where's the rest of it?' asked Bernstein the younger, pulling his favourite teen stroppy face. 'And what about the mayor, isn't he supposed to be giving a speech?'

'He's probably gone to the pub,' muttered Rawlings, still rubbing at his leg. Secretly he was beginning to wonder if the circulation would ever return to anything near normal. One thing he was sure about, there was no way he was going in the back of the Volkswagen on the way home. He'd make damned sure of that.

'Pub? Did someone say the magic word?' asked Bernstein the younger, dribbling in a way that would have delighted Pavlov.

'Oh no,' insisted Matlock as the sea-horse and the octopus hove into earshot. 'You're not going to the pub until after the dance. It's our duty to entertain.'

'I ain't dancing for four people. Especially when half of them are auditioning to be sushi.'

'You must,' coughed Matlock, sensing dissension in the ranks. 'We're booked to do it.'

'We're booked for tomorrow. Tonight we party.'

'Ahh, yes. About that booking,' asked Ray. 'Does it have a cancellation clause? Do we still get paid?'

'Money again,' countered Matlock, attempting to avoid the question.

'Look, I'm not a charity. I've got my expenses,' said Ray,

rolling another cigarette. 'Sooner they legalise this the better. It'll be cheaper.'

'Face it, nobody's coming,' tutted Rawlings. 'I vote pub. All in favour follow me.'

'No, you can't, you've got to dance,' pleaded Matlock, feeling the way of all sinking ships watching troops of emigrating rats.

'All right, guys, after three,' began Rawlings, turning his back. With the lightning speed of the terminally thirsty, a conga line formed and headed off in search of a hostelry.

'Come back,' shouted Matlock above the din of clogs on cobbles.

Unsurprisingly, he was ignored.

'Huh. Still, they'll be back later. Where else are they going to sleep other than my van?'

Unseen in the gloom of a faulty streetlight, a confused knight in shining armour stood on the heads of two four-foot-tall peasants. 'Always the same,' he muttered under his breath. 'Nobody runs a decent carnival these days. Even Notting Hill's gone to pot.'

Shaking his head, he turned and headed off into the backstreets of Camford, feeling like the only one at a cocktail party who'd turned up in bermuda shorts.

The conga line of morris men rounded a sharp corner and clattered to a sudden halt. 'Well, hello,' smiled Rawlings as he clapped eyes on the double delights of the Monocle and Asparagus and the tall brunette standing in the shadow of the signboard. He looked her up and down, admiring the lemon-yellow sheet draped around her shoulders. Actually, truth be told, he was admiring what was underneath.

'Bet she knows a thing or two about pelvic thrusting,' grinned Rawlings. 'Gentlemen, mine's a pint and I'll join you in a few minutes. After I have persuaded a certain woman not a million miles from here that she really does want to star in tomorrow's performance of "Sowing Seeds with the Fairest of All Virgin Maidens of Buxom Proportions".'

'God, he's full of himself, isn't he?' muttered Bernstein the younger.

'Full of something,' tutted Ray and headed off towards the pub.

Rawlings adjusted his neckerchief and drifted casually towards the woman on a shimmering of ankle bells.

39

As the last of the witnesses drove away up Jeroboam Hill and the drivers of a certain 'Chechnya'-grey BMW and a written-off fairground attraction were cuffed and led off down the hill, PC Sim began to talk.

'Not a bad idea, y'know.'

'What now?'

'Taking a vow of paranoia. Good idea.'

PC Plain shook his head. 'This should be good,' he grinned to Skitting. 'And the explanation?'

'Well, you'd never get any junk mail. Never have idiots ringing you up offering you time-share holidays.'

'He's got a point there,' agreed Skitting. 'And being a religious sect, you wouldn't pay council tax.'

'Yeah, and if no one knows your address then nobody would ever send you bills,' enthused Sim. 'In fact, the only contact you'd ever have with the outside world would be with people you want to talk to. Neat that.'

'A little too neat,' muttered PC Plain, his investigational nostrils flaring.

'And what's that supposed to mean?' chorused Sim and Skitting.

'Question . . .'

'Uh-oh,' worried Sim. 'Now we've done it. We've set him off.'

'Question.' Plain frowned. 'Just why would anyone actually want to remove themselves from so many mailing lists?'

'Because they're paranoid,' answered Sim with the singsong voice of one with entirely the wrong answer.

'Or because they have something to hide,' whispered Plain. 'Something very big.'

He pulled the keys to his handcuffs out of his pocket, unlocked the drivers and reclamped them around a convenient lamp-post.

'Hey, what you doing? You can't leave us here,' objected the BMW owner as Skitting followed suit.

'What you going to do about it? Call the cops?'

'This is an infringement of civil liberty,' shouted the driver, tugging at his cuffs.

'Wrong,' grinned Plain. 'It's a lamp-post. Now shut up or we might just forget to come back this way. Clear?'

The three men from Camford Constabulary turned and headed off back up Jeroboam Hill.

The once-proud owner of a certain fairground attraction shrugged. 'Fancy a jelly baby?' he said to his arch-enemy facing him on the other side of the lamp-post.

'Nah. Got a Murray Mint instead?'

40

It had been only a matter of three quarters of an hour since the mutinying men of the Matlock Morris Dancing Team had conga'd into the lounge of the Monocle and Asparagus, but already they were well into their fourth pint each. It was the uniforms, it must be. They gave one such a thirst.

'So, then I do this,' explained Rawlings, swaying as he shimmied aross the floor towards their newest recruit, Audrey Williams. 'I take out my stick and, well, that would be where you'd lose your sheet, see?'

'Oh,' she smiled, leaning against an oaken beam in the back room. 'And then what?'

'Well, after I've tied your wrists to the pole, 'cause we'll be using a maypole, see? After I've done that, which kind of represents the farmer's eternal bond . . . bondage to the fertility of the land . . . Cooo, is anyone else hot? . . . Er, well, that's the pelvic thrusting bit, see?'

'Would that be fast thrusting? Or slow, like this?'

The entire troupe of men watched as she writhed erotically beneath the sheet.

'Slow's good,' breathed Rawlings, his glasses steaming. 'Yeah, slow's very good.'

'Is that because it represents the rhythmic passage of the seasons and the cyclical nature of Mother Earth's sensuous fertility?' asked Miss Williams.

'Er, yeah, that's good enough for me. Whatever you say, just do slow—'

'So there you are,' came the voice of Bertrand Matlock as he entered the back room. 'I knew I'd find you disporting yourselves in some lewd manner. But this time you've really excelled yourselves. Disgusting. I don't know how many times I warn you about cavorting the night before a performance, but do you listen? Morris dancing is not just about the beer, it's a physical expression of man's unity with nature—'

'Beer's natural.'

'So's whisky. No preservatives in that.'

'You know what I mean,' hissed Matlock.

'Look, this is a dress rehearsal, okay?'

'That is a sheet,' pointed out Matlock.

'That's because you've got the costumes in the van,' answered Rawlings. He knew this only too well, having spent the entire journey surrounded by cardboard boxes full of them.

'And you expect me to accept her into my morris troupe?'

The men nodded hearty agreement.

'You promised,' answered Rawlings with just a little more desperation than he would've hoped for. 'In the van, you said—'

'That if you fulfilled certain criteria, we may perform "Sowing Seeds with the Fairest of All Virgin Maidens of Buxom Proportions".'

'Yeah, that was it. And here she is.'

'Dost thee deny that she is not indeed wondrous rare? A lily of glabrous shining? A mare of lilith quivering?'

'Your dad's lost it,' muttered Ranzo Ray.

'Tell me about it,' whispered Bernstein the younger. 'Embarrassing or what?'

Matlock frowned and decided to opt for Rule of Leadership Number Five – if in doubt, threaten and walk out. 'I am going to avail myself of a sparkling mineral water and when I return I want her out of here. Do I make myself clear?'

'But "Sowing Seeds"? What about it?' pleaded Rawlings, feeling every syllable of meaning deeply in his loins.

'Forget it. We don't have the music.'

'I'll hum,' begged Rawlings. 'Whistle?'

Ranzo Ray exhaled slowly. 'Now that I like. Kind of earthy that is. Primal.'

'Can't believe that bastard stitched us up again,' cursed Rawlings into his glass.

'And he promised me we could use Marillion. He promised.'

'The guy's an idiot.'

'Sometimes I think we'd be better off without him.'

'So do I.'

'I mean, he's just dragging us down.'

'Holding us back.'

'Stifling our creativity, man.'

'So we're all agreed, then?'

'Fol-derah down sheee nimh,' nodded Bernstein the elder.

'Ohh, it's so good to hear men in full agreement,' purred Audrey, holding on to the oaken beam. 'It's so . . . liberating.'

'Er . . . it is?'

'Really makes my pulse quicken.'

'It does?'

In the dim light of the back room no one noticed the crimson glow that was beginning to creep into the eyes of Miss Williams. Or the way her fingers started to dig into the very fabric of the beam. 'Men being decisive is just so . . . exhilarating. Just leave him to me, okay?'

In a flurry of sheet she cantered across the back room and out into the bar.

'Let's just go and see what costumes you have in that van of yours,' purred Miss Williams, lashing a surprisingly strong arm around Matlock's shoulders and leading him off into the Camford night air.

'Was it me,' began Rawlings a few moments later, 'or did anyone else hear hooves?'

'What you need, man, is more beer,' suggested Ranzo Ray, rolling another cigarette. 'And while you're at the bar, mine's a pint.'

'And mine.'

41

It could have been the ninth one that did it it, I suppose. Or maybe the tenth. I don't know, they all just started blurring into each other after a while. I mean, one martini is pretty much like another. So one's shaken, one's stirred; face it, who can tell the difference? What I do know is that Kirstee judged her timing just right. Any earlier and I would've screamed and run. But right then, after the day I'd had, well, it was almost perfect.

She was just there, all big hair and plunging neckline and that strange leather and herby smell. I saw her lick her lips. I was fascinated. Amazed that a human tongue could be so, well . . . moist. It glistened. All over. I don't know how it was possible but I actually heard Kirstee's tongue slip over her upper lip. Even above the music.

I knew what was happening of course. I'd expected it. Maybe not this soon, true, but it was bound to happen. Well, they'd had practice. And there was no point in fighting it. Not if I was to truly learn the power of temptation. After all, I was prime corruption territory. I'd just turned down the Daughter of God. The dark side was bound to be after me.

It was good it happened this soon, you know, whilst Audrey was still fresh in my mind. Comparisons were that much easier.

'I prefer the mystery,' I heard myself slur. 'Naked's nice. But it doesn't leave much to the imagination, does it?'

She giggled. I'm sure she giggled.

'Take you, f'rinstance,' I continued.

'Play your cards right and you might just get to do that.' She did that thing with her tongue again.

It threw me. I had to start again. 'Take you, f'rinstance, all that leather and laces and thongs'n'stuff. Interesting that is.'

'Oh yeah? How?'

'Makes you wonder, doesn't it? Makes you want to know just what's under there.'

'Simple answer,' she purred. 'Me. All of me.'

And then I noticed that my hand was on her thigh. Don't ask me how it got there. It just did. Look, I was dealing with experts here. Don't tell me Jesus wasn't actually tempted by the devil. He was just made of strong stuff. Either that or he wasn't quite as full of strong stuff as I was.

'Want to dance?' I heard her ask.

Well, how could I refuse?

Before I realised it, I was on the dance floor and writhing. I tell you, it felt weird. Like I was remembering how to dance from fragments of other people's memories. But there was something about the music that just got right inside of me. Deep into every major muscle group.

In moments I'd forgotten why I was there. Forgotten who I was. It was just Kirstee, me, the music and a dozen arteries full of martini.

It was odd, but things started to seem a little more pleasurable. Especially when I caught glimpses of admiring smiles from the rest of the bar. Well, I couldn't disappoint them, could I?

As the club's speakers exploded with the sound of Frankie's 'Relax', I reached for the bottom of my jumper.

I think it was when they saw my dog-collar that things started to go wrong.

42

Outside the Monocle and Asparagus, a woman wearing nothing but a smile and a lemon-yellow sheet halted in her tracks and homed in on the vibes emanating from the group of morris men. Her heart began to beat faster as she tuned into their needs and desires. Their one united urge. Her pulse quickened as she turned Bertrand Matlock to face her.

'They don't like you, you know.'

He looked up from the map in his hands. 'Which way is north?'

'They don't like you, you know.'

121

'That way, isn't it? And this is . . . er . . . wow. This is it. This is the spot. Right here!'

'Look, just listen, will you? They really don't like you.'

'I don't do this to be liked. I am their coach. Their leader. Their guru. I will reveal to them the ways of the underworl . . . er, underrated world of morrising.' He tried a thin smile and hoped she hadn't noticed his slip.

'How'd you like to give them a bit more freedom? Cut them some slack, eh, Bertie?'

'Impossible. There's . . . there's the traditions to consider.'

'Now that sounds awfully like an excuse to me.'

In the back room of the pub, eighteen inches away as the thought flies, the rest of the group were in deep discussion.

'Never even tries to book anywhere to stay. Have you noticed that? All the way to Tintagel, or Avebury, and never a stop in a hotel.'

'So that's why we always end up in that bloody van of his. I had wondered.'

'I bet he pockets the B&B expenses we give him.'

'Bound to. Dead cert.'

'And the petrol money.'

'And three-times-thirty tithes of our bond.'

All eyes turned to Bernstein the younger, eager for explanation of his father's pronouncement. 'And ninety per cent of our supposed appearance fee.'

'Bastard,' chorused the troupe. As one they stamped their feet. It was accompanied by a peal of ankle bells.

And at that moment, as the wave of hatred plunged through the wall, Audrey had her first hallucination. Or could it have been a trick of the light? Whatever it was, it looked as if her left hand sort of went a bit blurry and kind of faded out of reality for a moment. In its place was a large black scaly claw tipped with razor talons. She shook her head. It was shock, had to be.

After all, you can't expect to come out of a coma after eight weeks totally unscathed, can you?

'It's not an excuse,' defended Matlock, frowning at the woman who had the nerve to shake her head at him. 'Tradition is a very important part of morrising. And that's why I don't want you dancing tomorrow. Morris *men*, see? You, my dear, do not fit certain categories of that phrase.'

'You pulling the sexist card?'

'Of course not. It's tradition.'

Another wave of dark desires floated through the pub wall. This time they were strangely more coherent. Curiously more focused.

'Wonder how much money he's stolen from me? Couple of hundred. Thousands?'

'Or how many sleepless nights. That top bunk isn't comfy, you know? There's a lump just in the middle—'

'And then he refuses to get a new van.'

'Makes you want to kill him.'

'Yeah, string him up.'

'Throttle the bastard.'

And just outside, at that very instant, something very odd happened to Audrey Williams. In a flash of collapsing miracle, she vanished. Only to be replaced by nine foot of black scaly demon, eyes glowing like blacksmith's coals.

'Ohhh my . . .' began Matlock as she stepped forward. 'I was right. Er, look, you couldn't stay here and let the guys see you?'

'Whatever you want,' she croaked, nodding towards the back room as waves of murderous intent hit her. Her mind swirled with images of her hands tight around Matlock's throat. 'Anything you say, guys.'

'Look, if you feel that strongly about taking part I'm sure

I . . . I can be flexible. There's a tambourine I could lend you—' He never finished the offer.

Miss Williams closed on him, her body coursing with boiling urges, her muscles firing with inhuman strength.

'Ahhh, first contact,' he whimpered. 'So strong, so solid, so . . .'

Razor talons closed around his pale throat and lifted him effortlessly off the ground as his braces were ripped from his chest.

Thirty seconds later the sound of hooves was heard on the floor of the Monocle and Asparagus.

'Well, that's that,' announced nine foot of darkly demonic creature as it ducked into the back room and headed for a seat.

'Er, I think you have the wrong room, man,' said Ranzo Ray. 'There's carnival guys in the other bar.'

'Don't be silly. That's my cider there.' A quarter pint of liquid sat in a pint glass on a distant table.

As one, the morris men shook their heads. 'Carnival guys are in the other bar. Clear? That's waiting for our friend to come back.'

Audrey stopped in her tracks. 'This is a wind-up, yeah? I'm back. You were dancing with me not ten minutes ago.' She thrust her pelvis slowly at them. The effect was somewhat different than before. Probably something to do with the large tail which scraped the floor.

'Oh, God. How do they know?' coughed Rawlings. 'Cameras, where are the cameras?'

'Aud . . . Audrey?' muttered Ranzo Ray, pulling hard on his cigarette. 'That really you in there?'

'"In there"? What's that supposed to mean?'

'Didn't know we had costumes like that in the van,' muttered Ray, looking the nine-foot beast up and down.

'Costumes? What are you . . . ?'

'Or stilts. That how come you're so tall? Er . . . you on stilts or something?' asked Bernstein the younger, scratching his head.

'Isn't anyone going to buy me a pint? Tell you what, make it two. I've got a thirst.'

'If that's what Matlock was saving the money for,' began Ray, 'well, I could almost forgive him.'

'Must've cost a few bob,' added Bernstein the younger. 'Those scales look almost real. And the hooves . . .'

Audrey followed Bernstein's finger as he pointed to her feet. Or rather, where her feet should have been. Vertigo spun around her head as she stared down past shining scaly thighs which terminated in the type of large hairy hooves that a shire horse would give its eye teeth for.

'My legs . . .' squeaked Audrey in a way not normally associated with those of a satanic nature. 'And I only shaved this morning!'

'You think the legs are good, take a look at your tail.'

She turned and glanced over the horizon of her left buttock. 'No . . . No!' she screamed and galloped out of the room, realising in the nick of time that the ceiling was far lower than she had expected.

'Hey? Is Matlock coming back? Would you mind getting him a pint?'

As if by way of an answer, at that very moment a woman walking her Jack Russell screamed. Bertrand Matlock dangled ten feet above the pavement, a strange smile on his face. 'First contact,' he choked. 'I told them. "Here be beestees."' He kicked, struggled his last and quietly expired. He swung from the pub sign, bobbing gently from the braces round his neck, tongue swelling.

Death by Advertising

43

Three policemen stood beneath a pub sign and looked up at the gently swaying morris man.

'Suicide,' said PC Skitting with grave certainty. 'Definitely suicide.'

'And just what makes you say that?' tutted PC Plain.

'Well,' began Skitting, in a very I-was-hoping-you'd-ask-that kind of way. 'It's a hanging, see? Stands to reason. I mean, whoever heard of anyone murdering someone with their own braces?'

'Uh-huh,' grunted Plain, unconvinced.

'And another thing,' enthused Skitting. 'Look at his expression. He doesn't look like he was a man exactly bursting with *joie de vivre*. He was a morris man, for God's sake. That's only one rung up from trainspotter. Definitely suicide.'

'Answer me this, then,' challenged Plain. 'How'd he get up there?'

'Easy,' grinned Skitting. 'Ladder.'

'Which is currently to be found where?'

'Ah.'

'On the roof,' chipped in PC Sim. The others turned and stared at him. He took it as a cue for more information. 'It'll be up there.' He pointed vaguely. 'See, after using it to climb up to the sign and wrap his braces round his neck, he reached down, pulled up the ladder and, er, threw it on to the roof. Simple.' The silence was underwhelming. 'Okay, so what's your theory?' hissed Sim, glaring at Plain.

'Advertising.'

'What?' chorused Skitting and Sim.

'Nobody dies from advertising,' added Skitting.

'They do if it goes wrong. And in this case it has gone tragically wrong.'

'This I have got to hear,' tutted Sim, settling on to a nearby litter bin. 'I am sitting comfortably.'

Plain straightened the front of his jacket proudly. This he knew was going to blow their minds. 'Upon arrival at the site of this troupe's forthcoming engagement as part of the Camford Festival of Arts and Stuff, they were dismayed to discover that insufficient promotional material had been provided to secure the requisite crowds.'

Skitting nodded to Sim.

Plain continued. 'Strapped for cash and lacking sufficient time to mount a major promotional onslaught upon the Camford populace, they hit on the innovative idea of suspending one of their team from a prominent building in order to drum up support for their show.'

Reluctantly, Sim shrugged.

'Unfortunately, due to an ill-conceived and badly executed knotting of braces, which was almost certain to have been in part due to the consumption of alcoholic beverages, their attempt at self-publicity has ended in the tragedy you see before you.'

Skitting almost burst into spontaneous applause.

But Sim wasn't so easily swayed. 'And the ladder? Where's that, eh?'

'Ah.'

'There wasn't one,' grinned Skitting, siding proudly with

127

Plain. 'Being morris men they simply made a human pyramid under this sign, thus leaving no evidence.'

'No, that's gymnasts. Morris men can't do human pyramids . . .' began Sim.

'Well, how else did he get up there, eh?'

Sim opened his mouth feebly. 'How come you always get to the bottom of these things so quickly?'

'Ecstatically, my dear Sim. And now for the arrest,' grinned Skitting.

'Not so fast,' said Plain. 'So far my theory is just that. A theory. We need some extra vital information.'

'Er, we do?'

'And that information is to be found in there.' He pointed to the Monocle and Asparagus.

'Oh good, I could do with a pint.' Sim followed Plain towards the door.

'Er . . . what about him?' called Skitting, pointing upwards.

'He's going nowhere.'

Skitting glanced from the swinging morris man to the temptingly stocked bar. It was no contest.

44

When the history of disco is written and put to rest one item will stand head and shoulders above others as the cause of most frequent embarrassment upon the dance floor.

The ultraviolet flood.

Never has a lighting effect had such an ability to publicly point out dandruff on black velvet shoulders. Or turn innocent bra straps into neon nipple protectors gleaming blindingly through suddenly transparent blouses.

But embarrassment was one thing. For me it was almost fatal.

Without warning the dance floor was suddenly awash with UV and there, gleaming brighter than eyeballs and teeth and knicker elastic was my dog collar. It shimmered around my neck like a slipped halo.

All eyes turned on me as the music stopped. The silence was almost as deafening. But far less rhythmic.

'So, a priest!' hissed Kirstee, stepping away from me and placing knuckles on her hips. Her eyebrows arched into a cunning 'v'.

'Guilty,' I grinned sheepishly. It was pointless denying anything. But why should I deny the truth? After all, my faith would keep me safe.

'Kill him!' shouted a voice from behind the bar.

'What?' I coughed.

'Tear him apart,' sniggered a vast bouncer, eyeing up my major limbs.

'No, no, no. Wait a minute, you can't do that to me.' I was squeaking again.

'And why not?' hissed Kirstee, looking me up and down in a way far more calculating than I had seen her before.

'Well, I . . . I'll make a mess on the dance floor.'

'That's easily mopped.'

'Oh . . . Yes, I expect it is.' My head started going crazy again. I saw them carrying black body bags out of Il Diablo's. I swallowed uncomfortably. Body bags. That sounded very messy. 'Er . . . but . . . now I'm not trying to tell any of you how to do your job or anything, but . . . you'll have to hide my body.'

'Never been a problem before,' growled the bouncer.

'Tell you what.' I attempted to bargain. 'Why don't I save you the trouble? I just walk out of here and . . . well, *after* buying a few more rounds of course, and . . . I mean, think about it, all that lifting of dead bodies . . . well, save your back . . .'

'Can't do that,' whispered the bouncer, taking a step closer. I could have sworn he was dribbling. 'We made a vow, see?'

'A vow?'

The UV lit the bouncer's teeth beautifully as he edged closer and smiled with the charm of a piranha. 'To dispose of any more of the likes of you.'

'Lottery winners?' It was a desperate attempt but it just might work. I saw Kirstee shift uncomfortably. Shame the others weren't so easily distracted.

'No. Priests.' The crowd hissed the word in a remarkably well-drilled manner. Like they really meant it.

'Always coming down here they are, trying to show us the light, attempting to steer us all towards the path of salvation,' explained the bouncer. 'It's the name of the place I'm sure. Still, who cares why they do it. Not my problem. They come, we make them go. And in your case, that'll be permanently, see?'

'I'll . . . I'll never come back. I'll forget all about this place. Erase it from my memory. 'Il . . . whose? See, it's working already . . .'

'Left arm or right?' asked the bouncer. 'Which one d'you want to keep? Or should I just pull both and see which comes off first?'

'Look, you've got it all wrong. I only came in to find out the lottery numbers. I wasn't going to convert you or anything.'

'Ahh, but a vow's a vow.'

And then, through the murk of mounting panic, a brief moment of clarity appeared. It was out of my mouth before I realised. 'It won't stop them, you know. They'll send more. I don't report in and within twenty-four hours this place'll be swarming with nuns and vergers and . . .'

'He's right, you know,' said Kirstee with almost a sigh of relief. Could it be that among the crowd, she was actually on my side?

'And they'll be harder to spot. They'll have ever more devious disguises,' I added. 'Believe me, the things we priests can do with make-up is quite amazing.'

'He's right,' picked up Kirstee. 'This one we leave alive. Send him back to them as a message.'

'He'll just bring reinforcements. The whole Salvation Army'll be down here,' growled the bouncer.

'No, honestly. Would I lie?'

'There is a way to make sure they pay attention,' smiled Kirstee. I felt my heart miss a beat. Even without the UV she had a brilliant smile.

'Rip his ears off?' asked the bouncer.

'No . . . we need something with a little more finesse.'

'Every other finger?'

It was then I saw Kirstee's eyes light up. 'If there's any ripping to be done I know exactly what it is.' She stepped forward and plunged her hand into my trouser pocket.

'No, not the testicles,' grunted the bouncer. 'There's no point. He wouldn't use 'em anyway.'

'I'm talking about this,' scowled Kirstee, holding up my lottery ticket. 'A roll-over week. Thirteen million this is worth. This'll make them wince.' Theatrically, she held the ticket above her head.

'Not the only ones,' coughed the guy behind the bar.

But Kirstee ignored him, scrambling up on to a nearby table and grabbing a suitable beermat as she went. With everyone's attention fixed on her hands she tore the lottery ticket into a dozen worthless pieces. She sprang off the table and slapped the shreds of paper into the palm of my hand. 'You owe me big time,' she whispered close in my ear. 'Big time. Clear?'

For a moment I wasn't sure. After all, she'd just torn up a ticket worth an estimated thirteen million quid.

But then I was still intact.

So what? You could buy a hell of a lot of plastic surgery with an estimated thirteen million quid.

'Believe me. You owe me,' she hissed again before raising her voice. 'Now throw him out.'

It was moments later that I discovered just why bouncers are so called. I skipped three times across the street before rolling into the far wall in a crumpled heap.

How long I lay there I haven't a clue, but the ground was thumping to the sound of heavy bass by the time I risked opening my eyes. Nervously, I checked out my major limbs. Oddly my right thigh rustled as I ran my hand over it. The sound of denim and paper.

And there, in the palm of my hand, was the lottery ticket. It was miraculously intact. Nay, pristine.

Thirteen million smiled up at me.

'You owe me big time,' whispered the memory of Kirstee.

'Oh my God . . .' I began, and would have launched into a string of some of the more exotic psalms had not something very large come sprinting around the corner.

I looked at a pair of hooves and slowly my gaze travelled up the entire length of the nine-foot black scaly demon pointing an accusing talon straight at me.

'You bastard,' it growled. 'It's all your fault.'

45

Twenty-five feet below street level, a leather-clad woman shot the bolt in a cubicle of the ladies and squatted on the closed toilet seat. Quivering only very slightly, she pulled a palmful of paper shreds out from her bra and waited for her eyes to adjust to the dark.

'Oldest trick in the book,' she grinned to herself. 'Simple sleight of hand. Paul Daniels would be proud.'

And slowly, carefully, she attempted to reassemble the beermat. 'Sixteen, yes. Sixty-four, yes . . .' A squirm of doubt crossed her forehead. 'Sixteen sixty-four! No, what kind of a name is that for a lager!'

Spitting angrily, Kirstee exploded out of the cubicle. 'Double-crossing bastard. I save his life and this is how he repays me.'

The door to the ladies barely remained on its hinges.

46

The mayoral chair creaked. There was the slap of elastic against thigh and a pair of Marks and Spencer's finest knickers were tossed on to the carpet.

'You do your bra, will you?' muttered His Worship. 'Those clasps are a bloody nightmare.'

'Men. They never learn. Squeeze the straps together and they just pop open.'

'Rubbish. Never works.'

'I'll photocopy you a diagram tomorrow if you want.'

'It's a woman thing. Like shorthand and pastry.'

'And that's how come I can do it behind my back.'

'Of course. It's as genetic as wearing high heels. Just get it off.'

'And they say romance is dead,' tutted Delia, the secretary. With the slightest arching of her back and a brief flick of shoulder blades the stubborn clasps yielded.

'There's a remote control somewhere, isn't there? C'mon, admit it.'

'Just shut up and take advantage of me, or I'll start to feel guilty and have to do some filing or something.'

'You don't get overtime for that.'

'Is this more what you had in mind?' She knelt on the mayoral chair and settled expertly on to His Worship.

'Ohhhhhhhyes!' Almost immediately, the familiar creaking of the chair began echoing around the office.

And with theatrical timing, the phone rang.

'Get that, would you, it's ruining my rhythm,' groaned Keswick as his eyes rolled.

'Mayor's office?' answered the secretary with barely a twitch in her regular pelvic thrusting. 'No . . . I'm sorry, he's otherwise engaged . . . Disturb him? . . . Hmmm . . .' Expertly, she placed her palm over the mouthpiece and looked down. Keswick's lip twitched. 'Er . . . please hold,' she said into the phone. 'He'll be coming shortly.'

Fifteen short thrusts later and it was all over bar the panting.

'It's for you,' she said, handing him the phone as she dismounted and reached for her undies.

'Uhhhh?' grunted Keswick, wiping his brow.

'Ahh, Your Worship, PC Plain here, just want to talk to you about advertising, sir.'

'What?' The mayor's eyes rolled as his mind failed to focus on anything in particular.

'About this carnival, sir. What is the official position on self-publicity?'

'Er . . . I . . .' He stared across the room as Delia rolled far-from-secretarial stockings up her thighs.

'Is any allowed, sir?'

'No budget.'

'That's what I thought, sir. Thank you, sir. I'll deal with the body immediately.'

'Body?' Keswick sat upright. 'What body?'

The phone went dead.

'He's got a body?'

'Not jealous, are you?' grinned Delia, clipping suspenders demurely. 'I wouldn't be. He'll have to hand his in some-where. You can have me any time.'

'Er, yes, I suppose you're . . .'

'You don't sound too sure. Am I going to have to come over there and prove it?' She looked out from under her fringe and began unclipping her suspenders. Shedding underwear with every step, she crossed the office.

'But, a body . . .' The mayor stabbed 1471 and listened to the digital woman on the other end. 'Telephone number 096 . . .'

Across town a mobile warbled in the front bar of the Monocle and Asparagus. 'Plain here . . . Oh, Your Wor-ship, what can I . . . ? The body? Er, hanging on a pub sign, sir . . . That's right. Well, we can't at this stage rule out alcohol as part of . . . You want us to what? . . . Yes, sir. An honour, sir. Thank you, sir. Thank you so much, sir.'

Barely hiding a wriggle of a smile, PC Plain folded his mobile into his top pocket.

'What was that about?' asked Skitting.

'Beermat,' grinned Plain.

'You've got one.'

'No, Operation Beermat.' He settled back into his chair and folded his arms. 'Gentlemen, we have a green light.'

'I need to go to the toilet,' winced Sim.

47

'You bastard! It's all your fault!'

Frankly, I couldn't believe my ears. 'My fault?' I coughed. 'I'm the victim here. I'm the one lying in the gutter.'

'At least you can crawl out of it on your own knees. What about me, eh? Do these look like my knees?'

My mouth opened. I was convinced I was going to say something. But nothing came out. I was beginning to suspect that there had been something more than just martini in those martinis. Something hallucinogenic. Well, why else would I be imagining talking to a demon about knees?

'And what about these hooves? Try telling me they're mine, eh? You won't convince me.'

I shook my head.

'I used to have shapely ankles,' moaned the demon. 'Nicely turned out. Now I look like a bloody carthorse. And it's all your fault.'

'Would you mind taking your talon out of my nostril, please?'

' "Talon" he says. "Talon". No more fingernails for me. And I bet a quick manicure's out of the question now, isn't it? Why me, eh? Why d'you pick on me?'

'If I knew who you were then I—'

'Oh, that's right. Deny it all, pretend you don't know me. How quickly they forget. Look, pal, you were familiar enough with me this morning. Don't tell me all that's forgotten, eh?'

'This morning? But I . . .' Morning already seemed far too distant to remember with any kind of accuracy. 'Remind me just which bit of this morning you're thinking of.'

'The bit starting with "Jeezusmaryjosephandallthearch-angelsupinheaven" and carry on from there, right?'

'How do you know about—'

'You know, past the hamster and the cage and the fire and the lottery ticket and—'

'What do you want? What are you trying to do to me? You can't know any of that unless . . .'

'Unless I was there? Congratulations, you got it in one.'

'But . . . where's Audrey? What have you done with Miss Williams?'

The demon made a noise like a game show buzzer. 'Wrong answer. I've done nothing to Audrey. You are looking at her.'

'Ohh no, no, I really don't think I . . .' And as I shook my head, I guess I must have jolted some bits of understanding together. Either that or there was something very loose upstairs. Somehow it began to make sense.

They were at it again. The Forces of Evil were trying to headhunt me.

And this creature before me was their attempt at seducing me to the dark side.

I suppose I had to admire them, they were quite persistent. And they'd done their homework. They must have been watching me all morning. And for how long before that? I must admit it was a minor revelation to me when I actually realised that God didn't have a monopoly on the being-in-all-places-at-all-times thing. Made sense really. I mean, Lucifer must've learnt a few tricks when he was a decent archangel.

Good job he hadn't learnt how to create convincing images of womanhood.

This apparition before me was supposed to be the spit of Audrey Williams. And this time, instead of being the idiot I had been and losing her, this time I was supposed to follow her to the ends of the Earth. Or in my case, Hell.

For my continued health, it was time to play along.

'Oh Audrey, it *is* you. And about in there.' I pointed to the club. 'It wasn't my fault they threw me out. I didn't touch her. She made the first moves. Okay, so I was tempted, sure, but that was the whole point, wasn't it? No use having a temptation if you're not tempted. Am I right?'

'Just shut up and take me home.'

'Er . . . okay, whatever you say.' I struggled to my feet and began heading off towards St Cedric's.

'Home,' growled the demon. 'As in your place.'

'This is new. I thought you were supposed to take me to the top of the tallest mountain and do the "This can all be yours" bit.'

'Not right now, my hooves are killing me.'

48

A bored police officer yawned, took another sip of coffee and stared at the bank of CCTV screens currently offering surveillance on a host of known local trouble spots.

' 'Ere, Kev, look at this. Last chance to get in on the action, man.'

'No, I've told you, I don't want to.'

'C'mon, it's only a bit of fun. Give us a fiver and you can . . . Whoa . . . too late. And they're off!' A youth broke away from a group staggering down the road. He veered sharply to the left and headed towards a shadow.

'We're in pursuit,' grinned Frank, the other night officer, grabbing at a joystick and panning the camera. 'Guess Mama Salmonella's up to scratch.' A young man was doubled over throwing his guts up into an abandoned shopping trolley. 'Must've had the Quattro Botulismo Thin Crust.'

'You're sick,' muttered Kev, frowning at Frank, his superior by three days.

'Not me, mate. That's all his doing. Okay, we're going in.' He snatched at a small joystick and pulled focus. 'We have peppers, bread and . . . ohh yes, cabbage. Yes, we have a kebab.' Cheerfully, he ticked a sheet of paper.

Kev shook his head.

'Look, you've only been here two days. I tell you, this is the only way to fight the boredom,' defended Frank. 'By the end of the week you'll be in on the pavement sweepstake. Which currently stands at three pizzas, two kebabs and half a cheeseburger.' He stared at the screens. 'One more pizza and the kitty is all mine.'

'Wait a minute,' said Kev, suddenly sitting up and looking at his screen. 'Hey, I . . . I've got something.'

'Oh yeah? Pizza or kebab?'

'Someone's just been chucked out of a nightclub. Hey, and it looks like a priest.'

'What?' Frank looked over at Kev's screen. 'Ahh, ignore that, they always dress up weird in Il Diablo's. Don't know what they see in the place.'

'Hold on . . . is that the devil?'

'Nah, just *a* devil,' tutted Frank. 'Look, if they're not chucking anything up I'm not interested.'

Kev watched as the two figures in his camera walked out of sight. 'Hmmm, you could be right about this boredom thing. Oooh, hold on though, get an eyeful of her.' A tall leather-clad woman erupted from the doors of Il Diablo's and skittered to a halt. She looked up and down the street, her fists clenching angrily. In seconds she was kicking hell out of an innocent litter bin. 'She doesn't look very happy.'

'PMS,' muttered Frank. And then suddenly he sat upright. 'And what have we here?' A quick flick of joystick and a

grainy image of two figures quivered into shot. 'You wrestling with her or . . . oh yes.' A pair of knickers arced across
the screen. 'Oh yes indeed. Get in there, man!' With glee,
Frank placed a tick on another piece of paper. 'And I'm way
on target for walking away with the Bonking Bonus.'

Kev shook his head.

49

An air of feverish panic emanated from the pair of figures
deep in the basement of St Cedric's. Six dozen incense sticks
smouldered on shelves, filling the room with an almost
choking fog.

'Well? Are you done yet?' hissed Bishop Hutchinson with
the nervy impatience of a six-year-old on the first day of its
summer holiday.

'Just a few more and I'll be—'

'A few more? This has got to be right. Seventy-seven incense
sticks. Precisely seventy-seven, it's written here.' He jabbed an
irritable finger into a musty book. 'You remember?'

'Of course I remember,' grumbled Brother Lyndsey as he
lit another pair. 'You reminded me twenty seconds ago. Just
relax, I know what I'm doing.' He placed the glowing sticks
in another vase and lit three more.

'And the hundred and fifty-two candles, how are they
coming?'

'Brilliantly. One hundred and twenty lit.'

'What? But I've done forty-six. Quick, blow some out!'

'Look, just go and decant some Holy Water or something.
Leave the incendiaries to me. Otherwise I'll lose count and
then God alone knows what we'll end up with.'

'You don't have to tell me how particular these miracles
are. The setting's got to be spot-on.'

'Yes, well, just go and get the water ready. I've put the carafes out on the altar over there, okay? Three enough?'

'Plenty, plenty. This isn't a resurrection.' And so, checking things off on his fingers as he went, Bishop Hutchinson shuffled off towards a large marble altar draped in white linen.

Minutes later, having extinguished the extra candles and completed lighting all the incense sticks, Lyndsey knelt beside the bishop.

'All present and correct, Your Holiness.'

'Close your eyes and start swinging that burner. Slowly.'

Smoke rose in billows as Bishop Hutchinson began reading from the ancient text concerned with the re-establishment of a Vision of Immaculate Camouflage. A low and heavily accented chant built up within the candle-lit basement. To any observer it sounded primeval. Shrouded in the mystery of the Far East.

It was shattered by a sudden coughing fit from Brother Lyndsey.

'Sorry,' he choked a few moments later after a sip of water. 'Incense always gets the back of my throat.'

'Well, hold your breath and shut up,' hissed the bishop out of the corner of his mouth. 'This isn't easy with you coughing your guts up. Now, after three. Believe.'

And the chanting started again.

It reached the third canto and stopped.

'Are you concentrating?' scowled the bishop, squinting out of one eye.

'Who me? Ahh, well no,' confessed Lyndsey. 'I kind of drifted off there, sorry. It's been a hard day and that chanting, well, it's just like those hypnotherapy tapes I've got upstairs—'

141

'You won't have a room upstairs if we don't get this done. The boys in Rome frown on non-secret activities. Remember?'

'Ahh, right. Consider me in full belief of your abilities as of now. Only, one thing, can you make that chanting just a little less soothing?'

Hutch frowned and launched back into canto three with a definite turn of speed. He knew the attention span of his colleague. Especially at this time of night.

And upstairs, out on Jeroboam Hill, something began to happen. Much to the immense confusion of a flock of pigeons who were settling down in the relative warmth of the remains of room six, patches of the floor began to vanish. The bed disappeared and several dozen tons of worthless rubble apparently faded out of existence. Rafters blinked into nothingness and were followed by arteries of aging plumbing.

Quite simply, St Cedric's Hostel for the Less Than Perfectly Well rippled out of sight.

And it would have stayed there too, if it hadn't been for the tiny draught which happened to snuff a single candle in the furthest reaches of the basement. A couple of seconds each way and it wouldn't really have made much odds. But fate being what it is at times like this, the candle died during the establishment of a particularly delicate control sub-blessing.

Three seconds later, and the space formerly known as St Cedric's quivered into a perfect art-deco glasshouse, filled with exotic fernery and a few even more exotic marble statues.

It didn't stay there long.

Two and a half minutes to be precise.

The air shimmered and, as if by magic, a shopping mall appeared and a confused flock of pigeons took to the Camford night sky.

142

50

PC Skitting nursed the last warm dregs of another pint into the back of his throat and settled the empty glass on the table. 'I think it was a wind-up.'

'Nonsense, they'll be here.'

'You said that three pints ago,' tutted Sim. 'And it's your round.'

'Look, these things take time. You don't just jump straight into Operation Beermat without some preparation. Even SWAT teams think before they go in.'

'Never looks that way. Those Americans are trigger-happy, I reckon.'

Sheepishly, PC Sim raised a hand. 'Er, am I the only one here who doesn't know what Operation Beermat is?'

'No,' replied Skitting.

'There's the whole of the rest of the Camford populace who are blissfully unaware of it.'

'Er, that's good?' shrugged Sim.

Plain nodded with self-assured satisfaction.

'So you going to let me in on it?' begged Sim. 'I'll buy you a pint.'

'And me,' whispered Skitting.

Plain leant forward as if briefing secret agents on the brink of a mission. 'Put in its simplest terms, Operation Beermat is designed to mop up the unwanted elements in our local hostelries.'

'What, like fag ends in the urinals?' asked Skitting, missing the metaphor by a mile.

'Like them.' Plain pointed a covert finger into the back bar. The others stared at the morris men.

'I like pissing on fag ends,' mused Sim. 'Gives me something to aim at.'

'Yeah,' nodded Skitting. 'It's hell when you miss. Takes days to get the shine back on your boots.'

'Shut up,' hissed Plain through his teeth. 'I'm talking about the criminal element.'

'Mercury,' grinned Sim. 'Well, it's an element. All right, I'm listening.'

'Good,' tutted Plain and put on his lecturing hat. 'A couple of years ago, a report came out saying that one hundred per cent of all alcohol-related crimes involved booze in some way.'

Sim was impressed. 'Wow. That's statistics for you.'

'And so, after the injection of several million quid's worth of European cash, Operation Beermat was born. Specifically designed to combat crime in public houses, every bar in town was given a special number to call in case of trouble. Look.' Plain pointed to a sticker just above the till which was almost totally obscured by the numbers of local taxi firms.

Sim squinted and made it out.

> Operation Beermat.
> In case of trouble and stuff
> call 999

'Nice to know our European cousins are looking after us so well,' smiled Sim. 'And so clever of the mayor to use a number that most people are familiar with. There's too many phone numbers about these days. And e-mail addresses. I can never remember them. Slash this, at that, dot the other.'

'So where are they?' asked Skitting, trying his best to ignore Sim. Experience had taught him it was always best to. Ever since he'd failed to get to grips with level one of Abe's OddWorld, he'd had a downer on all things computational. Skitting shuddered as he recalled the dying days of 1999

144

when every other day had Sim wittering on about the millennium bug being nothing but a hoax to keep money-grabbing computer programmers in so-called work. The first quarter of 2000 hadn't been much better either. If only he could have had a pound for every time Sim had said 'I told you so' in that smug way of his . . .

'They're on their way,' whispered Plain. 'I'm sure of it.'

'Well, they'd better get a shift on,' tutted Skitting as he glanced at the clock above the bar. The bell for last orders rang.

'Hot in here, isn't it?' grinned Sim, looking pointedly at his glass.

'All right. The usual?' grunted Plain, heading for another round.

He failed completely to see the three men huddled in the shadow of the cigarette machine. Missed another who was currently camouflaged as a bar stool. And he happened not to hear the greased wheels of the team on the roof as they sped down the length of the telephone cable and headed for the chimney.

'Timegentlemenpleasehaveyougotnohomestogoto?' yelled the landlord on the dot of eleven.

It was the signal for action. Three flak-jacketed coppers erupted from the cigarette machine and a bar stool suddenly produced an assault rifle. Clouds of soot tumbled into the back bar as a crack unit abseiled in and landed, blinking. In seconds the morris men were surrounded, the barrels of loaded weaponry pointing at vital organs.

'Phone them and they will come,' smiled Plain, sipping at his pint as the first victims of Operation Beermat were frogmarched out towards a waiting van.

'You didn't get me any peanuts,' complained Sim.

51

It wasn't the best night's sleep I'd ever had. And the duvet proved it.

Currently, it was huddled in a heap at the side of my bed, lying there looking up at me as if I regularly beat it. I shivered, grabbed it and pulled it over me. My clothes tumbled over the floor.

'Ohhhh God,' I heard myself groan. It rattled inside my head, kicking through the debris of far too many martinis. 'Never again,' I vowed.

And then the memories of the night before fluttered to the forefront of my mind, chattering for attention like starving fruit bats. Lottery tickets metamorphosed into dying hamsters and cross-faded into leather-clad ladies of the night. And worse.

A large and particularly ugly-looking memory grinned at me. It seemed convinced that I'd been accosted by nine foot of black scaly demon.

'No way,' I tutted. 'That could *never* have happened, okay?'

Stubbornly, the memory lingered, hanging around with the charm of the last sausage roll on the buffet.

'Impossible. Things like that just don't happen. Nightmare, that's what it is. A nightmare. And I'll prove it.' I struggled to my feet, slid my toes into the backsides of a pair of large pink rabbit-shaped slippers and shuffled off to the kitchen.

For a moment I stood before the magnet-covered fridge, hand on the door. 'Well-known fact, nightmares are caused by too much cheese too close to bedtime, right?'

The memory shrugged. Unconvinced.

I tugged open the fridge. 'Tan-naah. Not a scrap of cheese. There y'go. Ate it all last night. QED.'

I slammed the door shut, whirled around and ended up

face to nipple with the blackest, scaliest demon I'd ever seen in my kitchen.

'And just what time d'you call this?' hissed the beast.

I backed hurriedly into the fridge door, barely noticing how cold it felt.

'Go away, you're not real. Imaginary. Click your heels and you'll be back in Kansas.' The rabbits made hardly a sound despite repeated collisions of heels.

Naturally, little had changed when I next opened my eyes. 'You're just a piece of cheese,' I panted. 'You're not here. I'm still asleep. Safe and warm in my bed.'

'You often dream of yourself in your kitchen?'

'Oh yes,' I insisted, eyes screwed shut. 'All the time.'

'And in your dream kitchen, just what are you normally wearing?'

It smelled like a trick question, but I was on it. 'Chef's coat, white. Chef's hat, white. Catering trousers, black and white squares, teatowel hooked in the right pocket.'

'And that's what you're wearing now?'

'Ohh yes. Absolutely. Five buttons down the front, hand-kerchief in the top pocket—'

'Open your eyes.'

'No thanks, I'm fine.'

'Open your eyes.'

'Nope. Can't do that in a dream anyway. You open your eyes and you're dead. Says so in all those meaning of dreams books and—'

'Open them or I'll rip your eyelids off!'

There was something about the tone of voice that made me suspect that maybe something wasn't quite right in the land of nod. After all, dreams never usually answered back. And I'd never had one threaten me. I obeyed. Well, I was fond of my eyelids.

147

'So where's the chef suit now, eh?'

I wasn't sure which was worse. Discovering that there was, in fact, nine foot of demon inhabiting my kitchen. Or the fact that I was wearing nothing but two pink rabbits in full view of the nine foot of demon currently inhabiting my kitchen.

I screamed.

My head hated me.

52

Away across Europe, deep under the banks of the Tiber, a tiny electrical contact was made. Microamps trickled into a control circuit, activated a heating coil and passed to earth, secure in the satisfaction of a job well done. On a shelf in the darkened office, a gallon of water was brought to the boil and a perfect measure of Blue Mountain beans were swiftly pulverised.

By the time the key was turned in the door, the office was filled with the distinctive aroma of freshly waiting coffee.

'Double cappuccino. Extra chocolate,' ordered the first man through the door. 'You?' He turned to his new colleague, an eyebrow of query raised.

'Er . . . oh, low-fat latté.'

'Wimp,' grumbled the elder of the two black-cassocked men. 'I'll have to wean you off that thin stuff. My mission, and I've already accepted it, is to have you supping double cappuccinos by the end of the month.'

'Is that an order?'

'Not yet,' grinned Cardinal Aguilera, and reached for the steaming mug which appeared from the automated machine. He paused with it between his hands, inhaling slowly, eyes closed as if in morning prayer. 'Ahhh, beautiful, don't you just love it,' he sighed and took a loving sip of his cappuccino. 'Perfect every time. One of His finer inventions, don't you think?'

Francisco, the novice, shrugged. Was this a test? His immediate reaction would have been to say yes. Obviously the cardinal liked whatever it was he was on about and Francisco already knew that the quickest route up the promotional ladder was to agree with whatever the boss said.

But he had heard the capital 'H'. This was Him they were discussing. One of His finer inventions. He looked at the vast black coffee machine. Surely the cardinal couldn't be referring to that, could he? I mean, God didn't invent technology, did He? This was some kind of test. What if he chose the wrong answer and said something blasphemous? Was worshipping technology still blasphemous? Did they still have the Inquisition hereabouts? They had lots of other weird things that no one outside ever got to hear of. So why not the Inquisition?

'Well?' asked Aguilera as the coffee machine gave birth to a low-fat latté. 'Taste that and tell me I'm wrong.'

Francisco felt his stress levels rise. Tell him he's wrong? Go against the cardinal? That was surely instant death.

The cardinal took a swig of his cappuccino. 'Ahhhhhh, *in nomine familia Rubiaceae, genus Coffea spiritus arabica.*'

Francisco's stomach knotted. Oh no, he was spouting Latin. He *was* testing him. But something didn't sound right about it. Something non-ecclesiastical. Something almost biological.

'Still,' mused Aguilera, 'enough coffee worship, He might get jealous. And there's nothing worse than a lifetime's curse before elevenses.'

149

Francisco breathed out. 'Just one question,' he asked as he picked up his latté. 'Did God invent the coffee machine?'

'Sometimes I wonder,' grinned the cardinal and headed for the answerphone. Absently, he flicked the playback button. Immediately a small speaker resonated to the sound of a panicking Irish accent.

'Oh, the shame of it all. I hate you not being in when I call. It's so degrading having to talk to a machine, you wouldn't believe. Just try it. Anyhow, if it wasn't important I wouldn't be telling you 'cause I hate answerphones.'

'Ho hum,' grumbled Aguilera. 'And the point of this is?'

'Now, just a call to inform you that the safe house here in Camford . . . well, it's not so safe any more. By the way, change that message. It's not friendly at all. Ciao.'

'What did he say?'

'Something about the message being—'

'The safe house! Get me the files,' hissed the cardinal, suddenly animated, suddenly forgetting about the delights of double cappuccinos. 'Over there. Under "s". Quick. Oh God, what time was that message left?'

The novice struggled across the office under the weight of a vast cloth-bound file. With a grunt he heaved it on to the desk, almost upending the cardinal's mug. 'Mind the coffee,' he hissed and dived into the file. 'Camford, Camford . . . ahh, here it . . . Uh-oh . . .'

He stared at the page, blinking at the two red ink stamps, each saying 'Active'.

'This is bad.'

'Er, what is?'

The cardinal dashed across the office, chanting low under his breath. In the far corner an ancient-looking baptismal font flickered and lit up. The water glowed as if a blue fluorescent tube had been dropped in it.

Francisco's eyes were suddenly wide with wonder as a menu of letters appeared a fraction of an inch above the water surface.

'What d'you think?' whispered the cardinal. 'Dial "M" for miracle?'

'Don't ask me. I haven't a clue what you're on about. I'm a novice, remember?'

'There are two of them,' muttered the cardinal, oblivious to Francisco's presence. 'If they were to fall into the wrong hands . . . Surely one little automiracle won't hurt.'

With expert fingers the cardinal pulled at the floating cross-shaped cursor, placing it firmly on the letter 'M'.

The water shimmered and a new menu appeared.

Francisco's jaw dropped as his eye caught the first few entries. Angels. Apparition. Ascension. There were more, but already they were a blur as Aguilera scrolled down towards the bottom. He halted the cursor over Visions and stared at a new menu.

'We don't want anything too attention-grabbing,' he muttered, flicking past the entire God section.

Francisco caught glimpses of entries. Face of God: Trad male caucasian w. beard / Single white female w. flowing hair / Female black African. Hand of God: Pointing / Beckoning / Thumbs up. Hand with Choir of Angels . . .

'No, no. Where's the undercover bit? Honestly, how are we supposed to stay secret with all of this showy . . . Aha. Now that's more like it.'

He stared at the section concerning Doves of Peace and selected Single White without Laurel Branch. 'Co-ordinates. Get me the co-ordinates of Camford. St Screed's.'

'Er, St What?' asked Francisco as he wrestled through the safe house file.

'Screed.'

'That's what I thought you said. Er, can't find it. Nothing of that name here.'

'But I was just looking at it. They changed the name. Some management consultants decided it was too old-fashioned. Now it's . . . it's . . . Cedric's.'

'Found it.' He turned the file towards the cardinal and listened as he chanted the numbers in.

Ten seconds later, high above the heads of the residents of Camford, a small dove shimmered into existence. It glowed with an oddly radioactive tinge as it hovered over a vast crowd gathered on Jeroboam Hill.

'Oh my God,' whispered Cardinal Aguilera as he peered down from the dove's-eye view. The crowd applauded wildly as a vision of the White House metamorphosed into a fifty-storey hotel complex in Las Vegas. The front lobby was filled with a troupe of leggy dancers wearing nothing but high heels and an ostrich-worth of feathers each.

A man in grubby overalls stood on a stable piece of pavement and argued into his mobile phone. 'That's what I said. I don't know when I'll get the truck out . . . Because right now it's a palm tree. Okay? You try getting a hawser round a palm tree . . . No, I haven't been drinking . . . Uh-oh. It's off again.'

There was a crackle of static and the Great Pyramid of Giza hove into view. Complete with local wildlife. The crowd went wild. And, much to her surprise, Kirstee joined in. Okay, so she knew very well this wasn't getting her any closer to a certain thirteen-million-pound lottery ticket, but it was quite amusing. Better than she had expected for part of the Camford Festival of Arts and Stuff.

'Right, that's it, I'm not going anywhere near it now . . .' continued the mechanic in the overalls. 'Because it's a camel, that's why . . . Oh, you'll give me cheap rates for personal injury cover, will you? Geez, you insurance guys are all the same . . . Yeah, I know you want this job done fast, you always want House of God jobs done fast . . . Look, don't you insult us hourly-paid guys. No, I'm not screwing you for extra . . . Hello? Hello?'

Kirstee's ears pricked up. '*House of God job.*' And a connection was made. It was a good place to start looking for a certain priest. She set off to find a back entrance, her spirits rising. She felt good about this; after all, any religious establishment that felt good enough to shell out money on such a spectacular show for the carnival was bound to have someone in there with a strong enough community spirit to pester the clientele of Il Diablo's. With a skip in her stilettoed step, she snuck off down a small alley.

Back in the coffee-smelling office under the banks of the Tiber, Cardinal Aguilera was shaking his head. 'God, the English. When they cock up they really do it well. Francisco, get on the phone and grab us the next two tickets on the first flight out of here.'

'Flight?' he coughed, ripping his eyes reluctantly from the screen. 'You mean we can't use something out of there? Y'know, a miracle?'

'I wish. Our job would be simpler.'

'We've got to go by public transport?' squeaked the novice with a quiver of disappointment.

'Trust me, it's quicker.'

'Why can't we take a short cut, y'know, nip across the sea like He did in Galilee?'

'You ever tried walking on water against a head wind? Two forward, thirty back. Not fun at all.'

'But there must be a better way.'

'You been watching too much TV. Blame Christ. Why He had that thing about walking everywhere I'll never know.

153

Fastest he ever travelled was on the back of a mule. Get me on a 747.'

Francisco shrugged and picked up the phone.

And for the first time in well over thirty years, someone made a call out of the office of the Vatican Deep Cover Surveillance Department.

53

You wouldn't believe quite how hard it is to concentrate on getting yourself showered when you know that one of Satan's chums is pacing about outside the bathroom door. Those little brass bolts feel flimsy at the best of times, but right then – well, I may as well have tried to keep the door shut with a damp hair stuck across the gap.

'Just how much longer are you going to be in there?' growled the beast, rattling the handle for effect. 'We haven't got all day you know'

'I'm drying my hair.'

'You could have done that sooner. I've been up for hours.'

I shook my head in a spray of water. That was all I needed. A self-righteous demon. It was going to be bad enough being seduced into the dark side. But by a self-righteous creature from the nether regions of hell? I shuddered and then resigned myself to the inevitable. I supposed it was part of the job. Necessary evil, so to speak. I mean, the army has to put up with being shot at. Novelists have to suffer the idiocy of critics. It was just one of those things that priests have to face, once in a while. The sand in the vaseline of an otherwise cracking job.

'Hurry up in there. You've already missed the best part of the day.'

'And that is?'

'Night. Of course.'

I knew I shouldn't have asked.

'C'mon. We've got things to do,' hissed the beast.

I combed my hair in the steamed mirror, took a deep breath and emerged to face my own personal demon. 'Things to do?' I asked, looking up its nose. 'Things like tempting me. Wrestling with my deepest vows. Challenging the very basis of my belief system.'

'Er . . . I was thinking of something more like breaking and entering.'

'What?'

'The bishop's office at St Cedric's.'

'How do you know about that?'

'Duh, stands to reason, doesn't it? There's a bishop in St Cedric's so he's bound to have an office.'

'No. I meant St Cedric's. It's supposed to be a secret.' My stomach grumbled and reminded me it hadn't had its break-fast yet.

'Look, it's no secret to me. I've just spent eight weeks in there.'

My head reeled. They'd been planning this for a long time. I was surely doomed. Unless . . .

'Look, can I have a quick bowl of Shreddies, only . . .'

'No, we've got to go now.'

'What's the hurry?'

'This is!' The demon pointed to himself hunched in the hall outside my bathroom, horns scraping the Artex. 'I can't go on looking like this.'

My mouth opened. Then closed. Then hung open again.

'You try looking like this. It's hell. Especially when I think back to . . .'

My jaw swung even slacker as a sniff of emotion flicked around the beast's nostrils.

155

'Yesterday I was beautiful,' it moaned. 'Okay, maybe not movie star, country chick drop-dead gorgeous, but hey, I could turn heads.'

'Still can,' I muttered. Fortunately it didn't hear. Or it just ignored me, saving such transgressions up for later.

'And I had hair. Real hair. Hair that Jennifer Aniston would be proud of. Not this!' It tugged at the tufts of curly fuse wire sprouting from around the base of its horns. 'I can't do a thing with it.'

'You could try beads. They can do wonders, you know. They can even make dreadlocks look nice. In certain lights.'

'I want my old hair back. I want to be my old self. You've got to help me get rid of these bloody hooves. Promise me.'

'But what can I do?'

'Get me into the bishop's office.'

'I . . . I can't do that.'

'You can. You've got keys to every room in that place.'

I took a step back. 'How do you know that?'

'I've seen them hanging from your apron strings. Look, I'm getting into that office, okay? And I'm doing it with or without your help. It's up to you.'

I scratched my head. There was some weird psychology going on here. This wasn't the type of temptation I would have expected from an agent of the underworld. *You get me into the office and I'll give you all the sex, money and strong hallucinatory drugs you can handle for the rest of your life!* Now that I could imagine. This was disturbingly different.

'But if I go in on my own, I assure you they're going to need to call a locksmith. These are bound to cause a stack of damage.' It flicked its talons.

And suddenly I almost felt relieved. That pretty much sounded like a threat. I could deal with that.

'All right,' I answered, aiming for a businesslike tone in my voice. I missed. 'I get you into the office and that's it.'

'Oh no. You've got to open the files as well. You try turning pages with these talons.'

'Fine. The office and the files. And that's it.'

'Right. Let's go, then.'

'Er, can I iron my dog-collar first?'

'No,' growled the demon and headed off slowly down the stairs. Each step was painfully slow. 'Bloody hooves,' it grumbled. 'Bloody stairs.'

54

Deep in the bowels of Camford Constabulary Headquarters, in the formaldehyde-smelling forensics lab, a body lay crumpled on a post-mortem slab. Its mouth hung open, tongue lolling limply. Its eyes were closed, lifeless. It was almost as if it was waiting to be opened up.

A knock on the door echoed around the lab, rattling off trays of shining instruments, rebounding from a thousand different organs floating in preserving jars. 'Special delivery,' called a voice through the frosted glass.

There was no answer.

'Special delivery. Hello? Anyone there?' And then lower, under a breath. 'Shit, shit, shit. I hate it when this happens.' He stared at the paperwork sellotaped to the stomach of the body bag. He knew the drill. If there was no answer he'd have to take the thing back. He looked back down the corridor and shuddered. Dragging that thing up the stairs was going to be a real pig. Of course, he could leave a note saying he'd left the delivery with the people next door, but somehow he didn't think that would go down too well. High street banks don't normally go a bundle on the deposit of cadavers. Unless they come with a significant cash advance.

He rapped on the door again. Still no answer.

On the offchance, he tried the door. Incredibly, it was open. But then why shouldn't it be? If anyone was desperate enough to want to steal something that was already days or even weeks dead, a mere lock wouldn't stop them.

The delivery man shoved open the door and wheeled the corpse in. 'Er, hello? The door was unlocked?'

And then he saw the body on the slab. His stomach writhed uncomfortably. Somehow he could cope with the one on the trolley before him. Well, it was packaged correctly. Black plastic body-bag. Kite mark, the lot. But that thing. Well, it was there. Uncovered. Dead.

At least it was until it coughed and sat up.

The delivery man was long gone before Doctor Boscombe found his glasses and vowed for the millionth time not to end a day in the office with IM and T's. There was something about industrial methanol and tonic that was frankly addictive. Slight twist of lemon in there too and before you know it one's become twenty and you're out cold on anything that looks vaguely bed-shaped.

He ran his fingers through his hair, groaned and noticed the delivery. Almost immediately his spirits rose, wrestling any trace of hangover into the back of his brain. 'What have we here?' he grinned, rubbing his hands together as he stalked across the lab. It was a rhetorical question. He knew exactly what he had there. And his fingers were already itching to get inside it.

With a grunt of effort he swung the dead weight on to the slab, unzipped the body bag and began cheerfully arranging his favourite implements.

'At last,' grumbled Bertrand Matlock, sitting bolt upright. 'I tell you, it's not pleasant in there. Dark. Smells of rubber. And something else I can't quite put my finger on.'

'Scalpel. Forceps,' muttered Boscombe with the lilt of a mantra.

'In fact, I don't know what I was doing in there,' continued the leader of the morris men. 'Anyway, I've got a troupe of chaps to chivvy into shape, so I really must away.'

'Pliers. Kidney dish.'

'Are you listening to me?' objected Matlock, glaring at the doctor. 'It's not nice to ignore people when they're talking to you. Bad manners it is.'

'Hacksaw. Gouge.'

'Leave those things alone will you and tell me how I get to Keswick Square. Is it far? Would you mind answering me, please?' He swung his legs off the slab and marched across the lab. 'Honestly, I'd expect such behaviour from a teenager, but you, sir . . .'

He reached out to tap the doctor on the shoulder. It was only as his hand passed clean through his shoulder blade that Matlock realised all was not well.

Boscombe picked up his tray of surgical goodies, turned and stepped clean through the man in the morris suit.

Matlock screamed. 'What's happening? What's going on? This is a dream, isn't it? I'm still asleep. If I count to three I'll wake up and . . . and . . . onetwothree!' Nothing in the lab changed.

Well, except for the dark shadow that was growing in the centre of the floor. It spread across the tiles, expanding like a malevolent fungus at full time-lapse.

Matlock edged away nervously. 'Er . . . do you know your floor's dissolving? Hello? Your floor? Don't you care about . . . Oh my God.' It was at that moment that he caught sight of the body on the slab. He stared in horror as he recognised it.

Casually, Boscombe flicked a tape recorder on. 'Post-mortem exam of John Doe, 359/12, I think. Remind me to check that. Er, preliminary examination reveals what appears to be a morris dancing costume.'

'What d'you mean, "appears to be"? It is one! And a very fine one at that. Tailor-made for me by . . .'

Boscombe grabbed a scalpel from his tray and spun it theatrically between his fingers.

'What are you going to do with that?' gasped Matlock, certain he knew very well.

And Boscombe's scalpel came down, its point hovering inches above the dead man's navel.

'No!' squealed Matlock. 'Leave him . . . me alone! You can't just start chopping me up. Don't I have to sign something?'

Blissfully unaware of the objections behind him, Boscombe readied himself for the first incision.

And there was a knock on the door.

'Go away!'

'Thought you'd say that,' answered PC Plain, stepping into the lab. 'Carry on.'

'What the hell are you doing here?'

'My body,' grinned Plain, pointing at the slab.

'It's my body!' objected Matlock. He was ignored.

'I found it,' continued Plain.

'And just why are you here, hmmm?' frowned Boscombe, looking surprisingly like a young Boris Karloff. 'You do realise that a post-mortem examination is not a spectator sport.'

'I've got this theory about why he died,' grinned Plain. 'It was a tragic accident.'

'You're right about the tragic bit,' tutted Matlock. 'But it was no accident. I'm telling you, I was—'

'An accident?' scowled Boscombe, looking from Plain to the body. 'And just how does an accident end with his braces wrapped around his neck?'

'I was murdered!'

'Publicity,' said Plain, sporting his most enigmatic smile.

'This should be good,' tutted Boscombe, folding his arms. 'Give.'

'He was an advert designed to attract thousands to their part of the carnival. Only he slipped and . . .' He mimed being hung.

'No! It wasn't anything like that!'

Boscombe shook his head. 'This is another one of your little jokes, isn't it? I mean, look at this chap, does he look like a morris man to you? He's way too thin.'

'Hey!' objected Matlock. 'I was getting quite good.'

'And another thing.' Boscombe produced a syringe from somewhere and jammed it into Matlock's arm. In seconds he had dropped a few cc's of blood into a waiting beaker. It failed to change colour. 'Thought so,' he grinned. 'No alcohol. PC Plain, this man could not have been a morris man. He had not been drinking.'

'Oh,' muttered a crestfallen constable.

'That puts paid to your advertising theory, eh? This man was killed by something else. Now if you don't mind, I have a post-mortem to perform.' Boscombe glared at the door. Plain got the message.

'You're right,' ranted Matlock. 'I was killed by something else. All nine foot of it!'

Boscombe picked up his scalpel again and advanced towards the slab. 'Now, where were we?'

'No, you can't do that!' squealed Matlock.

'He can,' came a voice which sounded as though it was coming from under a cupboard. 'It's his job.'

Matlock spun around and stared at the vast black hole which had opened in the lab. And then he heard the screaming. Countless millions of tortured souls wailed far, far away. 'What the hell . . . ?'

'Got it in one,' grinned the demon peering out of the hole. 'Very astute. You'll go far.'

'No, you can't take me. Not down there.'

'Oh yes? And why not? And before you answer, please consider that I have been at this job a very long time. I have heard a great many excuses.'

'You can't take me because . . . I'm not dead?'

'That's the thirteen billionth time out for that one. Answer me this, just who's that on the slab, eh? Look, just let go, you've already had fifteen minutes extra.'

'No, you can't.'

'Oh, what is it this time?'

'Er, them!' Matlock pointed at the ceiling, where a heavenly glow was widening. Hosts of angels chorused in the background as a golden light beamed down around the ceiling-mounted fluorescent tube.

'Bugger,' cursed the demon. 'Thought I'd beaten them.'

'Here I am!' called Matlock, throwing his arms wide. 'Take me.'

Behind him, blissfully unaware of the cosmic struggle currently invading the lab, Boscombe finally made his first incision.

Somehow, over the wailing and gnashing of teeth and the strains of angels, Matlock heard the scalpel slice through his body.

'No!' he squealed, whirling around and grabbing Bos-

162

combe around the throat. 'Leave me alone. That's my bloody body. Hands off!'

And above him the Gate of Heaven began to close.

'Wait, come back. Where are you going?'

'Not suitable,' boomed a pious voice. 'Can't have language like that up here.'

'No, come back. It's a mistake. Bloody's an adjective. Look at me . . . er, him . . . it! Don't leave me!'

'Tough titty,' grinned the demon in the floor, his talons closing round Matlock's ankle. 'Going down.'

'Bloody well let go,' shouted Matlock. 'Get your poxy talons off me, you bastard.'

The demon grinned. 'That's the spirit. Good bit of cursing's just what you need at a time like this. Tell you what, we've got some great new words down here. You'll love 'em. Love 'em.'

And with one final scream of protest, the floor closed.

55

We were out the front door and a hundred yards up the road before reality tapped on my shoulder. I caught sight of the two of us in a shop window and my heart sank. There I was, jeans, T-shirt and dog-collar. And leering down the road behind me was nine foot of demon, horns, hooves, the works. It was not, it had to be said, a sight you would normally see every day. Kind of conspicuous. And yet, curiously, nobody seemed to be batting the slightest of eyelids.

'Don't tell me,' I began. 'It's just me, isn't it? Only I can see you, right?'

'What?'

'To everyone else there's just me, a particularly worried-looking priest, dashing down the road, on his own. Nobody else in tow. Nothing. You are invisible, yeah? My imaginary friend?'

'What are you on about? I'm real.'

'Yeah, right. And, like, my imagination's working double time.'

At that very instant, a knight in rusting chain-mail emerged from the chemist. He moved slowly, standing on the heads of two four-foot-tall peasants. 'Neddy? Neddy, wherefore art thou, Neddy?' he called down the street. 'You, sir?' He stared down at me. 'Hast thou espied my trusty white charger, for I seem to have mislaid him?'

'What?' It was the best I could do. Well, face to face with my imagination, what would you do?

'In my quest to keep these peasants downtrodden, I have allowed my steed to stray. Hast thou espied it hereabouts?'

I looked at the papier maché peasants suffering underfoot and my left eye started to twitch. It was too early in the day for this.

'C'mon, mate, play the game,' whispered the knight. 'We're all in this carnival together, right?' He pointed to my collar, winked and raised his voice. 'Thou hast espied my trusty stallion? And where wast it headething? East nor-west?'

'Er, yeah. Followed by a yellow van,' I answered.

The knight scowled at me and headed off in disgust. As he drew next to the demon behind me he slowed down. 'Hey mate, word of advice amongst us tall people. Just watch it if you're going down the next left. Some of the pub signs are way too low.' He pointed to the plaster freshly stuck to his forehead. 'By the way, great costume. See you in the main procession later.' He raised his voice again and shambled off up the street. 'Citizens of Camford, hast anyone espied my

164

horse? Neddy, wherefore art thou? You, boy? Hast thou seen my Neddy?'

I shook my head and walked away as a three-year-old boy burst spontaneously into tears. It would almost be a relief to do a bit of straightforward breaking and entering after this start to the day. Okay, so I was sure that I could be defrocked for illegally entering the bishop's office but, hey, at least that was just an office, right? At least there was nothing too unexpected lurking in there. Just files and papers and office stuff. Safe.

I quickened my pace and the clatter of hooves rattled on behind me.

Less than ten minutes later and I turned into a small dark alley. 'And before you ask,' I said heading any demonic objections off at the proverbial pass, 'we are not going in the front way. Clear? They *would* notice you. It's their job. And besides, they're not doing anything for the carnival.'

I turned to the ground-floor window ahead of me and eased one of the tiny glass panels out of its frame. I'd noticed it was loose a couple of days ago during a particularly vigorous cleaning session and had meant to inform a glazier. Briefly wondering if forgetfulness was one of the minor sins and if so just what price the penance, I reached inside and eased the lower sash open. In moments I was inside, looking out.

'Well, we're here. C'mon.'

'I . . . I'm not sure if I want to,' whispered the demon, looking almost sheepish. It must have put a lot of effort into it.

'What? Where's all the "get me into that office or else"?'

'I'm scared.'

'Look, just get in here, do the job, get out. Couldn't be easier. Hutch'll never even know.' I began to wonder what was going on in my mind. That reverse psychology was happening again. Surely I hadn't just been persuading a demon to do a bit of breaking and entering?

'It's not that. It's . . . well, what I might find out. It could be that I am actually five foot eight of slender brunette and that due to some freak skin condition I just happen to look like this.'

'There are times when I really think English is not your first language. You do know you're not making any sense?'

'Look, I've been trying to explain. But . . .' The beast took a breath. 'Up until yesterday evening, I . . . I was Audrey Williams. I mean, I still am, I think. Does that sound confused?'

I shrugged as I mulled that one over. A day or two ago and the answer to that would've been a piece of cake. Right now, confusion was in the ascendant and destined to outshine Capricorn in a matter of moments. 'No more than anything else does today,' I sighed, trying to play down the panic rising inside me. Inside, my mind was racing. I was talking to a demon with some serious personality disorder here. 'You want me to open the files, or not? Maybe we could just go for a stroll round town together. You know, inconspicuous like. Hey, we could even find a quiet pub, watch the carnival?' I was impressed with myself, it even sounded sarcastic to me.

And then, in a moment of lucidity, a plan appeared. I mulled it over, cogitated for ooooh, a couple of seconds and decided that it was worth a try. There was going to be only one way of getting this demon off my back and that was to fight it with the only weapon I really knew how to handle. The truth. I pulled a bunch of keys out of the bishop's drawer and turned to the filing cabinet. 'Williams, wasn't it? Audrey.'

There was a nodding of horns.

166

A swift rattle of keys and the file was in my hand. I crossed to the window, barely keeping all the paperwork in the damn thing.

'It's . . . it's full,' gasped the beast after I'd persuaded it to open its eyes.

'To bursting. And what else did you expect? A suspiciously empty file indicating that your history has deliberately been eradicated as you are no doubt embroiled in some deadly plot?'

'Well, yes,' muttered the demon, sounding disappointed.

'And this assumption was based upon the singular lack of relevant information pasted upon the end of your bed, no doubt?'

'Actually, yes.'

I opened the file. 'Uh-huh. Well, sorry to tell you this, but you aren't Audrey Williams.' I waggled a sheet of paper importantly. 'Since she is five foot three, blonde, and weighs one hundred and twenty pounds. You on the other hand—'

'That's not right. Show me that.'

I shrugged and handed over the page.

'See, like it says here,' I continued. 'Five nine, brunette, one hundred and thirty . . . er. This one says you're . . . she's six one . . . hmmm.'

'Give that to me.' Talons snatched the file.

'You can't take that, it's—'

'Mine. Never heard of the freedom of information act?'

'Wait, come back.'

The sound of accelerating hooves rattled away down the alley. And with it went any chance of promotion. When the bishop found out about this I was doomed.

Maybe if I nipped down to the confessional now, got myself a complete absolution, maybe then I might walk away alive.

Or maybe I could just run away. Now. Disappear into the crowds. Fly to Rio.

I shut the filing cabinet and jumped out of the window, vowing that if I could just get that file back before anyone noticed . . .

Ahh, the triumph of naivety.

It was very short-lived.

I heard her clear her throat before she stepped out from a dark shadow in the alley. She stood, hands on hips, high-lights glinting off the curves of her leather-clad body. Somehow, just then, she made Michelle Pfeiffer's Catwoman look like a scrawny tabby. I almost purred. Almost.

'Now, about that lottery ticket,' she began, and I got the distinct impression that she hadn't tracked me down to invite me out for a sweet sherry.

'Er . . . You didn't just see a nine-foot demon run out of this alley, did you?'

'Don't change the subject. I know you. Talk.'

'Er . . . well, what about the Daughter of God? Five eight, brunette, mostly naked—'

'Talk.' Somehow a small mobile phone appeared in her hand. 'Or do I call the police and let them find out just why you were breaking and entering?'

'Er . . . can we walk and talk, only that demon *is* getting away and . . . Audrey, that's the Daughter of God to you, well, she might be getting cold and . . .' I shrugged as a gaze of harsh disbelief burrowed into my train of thought. 'Besides, the lottery ticket's back at my place.' I tried my best smile.

Fortunately, she didn't demand a strip search.

Offering a swift prayer that she wouldn't spot the ticket in my pocket, I hurried past Kirstee and off into the streets of Camford, wondering whether I was better watching out for nine foot of demon, or just simply watching my back.

56

Quite how long he had been queueing he hadn't a clue. But already it felt like eternity bordering on forever. It wouldn't have taken much to convince him that several continents had drifted half-way round the world in the time he'd been standing in that line of damned souls. But then time in Helian was like that. Designed to drag. You think wet Sunday afternoons are bad. They don't come close.

'Next,' came a grunt from a large kiosk.

The man at the front of the queue stared into space.

'I said next,' growled the demon, leaning out through the window. 'That means you.' It glared fixedly at the pathetic figure in the morris man suit. 'You!'

Matlock looked around. 'Oh, so you finally get around to me. Have you any idea how long I've been stood in this queue? Have you? I'd almost forgotten what language was.'

'I don't care. Name.'

'I tell you, I've seen glaciers move faster.'

'Name.'

'You want to get more staff on these kiosks. It'd be far more pleasant that way. You know, welcome people in with a nice cold drink. Has anyone told you about the heating down here? Bit warm, you know.'

'We're fond of warm round here. Name.'

'I noticed. And another thing, there's nowhere to sit down. My feet are killing me and as for the small of my back . . . Do you have chiropractors here?'

'We got everyone here,' grinned the demon. 'Now, gimme your name or you go right back there.' He waggled a talon towards the far end of the queue. It vanished into the heat-haze.

The morris man swallowed. 'Matlock. Bertrand.'

'That's better—'

'But I shouldn't be here. There's been a mistake. I should be learning how to play the harp or something now.'

'We don't do harp lessons down here.'

'I know, I know. I should be up there. My own private cloud. I could've convinced Him that "bloody" is an adjective. But, oh no, you couldn't wait that extra few minutes, could you? Selfish bastards. I'm here for the rest of eternity and you couldn't give me a few minutes to convince Him I was murdered. And by one of you lot. I mean, that's just insult added to injury that is. Like you need extra people down here.'

'What did you just say?' asked the demon, checking feverishly at the parchment in front of him. He was sure that there had been a memo about something recently. Something about keeping eyes and ears peeled for anything relating to unauthorised demonic activity topside.

'Er, which bit?' asked Matlock, suddenly surprised that something was listening to him.

'Between the selfish bastards and the needing extra people down here.'

Matlock thought for a moment. 'You mean the murder bit?'

The demon nodded and eagerly flicked a switch under its desk. In seconds, a vast red flag unfurled above the kiosk and a dozen heavyweight demons cantered to a halt, surrounding the area in a ring of black panting scales.

'You want to tell them what you just told me?'

'This place is far too hot, you know. And the queues—'

'No. The other bit.'

'Er, honestly? No.'

'It's an order. Matters of murder are important,' prompted the beast in the kiosk. 'Especially when . . .' he led.

'Especially when one of you lot did it,' added Matlock, his words tripping into the silence like blind lambs in an automated slaughterhouse.

'One of us?' mouthed the largest of the dozen security demons. 'You're comin' with us. Grab 'im.'

Far too many scaly forearms wrestled to snatch hold of Matlock and, screaming, he was dragged away.

'Very vigilant,' grunted the beast in charge and then he somehow melted through the lines of bewildered souls.

A few moments later Matlock was picking himself up off a vast expanse of alabaster flooring.

'So,' hissed Seirizzim, sipping gently from a cold lava. 'Murdered, were you? By one of us, was it?'

Matlock nodded nervously.

'Now, and think very carefully before you answer, just exactly where was that, hmm?'

Talonspotting

57

It's damned difficult trying to remain even remotely inconspicuous when you're running against the tide of people and you've got five eight of leather-clad womanhood hot on your heels, firing questions at you. Okay, so most of the gazes were probably heading her way and what with the way her hips looked in those trousers, frankly, I'm not surprised. They were probably an even split of lust and jealousy. For the first time in my life I began to wonder if women ever suffered from hip envy.

It didn't last long. A new line of questioning rattled into earshot.

'So breaking and entering? Isn't that against some vow or something?' she called.

'Shut up.'

'I mean, there's laws telling you not to break and enter and—'

I spun around. 'Just shut up about that, will you. I'll come clean when we get back to my place. Don't worry, I'll bare all.'

I felt the full force of a pair of elderly women glaring at me. The back of my neck felt like it had been out in the Sahara all day.

'No, it's not what you think . . . ' I began.

'He always says that,' grinned Kirstee lecherously. 'The Vatican told him to save fallen women. He's *so* devoted. You wouldn't believe some of the things he does for lap dancers.'

I heard a shriek of horror. For a moment I wasn't sure if it was the women, or me.

I turned and raced off up the street. I got three paces of acceleration before the front wheel of a twin buggy gouged at my ankle. How I didn't end up flat on my face I'll never know. I swerved past a pensioner and ran headlong into a clot of lager-louts, rucksacks stuffed with RedStripe.

'Watch where you're goin', vicar.'

'I'm a priest, idiot!'

'Yeah well, good job you didn't spill nothing on my favourite shirt.'

I looked at the ancient black tour T-shirt and wondered quite how he could tell. In less than two seconds I spotted traces of pepperoni pizza, chicken jahlfrezi and a hefty dose of chicken tikka masala.

'Good job you didn't get any of that on his dog-collar,' joined in Kirstee. 'Likes to keep it clean he does.'

'Don't start,' I begged.

'He doesn't like to talk about it,' she continued. 'Nearly got disbarred for breaking that guy's neck couple of years back. Not a pretty sight.'

'Oh yeah?' Three of them wiped their mouths on the back of their hands and squared up to me.

'Guys, go to the carnival while you can still walk,' she said, and then, as if it was some dark secret, 'Black belt. Eighth dan.'

'Just you watch where you're goin', all right,' came a mumbled chorus of disapproval and they melted into the crowd, thumping each other's shoulders. I barely heard the quartet of ringpulls as more RedStripe was conjured, as, fuming, I headed off against the growing tide of people.

Faces loomed into view and passed by unrecognised. I ducked and writhed between shoulders, skipped over three-year-olds strung between doting parents. And with every step I struggled to take it felt more and more wrong.

And then something snapped inside. A neurone misfired or something hit me on the back of the head, I don't know the details, just that one minute I was there in Camford High Street, the next I was . . . well, somewhere else.

Unfortunately, I was still wading against the tide of people. But this vision, if that's what it was, had them looking downtrodden, filthy. Clothes hung in rags from their tattered bodies. And all the time, as if it was an essential part of daily life, they wailed and gnashed their teeth.

'Get out of my way, you pitiful scum,' I heard myself hiss and watched in helpless alarm as a vast black forearm caught a dozen of them round the back of their heads. I stared at the talons before me and felt my stomach quiver as I picked an ear off. 'Er . . . Anyone lost this?'

'That's mine,' whined a toothless face in the crowd.

'Well, don't be so careless.'

And, with a flash of whiteout, Camford High Street reappeared.

'You all right?' asked Kirstee, and the comforting smell of warm leather licked at my nostrils. At least I think that's what it was.

'Er, yeah, fine. I . . . think.'

'Migraine, right? I've seen that look. C'mon, let's get you home.' She took my hand and pushed ahead of me through the crowds. I started to object, but . . . after a few steps it didn't seem worth it. Churlish really. And besides, she might start being loud again. And right then I wanted a bit of peace. What had I just seen?

'So just what are you, eh?' she asked suddenly.

'What d'you mean?'

'Well, you're obviously not a priest. So what are you?'

'How dare you accuse me of not—'

'Breaking and entering, remember? And just how many priests do the lottery? Thought you lot were against gambling? You know, like you're against anything else you've got to be over eighteen for.'

'That's not true. Morally, I've got nothing against driving.'

'That's seventeen.'

'Oh. Er . . .'

'You've never even played the lottery before, have you?'

I looked at her. 'How d'you know?'

'Call it intuition. Or the fact you hadn't a clue about rollovers. Am I right?'

'Yes. But you're wrong about the other thing. I am a priest.'

'Got I.D.?'

'No.'

'Ah ha.' She looked at me with a glint of triumph in her eye. 'Working undercover, are you? Who's it for? Church of England? The Vatican? You can tell me.'

'None of them. I'm working for Him.' I pointed upwards.

She looked up at the jumbo arching across the sky. 'You work for Richard Branson? Cool. Get me some CDs, will you?'

'No, I work for . . . oh, never mind. You'll figure it out. We're here.'

I opened a small gate and rummaged for the keys in my pocket as I headed towards my front door.

'You'd better not be lying about this lottery . . .' Her voice faded away as the rhododendron next to the door rustled and something unfurled from behind it.

'And just where have you been?' snapped nine foot of demon.

'Oh my God,' sighed Kirstee as she looked the creature up, down and up again. 'Look at the size of . . .' she breathed as she stopped her upward surveillance just short of its midriff. 'He a friend of yours?'

'Er, well, in a manner of . . .'

'Any friend of yours, pal.'

Before I knew it, my front door keys were rattling in her hands and she had disappeared inside.

'I hate her,' growled the demon. 'Just look at those hips. I could *never* get into those trousers.'

'Play your cards right . . .' called a voice from my front room.

'I'm not hearing this. I am *not* hearing this. Just get inside,' I ordered. 'And find something to wear.'

'What about me?' called Kirstee.

58

The blade of Doctor Boscombe's favourite scalpel glinted bloodily under the fluorescent strip for a moment. It hovered in anticipation before it vanished deep into the softer parts of one Bertrand Matlock, deceased. Expertly guided, it homed in towards the liver and, with an admirable economy of effort, sliced the organ free. Its job complete for the moment, it rested on its favourite stainless-steel tray, secure in the knowledge of a job well done.

Across the lab, a glistening liver was placed on a set of scales.

Boscombe grunted suspiciously. 'Normal.'

The scalpel barely contained its exitement as a patholo-gically correct latex glove gripped firmly around its handle and plunged it deep into the burgundy-hued organ. In moments a small sliver of liver was under a microscope.

'No, no. This can't be right,' frowned Boscombe. 'Can't be right at all.'

Shaking his head, he crossed to his bank of implements and, much to the envy of the others, selected a small but perfectly formed circular saw and headed for his client's knees.

Diamond tips met bone at two thousand rpm.

'No. No. No.'

The rack of surgical-steel tools looked on in cold confusion at a sight not normally witnessed in the Path Lab.

Doctor Boscombe was baffled.

'Just doesn't make sense,' he muttered to himself, stripping his gloves into the bin.

'Found anything?' asked PC Plain, closing the door behind him.

Boscombe spun around. 'I do wish you'd knock.'

'I did, but you were deep in, er . . . thought.'

'His name's Matlock. And the answer is yes. And no.'

Plain pulled his best interested expression.

'You don't have a mirror at home, do you?' asked Boscombe. 'It's not getting any more convincing. Any joy with the perfect pout?'

'Given up on that. But the Elvis sneer's coming on . . . don't change the subject.'

'Well, at least I know you're listening.' He sat down on the slab and looked at Matlock. 'Cause of death's easy. Ligatural suspension leading to subsequent terminal asphyxiation.'

'That's easy?'

'How about swinging for several minutes from a set of braces tied around his neck?'

'Got that. So what's the problem?'

'Why.'

'Who d'you think you are, Quincy?'

177

'Just between you and me, I think there's more to this than meets the eye. Look at this liver.'

'Hmmmm, must I?'

Boscombe ignored him. 'Normal weight. Normal size. No sign of anything even remotely resembling the chronic effects of many beers.'

'So he's got a healthy liver.'

'And his knees. Look here—'

'Ahhh no. I draw the line at knees. I've got a thing about them. And toe nails. I don't do legs well.'

'But this is a splendid knee. Observe the way I've sawn through the patella to reveal the inside of the—'

'Cut to the chase,' whispered Plain, eyes shut. 'The point is?'

'RSI,' announced the pathologist. 'Repetitive Strain Injury.'

'Yeah, well, you'd expect that with all that jigging about.'

'Exactly. So just where is it?'

'What?'

' Constable Plain, I am experiencing grave doubts that this man was in fact a morris man.'

'But the clothes. The others . . .'

'Here to put us off the trail,' whispered Boscombe.

Plain swallowed nervously. He knew he'd regret this, but . . . what the hell. He had to ask. 'What trail?'

'Murder.'

'And just what makes you think that?'

'Well, at first I saw these marks here and I couldn't decide just what they were.' With a struggle he turned Matlock over. Bone crunched, ligament wrenched and there was a dull thud. 'Hmm, sorry about that,' apologised Boscombe, picking Matlock's lower leg off the floor. 'Anyhow, these abrasions on his back, shoulders and upper arm.' He pointed to a host of thin nine-inch marks. 'At first I thought these

178

were made by a knife blade. But I've never seen a blade this shape. That curl. Fascinating.'

'A weird knife equals murder?'

'These marks were made by stiletto heels. Add this to the fact that this man is not a morris man and it can be nothing else but murder. A mafia murder.'

'Ohh, come on, in Camford . . .'

'Look at his black hair. He's an Italian, killed by the brothers of his lover whom he has betrayed and who had a habit of wearing stilettos. It was she who made these marks, kicking him whilst he was down.'

'You've been at the methanol again. I tell you, you need to get out more.'

'Good advice, constable. I was already planning to.'

'Why don't I like the sound of that?' said Plain, heading for the door.

'Because already you are anticipating the difficulty in swallowing your own words when I present more evidence supporting my case.'

'Yeah, right.'

And with that Boscombe grabbed his favourite mock-crocodile Scene of Crime bag and dashed off past Plain, heading towards the Monocle and Asparagus, where he was certain there was evidence waiting.

58

For the fiftieth time in half an hour, Kirstee changed position on my sofa. She kicked off her heels, wriggled into the lotus position and tossed her hair over the back cushion. She settled back, chest heaving against leather, as relaxed as if she was up to her neck in a frothing jacuzzi, arms draped along the tiles. And I could imagine her there, bubbles

179

running up the curve of her back, arching around her ribs and wrestling for pole position in the chicane of her cleavage. I was seconds away from calling up a jacuzzi installation firm when the image shattered.

She shook her head, tutted and folded her arms. 'I don't know why I bother. You haven't even looked up once.'

I was foxed until I saw the direction of her irritation. She glared daggers at the demon currently sitting cross-legged among a blizzard of paperwork. A pair of my largest boxer shorts were straining at the seams, barely holding together around his waist. There were other regions under considerably more strain, I was certain.

'Look at you, nose buried in paperwork,' she sneered. 'What's a girl got to do, eh?'

A nine-inch talon flicked over another sheet.

'This a fetish thing? Like the feel of office stationery? Well, I can accommodate that. I'm sure I could find something interesting to do with a few leaves of Basildon Bond. Or would you prefer some of that handmade unbleached rough stuff?'

I knew from that moment on I would never be able to lick an envelope in the same way again.

But there was no response from the floor. Not even a blink.

'Okay, I admit it. You're nothing like I expected,' she tutted. 'You always been like this, or is it just good PR? Thought the devil'd have a bit more pizzaz, bit more sparkle. More fire and brimstone about the place, y'know?'

I don't know quite how she did it, but somehow I was very aware of a pair of nipples grinning out across the room. I was sure they had appeared at the instant she'd said 'fire and brimstone'. That was muscle control to be admired.

'I'm not the devil. Just *a* devil,' muttered the creature on the carpet.

'And one who's interested in paperwork,' she snapped back. 'Isn't there something a little more interesting you'd rather be doing?'

'What?'

'Me,' announced Kirstee.

The demon shrugged with an effort, as if the weight of the world was on those vast shoulders. As if no one could understand the significance of those pages strewn on the carpet.

Kirstee sighed, squirmed off the sofa and knelt on the carpet. 'Just what is it about that lot? There's something going on here I don't understand. I tell you, no one has ever withstood me for that long. And that particular fact doesn't leave this room, clear? So come on, spill it. What are you staring at?'

'Call it a journey of discovery.'

She scratched her head. 'But who is this Audrey Williams?'

'You wouldn't understand,' sighed the demon with a dumper truck of melancholy on each vowel.

'I'm a good listener. Rest your head here.' She patted her chest. 'Tell me all about it and Auntie Kirstee will soothe away all your woes.'

'I doubt it.'

'Now look, I'm getting just a bit confused by all this. Shoot me down in flames here, but this just isn't right, is it? I mean, you should be torturing other people, not yourself. Look at you. C'mon, lighten up a bit.'

'How would you feel if you woke up yesterday looking beautiful and now you looked like this?'

'Define beautiful.'

Talons snatched a photograph of a sleeping woman and dropped it at Kirstee's knees. She was blonde, slender and only slightly comatose.

'Hmmm, natural. Not my type,' answered Kirstee.

'And now look at me.'

For the first time I saw Kirstee lost for words. Her mouth actually opened in the way goldfish do. Round and stupid.

The silence didn't last long. 'That . . . That's you? But . . . it can't be, I mean, your hair, skin, everything's so . . .'

'Tell me about it.'

Kirstee tossed back her head, slapped palms on her thighs and roared with laughter. 'God, sometimes I'm just *so* gullible. I saw you and I thought "Wow, what's this? A party animal from the other side? Tasty." And hey, it was a natural thing to think. You know, priests deal with your type all the time. Well, they do in *The Exorcist* anyhow. And who better to. They're trained in all that Holy stuff.'

I cringed, but she barely took a breath.

'But now I find out that you really look like that.' She wiggled the picture. 'I tell you, that is one cool makeover. And I've seen some in my time. Why aren't you out strutting your stuff in the carnival? First prize for sure that is. How d'you get the scales looking so realistic?'

'Guess.'

'No, come on, share. I could give you a few of my beauty tips.'

'I'm sure you could.'

'And you look so tall. I've always wanted an extra few inches. They little stilts or something?'

'Not again.'

'So where's the zip, eh? You can tell me.'

'I don't have a zip.'

'Geez, a suit like that must have a zip. Even Michelle Pfeiffer had a zip in her Catwoman suit. Velcro, then?'

'No.'

'You're not telling me that's body paint? You'd have to be

a shot-putter or something to have shoulders like that.' And in a flash she was up close and examining skin textures. 'Geez, you're so hot. It is a suit, and I bet it's hell in there.'

'In a manner of speaking. Yes.'

And then she turned to me, almost as if she'd just remembered I was there. 'You got any ice cream? She's burning up in here.'

'I, er . . . finished the last a couple of days ago.'

'Men,' she tutted and headed for the door. 'When I get back I want every little detail, clear? Meantime, what ice cream can I get?'

We both answered at the same instant. 'Baked Alaska.'

'You're joking, right?'

'The more baked the better, I'm feeling in need of therapy,' I answered in the moment before the door slammed.

59

In the dull duck-egg-blue surroundings of Interview Room Three, four people stared at each other across a table. A police tape deck hummed gently to itself in the corner of the room and recorded the silence.

PC Sim's attention wandered floorwards as a woodlouse trundled aimlessly towards the skirting board.

'C'mon, admit it, Bernstein, you did it,' growled PC Plain, planting his knuckles on the table.

'No, nay, never shall I be accepting of thine lies,' answered the ageing morris dancer wearily.

'Stop saying that,' moaned Plain, turning away and pacing the room. 'Why does he keep saying that?'

'Folk.'

Plain spun and glared at Skitting in alarm. He looked at the microphone on the table. 'Let the record state that PC

Plain dissociates himself entirely from that previous outburst of PC Skitting's and wishes to offer sincere apologies
to anyone who found it offensive in any—'

'I only said—'

'Yes. We all heard, and language like that should be—'

'Folk. Folk. Folkety folk.'

Plain's jaw fell limp as Bernstein the elder's face lit up. 'I
sense there's hope for you, young man.'

'Er, oh, thank you.'

'So, you *can* talk,' hissed Plain, waggling an accusatory
finger at the first suspect in the Matlock case. 'C'mon then,
spill. How d'you get him up there, eh? What d'you do with
the ladder?'

'I owneth not such a device.'

'I don't care who owns the bloody ladder, just tell me
where you hid it.'

Sim stared absently at the floor as the woodlouse trundled
up and over the back of one of its cousins. Barely slowing its
pace, it disappeared down a gap in the floorboards.

And deep in the darker recesses of Sim's mind, a line of
questioning started to hatch. 'What if they didn't use a
ladder after all,' he began, and all heads turned towards him.
'What if . . .'

Plain's eyes bugged with expectation.

'It was a human pyramid,' blurted Sim.

Before Bernstein had a chance to answer, the door was
kicked open and a man in long cloak and ankle bells strode
in. 'Right, that's it, you've gone too far now,' he declared and
placed his ribboned straw hat over the microphone.

'Just who the hell are you?' challenged Plain.

'Jed Z. Trewithers, legal adviser to the Guild of Ancient
Morrisers and Noble Maypolers. And this interview is over.
You were skating very close to the wind accusing any

honourable and registered affiliates of the Guild of using artificial aids in the pursuit of a dance or dances of paganistic origin, but human pyramid? Why, that's tantamount to suggesting gymnastics.'

Bernstein the elder turned pale and muttered something under his breath.

'But this is a murder investigation,' pleaded Plain.

'Precisely. And as such, I and my clients would expect, nay demand, that any lines of questioning be tailored to offer least insult. Mr Bernstein, this way, please.'

'Wait, where are you going? You can't just—'

Trewithers rolled his eyes. 'Of course, I almost forgot. This legal system of yours is so archaic. Ahem, Callum?' he called out of the door, and instantly a shadow fell across the frame. 'In here.' A waft of stale horse filled the interview room. 'Drop it there, would you, sweet boy.' He pointed to the table and headed for the door.

Three policemen stared at a cubic rectangle of straw.

'What in God's name is that?'

'Bale,' said Trewithers, ushering Bernstein out of the door.

60

Clutching his favourite mock-crocodile murder bag close to his chest, Doctor Boscombe wheeled around the corner of the Monocle and Asparagus. He halted beneath the gently swinging signboard and began his preliminary examinations.

The usual detritus of daily life passed before his expert eyes and was duly dismissed. He wasn't interested in chewing gum wrappers, pizza crusts and the odd raspberry-ripple-flavoured condom. Under different circumstances he would've been down on each of them like a shot. But today . . . well, a certain morris man's stomach contents showed no traces of chewing gum, pizza crusts or even raspberry ripple. And other tests showed that there had been little or nothing going on in the trouser department for the past few years.

He pulled out his trusty magnifying glass and peered hard at the ground. Much to his disappointment, the pavement showed little or no sign of struggle. And more to his dismay, there were no signs that stiletto heels had been worn in the vicinity for the past two weeks. He breathed a heavy sigh as his mafia love triangle murder theory took a step into the shadows of impossibility.

But then he saw it. It shimmered at the edge of the magnifying glass, flicking tantalisingly in and out of view. A four-inch mark on the pavement. The mark left by a hoof. And then he began to see more. A line of them heading towards a spot almost directly beneath the pub signboard. His heart quickened as his imagination filled in the details.

Matlock was hurled hard against a cold marble floor in painful slow motion. His check bounced against Italian polished stone, wobbling as spittle flew in all directions. The morris man looked up at the heels of his lover, her legs rising out of sight, shapely pillars of fishnetted alabaster. She raised her foot, stiletto heel glinting with deadly precision.

'Noooooooooooo,' squealed Matlock as the shoe stabbed Psycho-mad out of the sky. Sprays of red lashed across Boscombe's mind's eye in forensically incorrect volumes. Violins shrieked trills of horror. And he began to suspect that perhaps his recent Hitchcock binge may have been a bad idea.

But his mind's eye ignored him. Not even pausing for a popcorn break it plunged on. Matlock's limp body hung across the shoulders of a horse as it galloped wildly through the midnight streets of Camford. Hooves screeched to a halt, and a figure sat tall in the saddle strung Matlock up on the signboard. Laughing manically, the horseman spurred his steed away, cloak flapping in a way that would've had Zorro green with envy.

'That's how it was,' muttered Boscombe to himself. 'So, I trace the horse and I find the killer.' He grinned as a fortnight's course of equine pathology started to pay off. Dimly he recalled an afternoon spent at the Spanish Riding School in Rome where it was demonstrated that the ratio of hoofprint sizes across all four legs is unique to each horse. But was it left front over right back minus right front over left back or right front over left front minus . . .

It was only after half an hour's eye strain staring at the pavement that he realised he could only find two distinct hoof marks. Which must surely mean that either it was a horse whose front and rear hooves matched exactly, or this horse had only two legs.

Images of rearing trick ponies came and went in a flurry of derision.

It simply had to be the former. And what a unique horse that would be. He bent to take final measurements, blissfully unaware of the increasing noise behind him.

'Neddy, Neddy, wherefore art thou?' called a knight in rusting armour as he rounded the corner at the head of the carnival procession. A papier maché downtrodden peasant caught Boscombe a glancing blow and sent him sprawling. And a wave of revellers wheeled around the corner, cheering the local fire brigade in their charity fire-appliance push.

'My evidence!' cried Boscombe as a vast Michelin rumbled across his hoofprints. 'Get that damned fire engine off my—'

'Donation for Arsonists Anonymous?' asked a teenager in a flame-red cheerleader's costume. She thrust a bucket of loose change under his nose.

'Don't stand on my hoofprints!'

'Any donation of ten pounds or more gets a flame lapel badge. Want one?'

'Go away before I—'

Mercifully, Boscombe's threat was drowned by the distorted strains of 'Sugar Baby Love' blasting from the float of the Diabetic Cats' Protection League.

Desperately, Boscombe fiddled with a pair of callipers, measuring vital dimensions. Until a battered boot caught them and sent them flying into the gutter. 'Will you watch what the hell you're doing?'

'You talking to me?' slurred an unshaven man, swaying as he opened a can of cider. It was obviously not his first of the day. ''Cause if you're talkin' to me in that tone of voice I won't be pleased, hear?'

'Yes, yes. Just give me my callipers.'

'Your what?' coughed the man of the streets, knocking back a good half of the can.

'Callipers. I need to measure my hoofprints.' Boscombe's answer was buried under a coughing fit.

'Sod off,' cursed the man, and hurled his can at Boscombe.

'Why me, why today?' Boscombe whimpered, brushing eight per cent Scrumpy out of his hair as a large black limousine growled past at two miles an hour.

'Good to see people getting into the spirit of things at last,' said Mayor Keswick, peering out through the tinted windows. 'Always a good sign when folks are falling-down drunk. They never remember how bad the carnival is.'

Belching diesel fumes the limousine growled on, a banner waving in the breeze. Camford Council Cares Considerably.

61

Not a great deal had changed in the three quarters of an hour Kirstee had been gone. The demon on the carpet had shuffled the contents of the file and breathed heavy sighs and I'd done my usual trick of offering tea and sympathy. Well, actually it was coffee; I was clean out of tea.

Suddenly, the door was kicked open and Kirstee shimmied in, a large blue thermal bag in front of her. 'You could've told me it was so far away. I had to get a taxi.' She dropped the bag and, barely slowing down, headed for the kitchen. 'Plates?'

'Draining board under the . . .'

'When was the last time you did the washing up?'

I cringed and shook my head. Well, after spending all day at St Cedric's cleaning up after everyone else, the last thing I ever felt like was doing my kitchen. All right, I know that cleanliness is supposed to be next to Godliness, but in my dictionary screaming fits always came after an hour's dish-washing.

'There's mould in this tin of beans.'

'Just bring spoons.'

'They're all filthy.'

'Well, fetch anything that's clean,' I shouted and began unzipping the bag. In moments I was staring at a glistening heap of dessert therapy.

'Wouldn't call that baked,' grumbled the demon.

'Don't concern yourself with that,' I grinned, producing a small gas blowlamp from a handy drawer. 'Look, I got it for doing crème caramels, okay? It's the way all the best chefs do it, right?'

Scaly shoulders shrugged. 'Whatever you say. Just get it lit.'

I needed no second bidding. There was the crack of a lighting match and then the comforting sound of roaring butane filled the lounge. Ice cream charred in satisfying waves of cinder as I played the flame over dessert.

'What are you doing?' squeaked Kirstee as she stared at a good tenner's worth of ash.

'Finishing it off,' I answered. 'You know the way there's never enough mozzarella on take-away pizzas? Well, there's never enough "bake" on shop-bought Alaskas.'

'There's no Alaska left in that. It looks like something that was scraped out of the pits of hell.'

'Perfect.' And in a flash of blackness, the demon had snatched a chunk.

'There's something seriously wrong with you,' grumbled Kirstee, dropping the only clean utensils she could find into the charcoal.

For a brief moment I looked at the potato masher, the slotted ladle and the whisk and decided that it was probably a good job she wasn't joining us. Eating with a whisk was almost certainly a challenging task. Mind you, the others weren't much better. A handful of crunchy ice cream ground between my teeth.

And the nightmare flashed back. Hooves echoed off the marble floors and walls of halls illuminated by a dozen lava lamps. Sheets of flame battered at windows. And all around was the wailing of torment.

'I want to see those teeth gnashing,' screamed a demonic voice from somewhere. It was followed by the crack of whips and the rattling of heavy-grade chains. 'Gnash!'

And as soon as it had appeared it vanished.

I blinked and looked at my lounge.

To my left a demon licked at nine-inch talons and ahead of me a woman in leather shuffled papers on the carpet.

190

'Look, just what's all this lot about?' asked Kirstee, looking up from the paperwork. 'What's going on here?'

The demon looked at me.

'What d'you think's going on here?' I hedged.

'Well that's what I've been asking myself,' she said. 'I mean, I'm wondering just why you two have got this file containing a series of photos which tell a very interesting story.'

'Er . . . they do?'

She nodded and pointed to the row of pictures which she had arranged in date order. 'I was asking myself why someone would want to photograph themselves as they went through the whole catalogue of hair colours, black to blonde. I mean, vanity's a weird mistress, but I could understand if it was just that.'

I stared at the pictures and there sure enough was a series of gradually blonding images.

'But then I noticed the other stuff,' added Kirstee. 'The weight loss. A stone and three quarters a week. And I thought, hey, this some new Weightwatchers course? One that really works? And I was nearly impressed. Until I saw this.'

Her finger ran across a whole string of figures, one on each sheet of the hospital charts. And as I stared at the entries in the height columns my heart almost stopped. This woman had gone from being well over eight foot six to a diminutive five five. In eight weeks.

'And even her skin's gone lighter, look,' pointed out Kirstee. 'So, come on, what's the secret? This some weird plastic surgery experiment, eh? Is it chemical? Or enzymes? Yeah, that's it, you've bred enzymes to . . . no, wait, this is all to do with the human gene thing, isn't it? You've figured out what gene does what and . . . my God, you could make anyone look like anyone else with this. So who've you bred, eh? Copies of the Spice Girls that can sing? Or a million Robbie Williamses that retail for a couple of hundred quid each? Or . . .'

'I don't know what you're talking about,' I said through an ever-constricting throat.

'Yeah, right, you're bound to say that. "Didn't do it. Wasn't there. Plausible denial." Well, you are here. So come on, the truth.'

'I *honestly* don't know what you're on about. I could never understand all that science stuff,' I admitted. 'And besides, I'm a priest. I couldn't mess about with what people look like. We're all supposed to be made in God's image so messing about with it is plain sinful.'

'God's image,' spluttered Kirstee. 'Take a look around you and tell me just what God looks like if we're all made in His image.'

'Ahhh, well . . . He's got legs and arms and . . .' She had a point. And I was beginning to get a headache.

'Look, I can cut you a deal,' oozed Kirstee. 'I can forget about all of this if we can fix the right arrangement.'

'Er . . .' I just knew I wasn't going to like this.

'You can guarantee my lifelong silence in exchange for a couple of inches here and here.' She pointed to her breasts. 'Now throw in a bit of a tummy tuck and four inches on my legs, two above the knee, two below, and I'm shtoom for life. What d'you say?'

She took my stunned silence the wrong way.

'Look, I'm not asking for much here. I mean, it's not like it's hard for you. You can work miracles on the human body.' She stabbed randomly at the photos on the floor. 'Just work a few plastic surgery miracles on me. C'mon.'

'It's not plastic surgery,' I heard myself say.

'Well, whatever you call it. Just give.'

I began to shiver as understanding galloped towards the front of my mind. 'Not plastic . . . ecclesiastic.'

'What?' chorused the others.

'Don't you see? It all makes sense,' I enthused, not really knowing where to begin. 'I should've seen it all before. It's a miracle!'

I was underwhelmed by their response.

I found myself waggling the first and last of the photographs at them. 'This. It's a miracle. All that in eight weeks can't be down to normal science.'

'Sod off,' grunted the demon. 'Open your eyes. Take a look at me. What's miraculous about this?'

'Yeah, well. Could be a rejection. Or eczema? It's on the increase, y'know. Pollution or something.'

'I was beautiful,' wailed the beast.

'Are you sure that's you?' asked Kirstee. 'Could be a mix-up. It happens sometimes, you know, wrong wristband stuck on the wrong baby and . . .'

'I remember being beautiful. I woke up yesterday morning with blonde hair and blue eyes and . . . and . . . all of a sudden I look like this. Gimme that photo.'

I wasn't going to say no.

'Yeah, yeah, okay. Calm down, I only asked,' soothed Kirstee, standing up and edging towards the door as the demon stared longingly at the most recent picture of Audrey Williams. I barely saw the curl of Kirstee's finger urging me to follow. In fact, if it hadn't been for the fact that she kicked me in the side as she walked past, I doubt I'd ever have known she wanted me to follow.

In the hall, she stood close to me and began to whisper.

'Has that thing ever . . . and I mean even only once, ever spun its head all the way round?'

193

'What?' I answered, distracted by the pleasant musk of warm leather.

'Head. Three sixty?'

'Well, I've never actually seen—'

'Projectile vomiting? Messages across the belly? You know, "Help Me I'm Possessed" kind of messages?'

'What are you trying to say?'

'All right, I should've twigged earlier, but you know, the influence of Hollywood and all that. I thought they always just sort of turned green around the gills and floated above the bed sounding like they've got terminal laryngitis.'

'Who do?'

'The possessed. You know, those inhabited by inner demons from the other side. Satan's little helpers. Don't tell me you've never seen *The Exorcist*?'

I shook my head.

'*The Omen*?'

I shrugged.

'You must've seen something with gangs of zombies dropping flesh from every limb as they twitch their way through downtown America?'

'Does Michael Jackson's *Thriller* count?'

She slapped the palm of her hand against her forehead. 'Forget it. Just trust me on this one, okay? There's more than just her in there, right?'

'Is that why she's so tall?'

Again there was that palm-forehead thing. Strange. I saw her take a deep breath and count to at least eight and a half.

'Within the boundaries of St Cedric's,' she said in a curiously forced way, 'which of the following items are to be found? Crosses, Holy Water, Bibles, wooden stakes. A) All. B) None. C) Other.'

'Oh A), definitely.'

194

'Excellent.'

'What are you doing out here?' asked the demon, pulling open the lounge door. 'Not talking about me, are you?'

I have to hand it to her, the way Kirstee pulled herself together was remarkable. 'We think we know what's the matter.'

'You do?'

'It's an allergy.'

I knew she was lying but I couldn't do anything but forgive her.

'D'you feel itchy? Skin kind of rough? Feet uncomfortable?'

'Yeah? That's right.'

'Often happens with a change of washing powder,' she lied. 'Right, just come with us and we'll have you sorted in next to no time.'

Crossing her fingers, she stepped out into the street.

'Will I be beautiful again?' asked the demon, following.

'Of course,' smiled Kirstee. 'You have wonderful bone structure.'

62

A taxi swept up the curve of Jeroboam Hill and halted across the road from Ayers Rock.

'You sure this is the place?' asked a young man in a black cloak.

'Oh yeah, I've done this trip a hundred times today. Give it a few minutes an' it'll change,' said the taxi driver. 'Fifteen-twenty, mate.'

'How much?' whimpered the novice Francisco, trying to convert the price into lire.

'Pay the man,' muttered Cardinal Aguilera, stepping out of the car and staring at the infamous slab of Australia.

195

Carefully, he looked out of the corner of his eye. Much to his satisfaction the image shimmered. 'Huh, amateurs,' he tutted as Francisco joined him on the pavement and Ayers Rock metamorphosed into the Taj Mahal. The gathered crowd erupted into whoops of applause.

'The English,' grumbled Aguilera, 'so easily impressed by simple visual trickery.' He strode off through the crowd, Francisco hard on his heels.

After several minutes of shoving, cajoling and the careful deployment of elbows, the two men from the Vatican emerged and stood on the edge of what appeared to be a long thin pond.

'Over there,' pointed Aguilera, looking out of the corner of his eye.

'What is?'

'The front door,' grumbled Aguilera. 'Come on.'

The crowd gasped as he walked across the pond leaving barely a shimmer on the water. Expecting at the very least wet socks, Francisco followed. He stepped off the edge of the tiled bank and looked nervously down. Koi carp peered up from between his feet and a pike dived for cover. All around him he could feel eyes staring in admiration. And suddenly he had an overwhelming urge to skip off down the length of the water-way and spin around the statues, dancing and warbling 'Singing in the Rain' at the top of his voice. Fortunately for the gathered crowd, the Taj Mahal rippled in the Camford air and metamorphosed into Mount Rushmore.

'Hurry up,' snarled the cardinal, standing before the vast carved head of Abe Lincoln. 'Have you forgotten we've got a job to do?'

'But I've never been to India.' Francisco looked sheepishly at his feet and hurried across a few North American foothills.

'In here,' ordered Aguilera, grabbing his wayward novice

by the shoulder and hurling him up Lincoln's left nostril. He hit the ancient oak door head first.

'Use the bell,' frowned the cardinal, snatching at a large handle and tugging hard.

Deep inside St Cedric's, the sound of ringing doorbells froze Brother Lyndsey's heart. 'Oh my God,' he whispered in the candlelit basement. 'Who can that be?'

'How should I know?' whispered Bishop Hutchinson, his eyes wide with alarm. Two callers to the front door in two days was two too many in his book.

The bell rang again impatiently.

'Should I go and answer—?'

'They'll go away,' whispered the bishop in a way that sounded more like a prayer than a reassurance.

''Bishop Hutchinson?' called Aguilera through the distant letter box. 'Open the door. We will not go away until you do.'

'Guess that answers that,' shrugged Lyndsey.

'It . . . It could be a bluff.'

'Yes. And we'll never find out down here, will we?'

A distant peal of bells rang again. 'Open the door,' shouted the Italian.

The bishop looked at the floor. 'Go,' he whispered with resigned dread.

A few minutes and several dozen swings on the doorbell later, Brother Lyndsey was at the ancient oak door. He slid open a panel and peered out.

'At last,' hissed Aguilera. 'Now let us in.'

'Password?' asked Lyndsey.

'Look, I found the front door, that ought to be enough for you.'

Lyndsey tried his best to not look impressed. Even finding the front of the building was impressive while it was changing into famous landmarks every few minutes.

'Password.'

'The longer we stay chatting here the longer this place is a tourist attraction.'

'Password.'

'Holy Mother of God,' hissed the cardinal, turning red. 'All this way,' he muttered, 'to be stopped by an idiot . . .'

The sound of creaking hinges halted Aguilera's tirade in its tracks.

'It's actually "Blessed Holy Mother of God",' said Lyndsey, peering around the door, 'but that's near enough. Welcome to St Ced—'

'This way, isn't it?' asked Aguilera rhetorically as he strode past and headed off down the corridor, Francisco close behind. 'Second flight down?'

'Er, yes, but . . . wait for me,' panicked Lyndsey as he shoved the door to and shot the bolts back. It was the fastest he had ever locked up. In seconds he was sprinting after the two foreigners.

'Where are you looking for?' he called, gaining swiftly on them. The men in black cassocks swept around corners and plunged on down ancient stone stairs. 'How d'you know your way around?' pleaded Lyndsey. 'Been here before, have you? Before my time, was it? Only I'm sure I would have remembered a visit from . . .'

Aguilera ducked left and clattered down a short flight of steps into a large candlelit basement. 'Mind the fourth one down,' he said over his shoulder. 'It's loose,' he added, skipping over the step.

'How did you know that?' coughed Lyndsey.

'This it?' answered Cardinal Aguilera, halting before a large baptismal font. 'This your main one?'

'Yes,' answered Bishop Hutchinson, emerging from the shadows. 'You know how to fix it?'

'Of course,' said Aguilera as Francisco set up a small but well-stocked field altar. In moments a tiny incense burner was alight and swinging over the font. 'Hmmm,' pondered the cardinal, stroking his chin. Carefully, he opened a tiny bottle and took out a dropper. With an expert squeeze of the rubber handle a trio of oil droplets were floated on the water. He stared intently at the directions they moved.

'Hmmmm.'

'D'you know what's—?' began Lyndsey. Francisco slapped a finger across his lips.

'Hmmmmmm.' Aguilera pored through an ancient book he'd pulled out from beneath his cloak. 'Thought so.' He marched up to the baptismal font, crossed his fingers and kicked it swiftly on the side.

Outside, the bridge of the U.S.S. *Enterprise* vanished and turned into a row of dark and highly ignorable houses. The crowd's cheers were somewhat muted. They were disappointed with this latest incarnation.

'Fixed,' grinned Cardinal Aguilera, rubbing his palms together. 'Fragment of disbelief in your control sub-psalm. Nothing to worry about. Now, down to the real business. Is your kettle on?'

Hutchinson looked at Lyndsey. 'Tea?' offered the brother.

'You English, it's always tea. Have you never heard of cappuccino?' He clipped his field altar shut and strode out of the basement.

'But I'm Irish,' whimpered Brother Lyndsey, following the other three out.

63

The tape recorder in Interview Room Three whirred gently to itself as the voice of Ranzo Ray droned on.

'Well, I wouldn't really call it a motive, man. Y'know, it was more kinda like a kinda artistic difference in opinion, like. I mean, I believe that the future of morrising is, like, looking forward into the twenty-first century an' utilising the drum'n'bass culture prevalent upon other dance floors to its logical maximum, y'know, man? See, ten years ago people were like kindascared of the Ibiza-isation of music an' the steady increase in sounds of a more aerobics-oriented appeal, an' now the youth culture is dominated by it, see?'

Three policemen stared glassy-eyed at the dreadlocked and droning creature before them.

'The new dance craze is gonna be drum'n'bass'n'ankle bells, you'll see. It'll sweep the country on a wave of maypoling and raving and—'

There was a knock on the door. It took PC Plain a few seconds to wake up. He stood, trudged towards the door and stepped out into the corridor, eyes staring into the middle distance.

Doctor Boscombe grabbed him firmly by the lapels. 'Ask him about the horse. They used a horse I tell you.'

'Horse,' repeated Plain, trying to focus.

'I've got the evidence.'

'Got the evidence . . . Whew, have you been drinking?'

'I've seen it, and no.'

'You smell like an orchard.'

'It was an accident. Just ask him about the horse and where they've hidden it. I want to see it.'

'Uh-huh, and just why is that?'

'Just between you and me, this is my chance to really make a splash in the world of equine forensics.' Boscombe's voice dropped to the quietest of whispers. 'It's got two pairs of matching hooves. Unique it is. And I found it.'

'Matching hooves? When was the last time you took a holiday?'

'Nineteen seventy-five, and I'm not as mad as your tone implies. The horse; find it and you find Matlock's killers.'

PC Plain shook his head and re-entered the interview room. Ranzo Ray was still droning on. '. . . Indian folk music against a pounding dance-rooted rhythm track of such amazing skill and—'

'Where's the horse?' demanded Plain.

'This interview is over,' hissed Trewithers, the lawyer, tossing his hat over the microphone.

'What now? I only asked about a damned horse.'

'Implying that one was used. You should be aware that the use of performing animals within a morris-based structure of festival entertainment is strictly – and that *should* be underlined – prohibited. Am I clear?'

'But forensics have found hoofmarks.'

'Coconuts,' insisted the lawyer, standing and leading his client towards the door. 'Strapped to the feet of the lead dancer in "Sylvester the Stallion Comes a-Courting", trad. arr.,' he added by way of a much-needed explanation.

'And just precisely how tall are these coconuts, hmmm? Tall enough to allow one to conveniently attach a certain recently deceased morris leader to a suitable pub sign?'

The lawyer ushered Ranzo Ray out into the corridor, before whirling around in a flurry of black cloak and advancing towards the table. He slammed something down and stood angrily. 'Fetch us all a taxi. We are leaving.'

The policemen looked at the small piece of turned wood.

'No, you don't understand,' said Plain. 'When we say bail we don't mean the top of a cricket stump either.'

The lawyer glared at him and swept out dramatically.

'Idiot,' hissed Plain.

64

Cardinal Aguilera sniffed suspiciously at the contents of his mug.

'Cappuccino,' reassured Brother Lyndsey.

The cardinal's eyes narrowed. It was hot, it had froth, it had chocolate bits, but something wasn't quite right. It didn't smell like the cappuccinos he had at home. 'Hmmmm,' he growled, concluding that perhaps his favourite beverage simply didn't travel well. He took a sip.

And spat it across the room. 'What in God's name is that? Are you trying to poison me?'

'Ahh, guess it doesn't work with Earl Grey, then,' shrugged Brother Lyndsey.

Aguilera delivered a withering stare and poured the remains of the mug into a suitable aspidistra.

'Now to matters more useful. Francisco, the bowl.'

Obediently, the novice tugged a wooden bowl out of his rucksack and handed it to the cardinal. He then pulled a large canister out and began pouring the contents into the bowl.

'If you'd wanted water you should've just asked,' said Brother Lyndsey.

'You don't get this from any domestic tap,' answered Aguilera, his voice heavy with importance.

Lyndsey tapped his nose. 'We've got the hard stuff here.'

'Not like this you haven't. Field issue, hundred and fifty per cent overproof Holy Water. The best there is.' It fizzed gently.

'And just what are you hoping to—?'

The cardinal hissed for silence, closed his eyes and began an almost inaudible chant. In seconds images began to appear in the bowl. They swirled in a way guaranteed to produce vertigo in all but the most seasoned of Harrier pilots looking down over rooftops and a gradually dispersing crowd.

'And now we wait,' announced Cardinal Aguilera, staring into the dove's-eye view. 'Francisco, is there any coffee in that sack of yours?'

'Er, no, I didn't pack any,' answered the novice with a shrug.

Aguilera muttered under his breath for a few moments in High Latin. 'Are you sure?' he asked.

'Yes, I'm quite positive that—'

'Take a look,' insisted the cardinal.

'Now how did that get in there?' wondered Francisco, pulling out a packet of fresh-roasted Blue Mountain specifically ground for all cafetieres.

65

I ducked into the alley at the back of St Cedric's and headed for the window. In moments I'd pulled the tiny pane of glass out, flicked back the catch and was shoving the lower sash upwards.

'Still can't believe that you've never seen *The Exorcist*,' said Kirstee, scrambling over the windowsill after me. 'I thought it would've been essential viewing for you guys. You know, like all rookie fighter pilots are shown *Top Gun* and soldiers get to see *Full Metal Jacket*.'

'And all wannabe space pilots get shown *Apollo 13*?'

'And novice priests get to see possession up close and personal in a little girl's bedroom.'

'Well, it's not part of the training,' I said and broke into a whisper. 'In fact, is this the right time to tell you that I haven't the foggiest idea what to do?'

'That's why we're here,' frowned Kirstee. 'There's bound to

be instructions kicking about somewhere. Maybe even an educational video or two. Where would they keep that kind of thing?' Kirstee stared around the office at the wall-to-wall filing cabinets.

I shrugged. 'Under "E"?'

'Just one thing,' came a voice from behind me. I turned and looked out of the window at the demon.

'What now?'

'Well, it's just . . .' It looked suspiciously at the back of its scaly hand. 'How can I be sure this is eczema?'

I shook my head and found myself wishing that lying came easier to me.

'How can you be sure it isn't?' asked Kirstee.

I watched as the beast scratched its head.

'See?' Kirstee jumped in. 'Itchiness is a sure sign.' I saw her fiddling with her fingers behind her back. There was a barely audible snap and, with the confidence of a nightclub magician, she apparently picked something off the window-ledge. 'And flaking is the clincher.' She opened her hand and there in the middle of her palm was half a black-varnished false nail. I had to admit it looked uncannily like a demon's scale.

'But . . .'

'Well, if you want to keep flaking just stay right there.' She turned to me. 'C'mon, let's go. Leave it to spend the rest of its life itching and scratching and having aching feet and . . .'

'No, I don't, it's just . . . Well, this place gives me the creeps.'

Kirstee frowned. 'Look, just 'cause you've come out of here with a skin complaint doesn't mean you can't trust the people who work here. I mean, this guy wouldn't lie to you, would he?'

'Not if he really was a priest,' hedged the beast.

'You don't believe me?' I complained.

'Well, I've never seen any I.D.'

'Just look at him,' answered Kirstee. 'Would anyone who isn't a priest wear one of those?' She pointed to my dog-collar.

'That's not exactly an answer.'

'All right, all right,' hissed Kirstee. 'I'll dig out his personnel file. Okay if he keeps looking for something to help you?'

The demon nodded. Well, it had little choice against the persuasive nature of Kirstee. I was certain that if she set her mind to it she could persuade the Pope to try ecstasy. I know I'd find it hard to refuse her anything.

I edged closer to her. 'Tell me one thing. Why are you doing this?'

'Eh?'

'Why didn't you just take the lottery ticket from me and run. You haven't even asked about it for the past few hours.'

'Oh, that.'

'Don't tell me you've lost interest in an estimated thirteen million—'

'Shut up.'

She hissed the word. Angry. The anger of terror.

'I only asked. You seemed sort of keen on it before.'

'Can't have it. Not yet. Not until . . .' Her eyes glanced quickly over her shoulder towards the window. 'They never give up,' she whispered, barely hiding a shiver. 'It's seen me. Knows me. It'll haunt me for the rest of my life. "It's behind you!" "In space no one can hear you scream." "They're here." How can I enjoy spending an estimated thirteen million when I know that maybe not today, but soon and for the rest of my life, it'll be back to haunt me? They always come back.' She looked down at the floor, trembling. 'They can chew through barbed wire, y'know.'

'But what's that got to do with you?'

'Happy endings.' She stared at her toes. 'Never get a happy ending until everything's all back the way it should be. "Never feed them after midnight and don't get them wet." And . . . and even then they can come back in the sequel. "Just when you thought it was safe to get back in the water." I buy a house it'll be haunted. The Porsche is possessed. Gold necklace reanimates and strangles me. No, it's got to go.' She flicked her eyes back towards the window. 'And you can't use an axe. They never work. Oh, you'll be fine for a few years, maybe even a decade, but somehow all the bits will find their way back together again and once it's got its strength back it'll come and find me.'

'That's just in the movies, you'll be—'

'Don't say it. If you promise me I'll be all right then I might as well kill myself right here. That's a signed warrant for misery, that is.'

'All right. But they're just movies.'

'You say that. But where do the ideas come from? I'll tell you. Personal experience. Oh, it might not be exactly the way they film them. "The names and places have been changed to protect the innocent." But they're real. People disappear every day.'

'Have you found anything?' called a voice through the window.

I saw her shoulders tighten. And I'd lay bets her stomach squirmed into a dozen of the least seaworthy knots.

'Patience,' I answered. 'There's a lot of files in here.' My eyes never left her. They couldn't. I was sure that if I blinked she'd disappear, vanishing behind the nearest suitable sofa, convincing herself that if she couldn't see them then they couldn't see her and they'd go away. Until the next episode.

I found myself gripping the handle of the filing cabinet. It was the only way I could stop myself from grabbing her, wrapping my arms tight around her and offering her all the comfort I could give.

'I've got to deal with it before I get the ticket. Besides,' she whispered, 'I think we make a pretty good team. I mean, you're not really everything I want in a man.'

'Let me guess, you prefer taller and darker.'

The slightest whisker of a grin trembled at her lip.

'I could wear heels,' I offered.

'You'd have to do more than that.'

'Sunbed? Work-outs? I could lose a few pounds.'

'Not the only thing you'd have to lose.' And she pointed to her neck. 'Guys with dog-collars are just so bad for my image.'

Before I had the chance to answer she had taken a deep, calming breath, pulled a large file out of the drawer and slapped it on to a suitable desk. 'Found it. Jacob MacFadden. Priest. This is your file.'

It was strange, I suddenly felt very nervous. Exposed.

She tipped up the file and my life spilled across the table. Photos, CVs, certificates, letters on headed notepaper.

'Is this what you're looking for?' asked Kirstee, snatching a letter from the heap and thrusting it out of the window.

The demon read out loud. 'Dear Jacob, I'm pleased to offer you the post of hygiene supervisor here at St Screed's Hostel for the—'

I waggled a finger in my ear. 'What did you say? Post of what?'

'Hygiene supervisor at St Screed's Hostel for—'

'Let me see that.' I snatched at the letter and stared at it. Questions wriggled in my head. Why was that name so familiar?

'Thought this place was called St Cedric's,' said Kirstee.

'It . . . It is,' I coughed feeling very unsure about it.

'Weird typo.' Kirstee wriggled her fingers as if imagining typing the two words. 'Almost a crypto-anagram.'

'A what?'

'Oh, I studied crosswords for a while. But the nearest anagram of Screed is Sedrec.'

'Spelt like that?' I held up a job application form filled out in my name. She looked at the coat of arms and nodded.

'Is it normal to change the names of ancient hostels?'

'Not unless there's something bad about the original,' I answered. 'There was a small chapel in South Wales devoted to Saint Shagwell. The parish council changed its name in the early sixties claiming that it was the fault of the English for mistranslating the name from the original manuscripts written by the fourteenth-century monk Guto Ab Siadwell. Personally, I think they made the monk up.'

'Er, I don't think that's the only made-up thing around here,' said Kirstee, looking up from the pile of papers from my file. She pointed to the application form. 'Your hobbies were white-water rafting and skyboarding?'

'Yeah, well, everybody makes something up for that bit. Drinking and playing cards doesn't cut the mustard most of the time. But that's history now. I am a priest and that proves it. The application, the letter of offer . . . what more d'you want?'

'Letter of acceptance,' growled the demon.

'Oh come on, I'm here, aren't I? I'm wearing the collar. That *must* prove something.' I looked to Kirstee, desperate for some kind of support. She seemed distracted, staring at the wad of documents in her hands.

'Uh-huh. Just one last thing,' she asked, holding the papers to her chest. 'How tall are you?'

'Five er . . . well, I don't keep much track of . . .'

'Weight?'

'Thirteen two.'

She scowled at me suspiciously.

'All right. Thirteen five. Thirteen nine,' I admitted. 'But I've been losing it. And if I cut out the Guinness and the pizza I can lose a bit more.'

'Like the twelve stone you've already lost?'

'What?'

'And the three and a half feet?'

'This is no time for joking about . . .'

Kirstee shook her head as she laid out the series of metamorphic photographs and turned over the cover of the document file. I read the words up to where she had them covered by her hand.

Name: Jacob MacFadden. Occupation: Hygiene Supervisor. Status: P . . .

'There.' I pointed and sensed that my voice was getting shriller. 'P for priest! That's it, isn't it?'

She tutted once and lifted her hand.

I stared in disbelief at the rubber stamp across the flap of cardboard. In the box marked Status was the single word 'Patient'.

'No. No. No. That can't be . . . Not right at all . . .'

'It's true,' said Kirstee.

'Oh my G . . .' And for the first time, I couldn't say it. The words caught in my throat.

And there wasn't enough time. Almost before I could breathe the door was pushed open and three men in black cassocks swept in.

'Makes interesting reading, doesn't it?' grinned a vaguely Italian-looking one.

I felt my mouth open and close a couple of times before panic grabbed my legs and hurled me towards the window.

'There is no escape,' shouted Bishop Hutchinson.

Unfortunately, he was right. The window was blocked by the demon as it scrambled in from the alley.

'What are you doing?' I squeaked. 'Run! That way.'

Black scaly shoulders shrugged. And in a moment I understood.

The alley was blocked by another black-cassocked man. But this one was armed. I stared down the barrel of a large and extremely powerful-looking weapon. Sights bulged from the top, handles protruded from all over and little red lights pulsed ominously. It was only when I spotted the filling nozzle that the illusion was shattered. In a flash I recognised it as a pump-action water pistol.

His finger trembled on the plunger. 'Don't make me use this,' he threatened.

'I'm not scared of that.'

'Should be. It's filled with Holy Water. Please don't make me use it, I really hate picking up scales.'

There was a clatter of hooves as the demon leapt through the open window.

'Situation contained,' grinned the Italian-looking one. 'Take them below.' With a flurry of cassock he produced a scale model of a Walther PPK, perfect in every detail other than its preference for liquid bullets.

I tried to catch Brother Lyndsey's eye as I was led past. 'Look, if this is about the fire in room six and the damage to the carpet, well, I was going to explain but—'

The butt of a water cannon nudged at my ribs. And I began to suspect that perhaps this was about something a little more serious. A little more secret.

Doing Delilah

66

There are times and places when being right is good. Pub quizzes. Placing bets on the Grand National. You know the sort of thing.

And there are times when being right is really not what you want.

I had suspected that there was more to the sudden appearance of certain black-cassocked chaps than a simple reprimand over a bit of burnt carpet in room six. Little things gave it away. The way we were rounded up and frog-marched down through the lower levels of St Cedric's. The way we were ordered into a room I had never visited in my entire time as hygiene operative. And, for me the clincher, the way we were all chained spreadeagled to vast slabs of ironmongery hanging from the wall.

The only person who didn't seem overly concerned about our state of affairs was Kirstee. She writhed against her shackles, flexed her wrists against the cuffs and actually seemed to be enjoying herself. 'You haven't got one of those big metal collars with a padlock at the back, have you?' she asked. 'Only I like those. They always feel so very secure.'

I saw Brother Lyndsey's jaw drop. Well, he didn't exactly get out much.

'I take it that's a no,' tutted Kirstee. 'Typical. Just typical of

211

men today that is. You've spent so long getting in touch with your feminine side that you've all forgotten how to give a girl a good time. Have you any idea how long it is since I had a really good satisfying shag? Have you?'

'That kind of language does not impress us,' hissed the Italian-looking one.

'I mean, that's not to say I haven't had my fair share of—'

'Enough!' snapped the cardinal, slamming a fist on to a table. A host of ancient religious articles rattled precariously. 'We are not here to discuss such pleasures.'

'And just why are we here?' It was out of my mouth before I realised.

'Ahhh, such curiosity.'

'And just who the hell are you anyhow?' I must admit even I was surprised at my using the 'H' word. And as for my tone of voice, well, Kirstee winked at me and did that thing with her tongue again.

'Who am I?' grinned the man in the blackest cassock. 'Well, I suppose it is only fair you know the name of your executioner.'

'What?' The outburst came from at least five different mouths.

'I am Cardinal Aguilera of the Vatican Special Forces, Counter Insurgence Chapter. Codename "Deep Duvet",' he answered, pacing the floor in true dictatorial style. Hands in the small of his back. 'I came up with that name myself. There is no better cover, see?'

If he was expecting applause he didn't get any.

He hid his disappointment well, pacing slowly up and down in front of us. 'Now, which of you is the demon, eh?'

'Guess.'

'I meant of those two,' hissed Aguilera, glaring at nine

212

foot of beast chained to the wall. 'Is it the girl with the carnal passions? Or him? The one behind it all. The ringleader?'

I felt him looking me up and down, convinced that he was quite capable of seeing through to my very beating heart.

'What d'you mean, "behind it all"?' countered Bishop Hutchinson. 'That makes it sound like some kind of conspiracy.'

'There's always some kind of conspiracy where demons are involved. It's their nature,' insisted Aguilera.

'No, these are different. They're under our protection. They're innocent.'

'Oxymoron,' tutted the cardinal.

'Who are you calling—'

'Impossible contradiction. Like military intelligence. Attractive politician. Interesting trainspotter.'

'Athletic golfer,' joined in Kirstee.

'This isn't word association.'

'And it isn't execution time,' challenged the bishop.

'Hear, hear,' I shouted and received a poisoned glare from the floor.

'This operation terminates here!'

'But you can't. Witness protection schemes don't end that way.'

'You call this protection?' snapped Aguilera, advancing on the bishop. 'Protection implies a certain degree of tact, of cover, of security. You not only expose this safe house to the world but you turn it into some kind of tourist attraction. Have you any idea how long we had to wait for a taxi to get here?'

'That was a mistake. You said so yourself. Bit of disbelief in the sub—'

'A mistake that has cost this entire operation. We're into damage limitation now. So, which of those is the other demon?'

And for the first time in several confused minutes, Francisco the novice spoke up. 'Er, I'm having trouble with this,' he began, his eyes fixed away to my left. 'Are you actually saying that . . . er . . . that that is actually an actual real live d . . . d . . . d . . .'

'From the very pits of hell,' confirmed the cardinal with the tone of voice normally used by big game hunters talking about tigers bagged in foreign climes.

'You insulting my home?' growled the demon. 'It's all right once you get used to the smell. And the wailing of tormented souls. Oh, and the gnashing teeth. That gets kind of irritating.'

Francisco was scratching his head. 'But it shouldn't be alive here.'

'That's what we're here for,' said the cardinal. 'In a few moments from now it won't be.'

'No, I mean . . . it should be frozen. Aren't they supposed to live at—?'

'Fahrenheit 666 – the temperature at which devils are happiest,' interrupted the cardinal. 'But not essential for life. They're actually far more adaptable to ambient fluctuations than any of them think. After a couple of days of shivering, they invariably pull through. But I shouldn't be saying that in front of two of them, should I? If secrets like that get out we'll be invaded by the damned things come next summer. They cannot be allowed out of this room with information like that. You hear me?'

I watched with mounting concern as he snatched the largest weapon off the novice.

'So, who's first?' he asked, training the sights on the three of us in turn.

'Ooooh, watersports,' giggled Kirstee. 'Me first.'

Aguilera's eyebrows angled towards dark suspicion. 'This some kind of ploy? Or have you really no idea of the way anything other than the purest flesh melts under a few drops of this stuff?'

'Except for the scales,' added Francisco. 'I hate having to clear them up. Of course I've never actually seen an actual execut . . . er, exorcism, but . . .' His voice faded under the angry gaze of the cardinal.

'Let me see, I know one of them was a woman,' mused Aguilera thoughtfully.

'How d'you know that?' coughed the bishop.

'Just call it divine inspiration,' grinned the cardinal. 'Or could it be that we in Rome do know what goes on in our safe houses? I must admit to being surprised at the fact that you two could be capable of such a feat. Can't repair a simple non-motile general illusion but you can turn beast into beauty. Clever.'

He marched up to within inches of Kirstee and peered intently at her through the corner of his eye. 'Hmmmm, so is it you? Or you?'

I stared back at him, concern gnawing at the ankles of my sanity. Surely I would wake up soon. I'd hit my head. I was still in the street across from Il Diablo's. I'd come around in a minute. Wrong.

'Does the so-called priest get both barrels?'

'I am a priest,' I wailed. It wasn't as convincing as I'd hoped. 'I've taken my vows and . . .'

'And what vows were they? I shall gather about me the evil scum of the Underworld?'

'No.'

'Or I shall indulge my carnal fantasies to the fullest using leather-clad vixens?'

'No,' I insisted, feeling somewhat red about the cheeks. How did he know that? Okay, I hadn't actually indulged, but boy, there were fantasies aplenty.

Kirstee looked across at me and winked. I'm sure she could tune into my thoughts at times.

'He's not my type,' she declared.

I was gutted.

'Ohh, such an act of loyalty,' applauded Aguilera, lining the barrel up on her. 'Which vow's he got you under, eh? Lust or scum? Hex or sex?'

'Leave her alone,' I blurted and the barrel swung my way again. 'You can't talk to her like . . .'

'Of course, it could equally be you,' scowled the cardinal. 'Hiding a renegade demon under the disguise of a man of the cloth is rather inventive. And employing him here. Subtle. Get him to check in every day without him ever suspecting a thing.'

'Yes, I must confess I was dead chuffed when I came up with that one,' smiled Brother Lyndsey, buffing his finger nails on his chest. 'And it's a way of avoiding unwanted attentions. Most people won't let themselves get anywhere near a member of the clergy unless they really have to . . . Oh dear.'

The expression on my face must have been wild. I've never seen Brother Lyndsey go so white so fast before. 'You're telling me I really am a . . .'

'Look, it's not quite the lie it sounds. Honest. It was for your own good. Seirizzim would never have let you tell anyone about the hamst–'

'Shut up!' squealed Aguilera.

'Hamster,' I whispered, my throat constricting with alarm.

'Where?' shrieked the beast on my left. 'Where is it? Don't let it anywhere near me.' Chains rattled as it searched the dark shadows at its hooves.

'So what else is a lie?' I shouted, my heart pounding with anger. 'My vows? My beliefs? My work?'

'Ahh, now that's real. See, it's a big place for just the two of us to keep spotless.' Brother Lyndsey attempted a grin.

'What about my life?' I wailed as fragile memories began to erode before my eyes. 'My whole life is just a lie?'

'Well, not all of it. Okay, I made some of it up but, well, your ordination day, that was mine, and the kitten you got on your fifth birthday, he was—'

'Yours!'

'But we can share it. He's dead now anyhow. Hit by a forty-tonner in 1983—'

'What? Why didn't you tell me? Skittles is dead?' I heard myself wail.

'No, no, Tickles. I called him Tickles.'

And waves of black anger writhed within me, racking at my body, clenching every muscle fibre. 'Not only have you filled my mind with lies but they're not even right!'

'Skittles, Tickles, it's not *that* much of a difference,' whimpered Brother Lyndsey. 'Look it's not easy translating through the High Latin, y'know.'

'I don't need excuses!' I roared. And something snapped. I wasn't sure whether it was my temper or the chains that went first. But suddenly I was marching across the room, trailing jangling metalwork from every limb.

'Hold it right there!' ordered Cardinal Aguilera, looking strangely small. I peered down at him. 'This is loaded,' he announced and shook the gun. It sloshed ominously.

'Off with his head!' enthused Kirstee behind me, writhing like a lap dancer.

The cardinal's finger trembled on the plunger. 'One step closer and I'll . . .' His knuckles turned white as he clenched his fist hard. 'Die, you spawn of Satan!' I saw the flash of red LEDs and heard the whirr of Duracell-charged pumps.

And the pain didn't come. He either missed or . . .

217

'It didn't fire,' wailed the cardinal, pumping with all his might. 'What's wrong with this damned thing? If we've been issued with Korean-made stuff again I'll . . . What do they know about religious assult rifles, they're Buddhists.'

'Er, this is the bit where we make a run for it,' observed Kirstee from her wall hanging. 'Like in the movies? Y'know, just at the start of the last ten minutes, just when you think it's all over, the heroes get their lucky break.'

'What are you on about?'

'She's right,' said the other creature shackled to the wall. 'Never look a plot device in the mouth. I'm out of here.'

Muscles rippled under scales and, with a rupture of metal fatigue, the beast was free and out the door. Chains clattered to the floor.

'Come back and be killed!' wailed Aguilera.

I looked from the shattered door to the baffled clergy.

'Er, time for the knight in shining armour,' prompted Kirstee. 'All right, shining scales are fine by me. Let's go.'

The cardinal thumped the body of his gun. 'Work, damn you!'

'Look, just get me out of here, will you,' shouted Kirstee, tugging at her chains. 'These guys are really not my type and if I stay here much longer I tell you I'm going to get *really* frustrated. You hear what I'm saying? Get your scaly arse over here and save a girl from a really boring time. Comprendé?'

Now I was certain I was hallucinating. She was talking foreign. I lurched across the room, snorting, my breathing somehow suddenly very horsey.

'C'mon. C'mon,' urged Kirstee. 'No, careful with the cuffs, don't snap them. No, don't pull so hard, my ankles are delicate. Just pull those chains there and there and . . .'

In moments we were out the door.

And behind me the echoes of accusation began.

'Damn this bloody gun. I told them changing suppliers was a false economy. Save a few quid here and what happens . . .'

'Er, Cardinal, the safety valve?'

'What about it?'

'It's closed, isn't it?'

'Who said anything about safety valves? Where's the safety valve status light, eh? Cheap crummy Korean . . . And I don't know what you two are looking so smug about. It's all your fault they got away.'

'Our fault? You had the weaponry.'

'And you, as bishop of this place, have the responsibility to ensure that all fixtures and fittings are in correct working order. When was the last time you had those chains serviced, eh? Tell me. And you'd better have the paperwork to prove it.'

67

In an echoing marble hall, a nine-inch black talon stabbed on to a sheet of parchment.

'There, you say?'

'Of course. How many times do I have to tell you?' tutted Bertrand Matlock, recently deceased. 'I was killed in Camford. There, just right where you have your finger . . . er, claw.'

'Talon,' corrected Seirizzim.

'I must say, you're aren't quite as tall as I'd expected. The Guides say you're at least ten six, but you look more like nine eight to me.'

'Human measurements are fallible. Things tend to look bigger when you're scared.'

219

'So, just for the record, when was the last time you went walkabout, as it were?'

'Colonel? Are the troops ready?' called Seirizzim, drawing himself up to his full height and staring at the door.

'Tintagel in 1976, wasn't it? September. No, August. It was a hot summer. All those ladybirds.'

'Colonel! Where's my squad?'

'Go on, you can tell me. Yes or no? Or . . . no. It was Scara Brae in 1985. Yes, of course. That was picked up by five trawlers off the Orkneys. And, coincidentally, corresponded to a significant and so far inexplicable power drop in Dounreay. That *was* you. So does it take a lot of energy to go topside? Y'know, you syphon it off like the Silurians do, and—'

'Colonel!'

Seirizzim breathed a heavy sigh of relief as the sound of hooves echoed to a halt outside the door.

'Bring them in. Please!'

'Or did you pop up at the Droia Stone near Llanfairfechan in Caernarfonshire during the last Summer Solstice—?'

The doors were thrust open and a squad of four creatures marched in.

Matlock's jaw fell open as he stared at the abominations before him. They stood well over ten feet and bulged in matt black. A halo of inchoate fur shimmered around where their faces should have been and trimmed off a hemline just below waist height. One of them took a step forward and muttered something. It sounded as if it had come from beyond the grave.

'What? Say that again.'

'Or you could try hand signals if . . .'

To Matlock's surprise, the thing raised a bulky hand and began feeling around its face. There was a rustle, the undoing of bits of webbing and the halo of fur opened.

'I said, "Squad reporting for duty, sah",' panted Colonel Tumor from the depths of his hood. 'All prepared for sudden temperature plunge.'

'And that'll protect you for how long?' tutted Seirizzim.

'If Fahrenheit-Celsius conversion is as the prisoner told us, then we can expect to survive for a maximum of twenty minutes. But, sir, are we able to trust him? This talk of weather and . . . what was it he said . . . rain? Liquid water? This cannot be true?'

'Do not concern yourself with such things. There is a better way. Follow me.'

Seirizzim headed for the door, four pairs of muffled hooves following him.

'Oh, and Colonel, tell your men to remove their insulation before they pass out. I believe I already hear their hooves sloshing in boots of sweat.'

'Yes, sir. And that's after two stops for drainage, sir.'

Matlock watched as the door slammed shut. He looked around him and grinned.

'Seirizzim's own front room. Wish I could tell the lads. They'd be well jealous.' With an effort he struggled up on to an oversize marble swivel chair and dangled his legs over the edge. 'If only they could see me now.'

68

Doctor Boscombe's tongue licked feverishly at the corner of his mouth, writhing like an eel in a sack. It was something that happened whenever he was concentrating hard. That and the tuneless humming.

He flexed a pair of forceps and picked up a perfectly

trimmed cocktail stick. He dipped each end in a tiny droplet of superglue and, under the watchful gaze of his bulging magnified eye, settled it into position.

A few seconds later his humming changed key to a major of expectation as he picked up a mesh of cocktail sticks and carried them across the lab. Four dabs of glue later and a one-hundredth-scale model of a certain local pub sign was in position on the cardboard box which was currently standing in for the Monocle and Asparagus. It was perfect in every detail, even down to the dodgy bit of pointing above the front window.

All that was missing was a victim.

A plasticine Bertrand Matlock complete with elastic band braces strolled in and stopped under the pub sign. And scenario number one sprang into action.

An orange plasticine man on horseback galloped in brandishing a polo mallet. Boscombe moved each limb fractions of an inch and photographed each instant. The horseman caught 'Matlock' behind the knee, knocking him to the floor. He spun his horse, lassoed the prone victim and hauled him up on to the sign.

Boscombe peered hard through his magnifying glass and frowned.

'Nothing,' he muttered to himself, homing in on Matlock's upper arms.

And scenario two entered stage right.

The horseman galloped in, felled the victim and wheeled around. A purple figurine sprang down and set about the prone Matlock with ninth of an inch stiletto heels. In a matter of frames the horseman had hauled the victim up on to the pub sign.

Boscombe's eye squinted at the scene and in particular at the upper arms of the swinging lump of plasticine. It didn't

222

look impressed. 'Wrong angle,' he grumbled. 'None of the marks are the right angle. Right shape though. Hmmmmmmm. Time for number three. Getting more unlikely as time goes by.'

He repositioned his orange plasticine victim beneath the pub sign and opened a shoe box. In moments he had his latest suspect on the move. It stalked across the scene, frame by frame, covering inches with each stride. It halted, snatched Matlock and bodily hoisted him up into the one-hundredth-scale Camford sky.

Boscombe fired the last frame on the camera and peered at the upper arm. 'Oh my God. That's it . . . almost.'

He stared at the stilted assassin and scratched his head as he began calculating fulcrum positions and swivel angles and—'

'Of course!' Feverishly, he wrenched off the tiny stilts, snapped them in half and reattached them to its legs and arms. 'That's it,' he grinned. 'That's it!'

And as he reloaded the camera, he tried desperately to ignore the questions nagging at the back of his mind. Just what stood a good seven foot at the shoulders, had claws and walked about on hooves?

Somehow he began to suspect that certain unimaginative police officers would have a great deal of difficulty taking any of this seriously.

69

Acres of expectant faces stared back from a couple of hundred tables as dozens of waitresses plied them with Napa Valley white.

'Do "Delilah"!' squealed the Republican candidate for South Carolina.

'Did I hear a request?' asked the man on the stage, with an accent normally associated with valleys on the far side of the Atlantic. Mining valleys.

The crowd went wild, hammering cutlery on their tables. Somehow, out of the tumult a chant developed. De-li-lah. De-li-lah.

Tom Jones nodded to the band and for the second time that day Las Vegas rocked. He spun on his heel, grabbed the mic and everything went black.

'Hey! That can't be it!' objected the demon on the couch, sitting up. 'I paid for a full day's possession. That's twenty-four hours. That includes the after-show party, right?'

'Wrong,' hissed Seirizzim.

'But I was doing "Delilah". You can't throw me out in the middle of–'

'I can and I have.'

'Why, why, why?' he sang.

'None of your business. Out. No encore,' snarled Seirizzim.

And three of the larger demons flung him out of the heat-purpled front door of the Transcendental Travel Company Ltd.

'Er, c . . . can I help you?' asked a harassed-looking bookings agent. 'Are you perhaps looking for that perfect holiday?'

'Holiday? Oh no, this is business,' grinned Seirizzim.

'Business? But . . .' The bookings agent scratched between her horns. 'I'm not sure that's what you're supposed to do with possessions. It's the simple pleasure of living vicariously off another party which normally attracts one to a possessional holiday. No decisions needed, you see? Just go with the flow. Gives the brain a rest.'

'My squad don't want to rest. They want a change. That's as good I hear.'

'Er, well . . .'

'You have spare capacity,' suggested Seirizzim, looking around at the empty couches scattered around the travel lounge.

'So how many will be in your party?' shrugged the bookings agent.

'Four.'

'And you have a particular destination?'

'Oh yes.'

The bookings agent winced nervously as she looked up at Seirizzim's widening grin. 'Do come into my office,' she swallowed.

70

Everything around me felt weird. Familiar surroundings felt like they'd taken a shift to the left. Wallpaper was a slightly different colour to how I remembered it. And my shoes didn't fit any more. I felt nothing could be trusted.

And especially not the photos stuffed in a shoe box hidden under the bed. A bed I wouldn't even fit into now.

I stared down at the box of pictures framed between my hooves and felt like I was staring at a complete stranger's life. A small black and white kitten peered curiously out of a glossy photo. 'Skittles,' I heard myself whisper before my talons screwed the thing into a ball. 'Who cares, it's just road-kill now.'

'That's a horrible thing to say.' Kirstee's voice floated over my shoulder. I didn't look up.

'Just another stitch in a tapestry of lies.'

'Uh-oh, he's getting poetic. That's always a bad sign.'

I stared at a fuzzy focus shot of a priest posing in front of a wisteria-coated abbey. The cross he was holding burned into the back of my eyes. Until I tore that to shreds.

'I could get bored watching this,' said Kirstee.

'Yeah? Well what am I supposed to do? Up until half an hour ago I was convinced I was a human being. Now look at me.'

'I'm looking.'

'Okay, so it wasn't that great a life cleaning up after other folk, but at least it was honest. At least I was human.'

I shredded another shot of my fictitious ordination.

'There are advantages.'

'Name one.'

'You don't need to get scissors to destroy photos. Those talons do the job perfectly.'

'So, I can hire myself out as a document shredder. Whoopie-do.'

'You could. Or what about a hedge clipping service? Look at the happiness that brought Johnny Depp. Of course, that wouldn't be a fraction of the happiness I could give him.'

'So that's two advantages. But what about the down side? I don't know who I am. I don't know where I fit in. I . . . I don't know anything about me any more. And none of my clothes will go anywhere near me.'

'Who says that's a problem? I can live without your clothes. Cassocks are *so* passé. And as for dog-collars . . .'

'But they made me,' I sniffed. 'Clothes do that for the man.'

'A tissue of lies. A web of deceit,' she answered. 'And I warn you now, I can out-cliché you for sure.'

'I can't do anything right any more.'

'Shut up,' she whispered. 'You saved me from those madmen.'

'Just returning the favour.'

'So we're even, huh?'

'Guess so. But what makes you want to be even with this?'

'Oooh, little things,' she whispered, and for the first time I

226

became aware of the gentle clinking of chains behind me. 'Like the fact that, judging by the way you went through various doors, pulled massive amounts of hardware off walls and carried me all the way back here without stopping for a break, I guess that makes you, what, four hundred and twenty pounds of pure muscle.' I could feel her gaze on the back of my neck. 'And I kind of like that in a m . . . my partner. It makes me feel secure.'

'You're just saying that.'

'Why would I do that? You're my hero.'

'Or is it because you've been chained to that portcullis for the last few hours and you're feeling horny?'

'Well, yes, but . . . I mean, look at you. Tall, very, very dark, and handsome in a devilish kind of way. What more could a girl want?'

'When you put it that way . . .'

I turned and looked at her spreadeagled on half a ton of ironmongery. She smiled. 'Help,' she whispered. 'I'm trapped.' And, as if to prove the point, the chains around her ankles rattled ever so slightly.

'And just what is it you want me to do about it?'

'My nose is itchy,' she cooed, as warm and dark as cream of mushroom soup. 'You couldn't just . . .'

I leant over her, flicked out an index talon and reached for her nose. 'Anywhere in particular.'

'Closer. Closer.'

I never reached my target. With a creak of leather she shifted her head and suddenly my claw was in her mouth. I felt her tongue curl tight around my talon, felt it squeeze, warm and moist, and at that moment I didn't want it to be anywhere else. Especially when I heard her moan. Small, quiet and so powerful. She moved under me and the smell of warm leather stroked at my nostrils.

And as her tongue snared another of my talons I heard the sound of something unravelling. I couldn't believe my eyes as I looked down. The single zip which ran down the full length of her body was slowly undoing. It moved an inch at a time as she squirmed against her bonds. A seductive snake shedding her entire skin.

I couldn't peel my eyes away. As the well-oiled zip purred way past what could be considered a neckline, I realised I was hooked. Fascinated. And then other zips joined in. A pair travelled off down the length of her arms and two others slid down the entirety of her inner thighs and calves and on towards those ankles of hers.

She smiled up at me and, with a final wriggle, she was naked.

'Oops,' she whispered and kissed the inside of my wrist. 'Can't think how that happened.' Her tongue slithered off up the inside of my forearm. 'You're so hot.'

'Ohhhhhhhhhhhhh.' It was all I could say.

'And I feel so very cold. You couldn't just . . .'

I needed no second bidding. I pressed my body against hers, scales on skin.

'Ohhhh yes, that's better. Much better,' she whispered, and began to move in ways I'd only previously fantasised about.

71

If tape recorders had fingers the one in Interrogation Room Two would have been drumming them with boredom. It had heard it all before.

Yes: Matlock was dead.

Yes: there were a bunch of morris men in town.

No: they say they didn't do it.

No: PC Plain had no new angles in his investigation.

If the tape machine had actually paused, rewound and

thought about this last point, it would have realised that it was wrong. So far the questions had all been the same as the previous abortive interrogations, except for the subtle change of personnel. PC Plain hadn't said a word. That had all been Skitting's pleasure.

But all that was about to change.

'Okay, enough is enough,' announced Plain, and everyone shook themselves awake. 'No more beating around the houses. Let's get straight to the heart of the matter. C'mon, confess, we know you did it.'

'What?' coughed Rawlings with a jingle of bells. 'I didn't. I . . . I've told you.'

'Yeah, well, we've done a bit of digging and that kind of thing just doesn't hold the water it's printed on, see?'

All eyes turned on Plain, confused.

'We know about your past, Rawlings. We know about your time.'

'What time?'

'Behind bars,' hissed Plain, knuckles on the desk, shirt sleeves rolled up.

'Oh, you've been doing your homework,' said Rawlings, looking at the table.

'Care to tell us about it?' prompted Plain, pacing the room.

'Look, I needed the money, okay?'

'Aha!'

'It's never been easy being a student but, well, ever since the government changed the entire cash-flow system relating to the provision of financial . . .'

'Get to the point!' snarled Plain, sensing he was getting closer to the truth.

'Look, I only did it once. And I hated it.'

'Once. Twice. A crime is still a crime. And you're going down for it again.'

'Going down for what?' squeaked Rawlings. 'It's not illegal to work behind bars, is it?'

Plain stopped in his tracks, spun on his heels and snatched at the dossier on the table. He fumbled with a pair of glasses and squinted at the tiny type.

'Look, if I'd known that the supply of alcoholic beverages was . . .' pleaded Rawlings.

Hurriedly, Plain dropped the paperwork on to his chair and pulled what he hoped was a reasonable if sceptical face. 'Yeah, well, that's history. But we know about the rest of your past. Eh, "Fingers"?'

Rawlings scratched his head nervously.

'We know all about the Mother's Day Massacre of 1976 when twenty-seven sales assistants in card shops rioted and were mercilessly gunned down by . . .'

'I was ten years old in 1976,' whimpered Rawlings.

Plain looked suspiciously out of the corner of his eye and peered at the front of another dossier. 'You saying you're not Frankie "Fingers" Rawlings?'

'No, I'm not.'

'Oh.' Plain grabbed another file. 'What about Louis "The Forks" Rawlings, wanted for the Father's Day Firebombing of 1977?'

'Nope.'

'Vernon "The Fringe" Rawlings?'

A shake of his head and another file vanished.

'Algie "Scarf Ace" Rawlings, famed for his penchant for using a variety of neck warmers in a series of spectacular murders?'

Rawlings shrugged and the last file disappeared.

'Secretaries,' tutted Plain. 'You ask 'em to do a job . . .'

'So what happens now?' asked Rawlings after a few minutes' worth of embarrassed silence.

230

'Well, don't ask me,' sulked Plain. 'Not my fault that a perfectly useful line of questioning doesn't come up with anything.'

'So am I free to go?'

'Well, er . . .'

'Not so fast,' declared Doctor Boscombe, bursting in through the door at full tilt. 'Nobody is going anywhere until they've seen this.' He slapped a freshly printed Compu-Fit picture on to the table and glared at Rawlings. 'Recognise that?' he demanded.

Plain took a glance at the picture and rolled his eyes towards the ceiling. 'And just what's that supposed to be?'

'Our murderer,' answered Boscombe, his eyes fixed on a baffled Rawlings.

'Er, Doctor, I have the distinct feeling that you have been at the formaldehyde again,' observed Plain.

'Nonsense. Nonsense. I'm perfectly, er . . . at one with my faculties.'

'But you don't seriously expect anyone to admit to having seen that.'

'And just why not, hmmm?'

Plain slid his arm around Boscombe's shoulder. 'That is a picture of a creature with horns and scales and the type of expression which only something from the nether reaches of Hades would wear. Am I right?'

Boscombe nodded. 'But the hooves, you see. One pair. Upright bipedal. I should have seen it sooner.'

'You should have seen a therapist sooner.'

'No, no. It fits. It all makes sense – they were working together. Them and it and . . .'

There was a jingle of irritated wrist bells as Jed Z. Trewithers slammed the illustration back on to the table. 'If you are in *any* way insinuating that a practising team of

231

morris men is in league with creatures from the nether reaches of Hades then I am out of here. With my client, of course.'

'Excuse me,' said Rawlings, finally getting a decent glimpse of the paper causing the controversy. He was ignored.

'If you are in any way linking the pursuit of morrising with that of other paganistic rites including devil worship or even simple admiration, well, I shall have no choice but to sue,' ranted Trewithers, his cloak flapping imperiously.

'Excuse me?'

'I have heard of such opinions amongst the law makers in this country but never have I encountered it with such blatant—'

'Excuse me. Er, can we do a deal here?' asked Rawlings. All eyes turned on him.

'Deal? What you got?' grinned Plain, leaning on the desk.

'I give you a name and you let us go? Charges dropped?'

'Depends on whose name it is, doesn't it?'

Rawlings's finger shook ever so slightly as he pointed to the face on the CompuFit.

'Now you're talking,' grinned Plain.

'Spill,' begged Boscombe.

'We go free? No record.'

'Yeah, yeah. Whatever. Gimme the name.'

All eyes were drilling hard into Rawlings's skull as he took a breath. 'The name you want is . . . Audrey,' he said. 'Audrey Williams.'

'Take him away. Lock him up,' snarled Plain.

'Throw away the key!' screamed Boscombe.

'Wait, you can't do that,' shouted Rawlings as Skitting and Sim frogmarched him towards the door. 'You promised.'

'That was before you started taking the piss. Audrey Williams indeed.'

'It's true. She told us.' Rawlings's objections echoed down the corridor.

'He's holding out on us,' mused Boscombe, rubbing his chin. 'Cancel their evening meal and turn up the heat, they'll snap. I know they know who that is. And they know that I know that—'

'Doctor?' began Plain. 'Shut up.'

72

Tony Keswick strode wearily out of the lift and headed towards his suite of mayoral offices. 'All that waving is *so* exhausting, don't you think? Still, it's good to see the populace with smiles on their faces. They do like it when their civic leader is amongst them.'

'Oh yes, Your Worship,' chorused the entourage of faithful assistants.

'Excellent,' grinned the mayor and turned on Haskins, Deputy-In-Charge of Funding Outsourcing. 'And since they enjoyed revelling in the sense of community, we'll just hike their community charge. Thirty-five per cent should do.'

'Consider the paperwork already done, sir,' grinned Haskins and headed off towards his office.

'Meekins?' called Keswick and in an instant the Staff Improvement Liaison Officer was at his heel. The mayor held his wrist and pulled a pained but noble expression. 'I feel that my ability to wave is not up to the perfection required by my public. Arrange for some training, will you? Three weeks in the Bahamas?'

'Of course, sir. Consider it booked.'

'Now, the rest of you. Back to work!' he ordered and stepped into his office to the sound of feet clattering towards their relevant places of work. He strolled up to his window and peered out at the throngs of revellers trying to find something to revel at.

'Ahhh, my public. So gullible. I tell them there's a carnival and they have one. Who needs to book anyone?'

'Such civic leadership is the envy of all,' smiled Delia, the secretary, licking the end of her pen. 'Is there anything you wish me to take down, Your Worship?'

'Hmmmm, now let me see. Ahh yes, take a letter, Miss Harris.'

'Is that before or after I bring you a nice fresh gin and tonic?'

'Oh, after, of course. And, er, you couldn't just warm up a pot of massage oil, could you? My feet are killing me.'

Delia winked. 'Consider it done,' she smiled and slid into another office.

She was half-way across the polished sycamore flooring when the spasms hit. She shuddered to a halt, grabbed at her head and doubled over. 'No, no, no. Arghhh, the prawns . . .' she gasped and collapsed. Sweat bubbled across her brow and her breathing rattled uncontrollably. It was the type of fit that would have had any red-blooded male running across the room ready to loosen any tight clothing and prepare for chest massage.

They wouldn't have had a chance. Almost as soon as it had started she rolled on to her back, stared at the ceiling and grinned as she ran her hands over her body. 'Ooooh, nice,' she said in a voice strangely deeper than before. She jumped to her feet and, wobbling on her heels, crossed to a mirror and began playing with her hair.

'*Report*,' hissed a voice in her head. '*Captain Tumor, report!*'

'Good choice,' grinned Tumor, flicking Delia's hair over her shoulder. 'Only disappointed I hadn't the chance to send myself on "Feminine Wiles: Tactical Deployment of. Part Three." Could have been handy.'

'*Just get on with it. The others are on their way.*'

'Aye, sir,' she hissed, saluted and headed off to a small oil warmer and turned it on. In seconds she had thrown together a large gin and was wobbling back into the mayoral suite.

'Ahh, there you are,' smiled Keswick, spinning idly in his favourite chair.

'Who else did you expect? Your gin.'

'Delia, your voice sounds a little, well, hoarse.'

'All that cheering I expect. Mind if I . . . ?' She pointed to the glass.

'Er, no. A small sip will probably . . . oh, you've finished it.'

'There's another already on its way.' And she wobbled out of the room just as the door was pushed open and Meekins swaggered in.

'What are you doing here? I didn't summon you.'

'About this community charge thing,' he began and settled himself opposite the mayor. 'Gimme one good reason why I should do it, eh? I mean, have you any idea of the paperwork that'll involve? Have you?'

'Meekins, you'll do it because I've told you to.'

'Not today.'

'What are you? This . . . this is insubordination.'

'No, it's not,' countered Haskins, stepping into the office and closing the door behind him. 'More like a little bit of favour swapping.' He pulled a chair over and sat next to Meekins.

'Delia! Delia! My staff are revolting.'

'Charming,' tutted Meekins as the secretary entered carrying a tray of drinks and a steaming bottle.

'That's nothing you didn't already know,' she grinned,

placing the tray on the table. 'Help yourself, everyone.' She grabbed a pint of gin. 'Hate short measures, don't you?'

'What is the meaning of this?' fumed Keswick. 'This some kind of joke?'

Three heads shook.

'Look, I'm going to call security if you don't stop looking at me in that malevolent sort of way.'

'Go ahead,' smiled Delia.

She watched as he reached for the phone, picked up the handset and pressed '9'. He scowled, hit the cradle and tried again. It took him four more attempts before he gave up. 'All right, so I don't know the number. That is your first victory. The only victory, I might add. Now, what d'you want? More pay? Better holidays?'

'Like the private said,' answered Delia, waving a hand towards Meekins. 'We want a favour.'

'I . . . I don't do favours,' sweated Keswick, nervous now he'd heard the word 'private'. That smacked of military. And weapons. And pain. He wasn't good with pain. Well, not his own anyhow.

'You will do this one,' smiled Delia, standing and picking up the steaming bottle on the tray. There was the slight sound of sizzling. Slowly, she headed around the back of the table and began unscrewing the lid. 'Your feet still hurting?'

'Er . . . I . . . Why do you ask?'

'This is the perfect temperature,' she grinned and nonchalantly poured a capful or so on to the floor. Steam rose in a cloud and the smell of burning varnish followed. 'Few minutes of this and your feet will never bother you again. Well, except in the nightmares where you dream about tap dancing at the Royal Albert Hall, of course.'

'All right. All right. What's this favour?' he spluttered, snatching for his pint of gin.

'We want you to find someone for us.'

'Find someone? Er, don't private detectives do that kind of thing?' Keswick's knuckles were white as he clutched at his glass. 'I can give you some names. Tell them I sent you, they'll give you good rates.'

'They take too long. My boss is keen to get a swift conclusion to this matter.'

'Well, how can I possibly help you out with—'

'Room 101,' said Haskins, picking his teeth with a letter knife.

'What? How did you know—?'

'I implemented it, remember? In the spring of '98.'

'But . . .'

'Look, Tony, you don't get any choice in the matter. You either come with us, or we take the parts we need to get through the security retinal scans. Your choice.'

Keswick blinked nervously as Haskins twirled the letter knife between his fingers. 'Lead on,' he sighed.

73

I felt like I was floating, adrift in that half-world between awake and asleep, clammy, sweaty but feeling wonderful. Eyes closed, I lay on a raft tugged by the currents of the ocean. Distant seagulls whirled above me, curly 'v's spinning on hidden thermals. Cotton wool clouds slid silently across the perfect blue.

And, in the distance, an ominous triangle cut through the waters.

'No,' I moaned.

As if it had heard me, as if it sensed me, it turned and accelerated, a bow wave growing at the front of the fin. And the sunlit sea began to seem far less welcoming. Especially as yards of kelp rose from the fathomless depths and pushed through the slats of the raft. They twisted tight around my wrists, wound around my ankles. In seconds I couldn't move. Out of the corner of my eye I saw the fin razoring through the sea. And silently it dipped below the surface.

'No, no.' Silence enveloped me, kelp tightened around my chest. Squeezing.

And the water shattered into chandeliers of terror as the shark powered into the air, arced on a trail of rainbows and plunged back towards me. Soulless eyes fixed on me as rows of diamond teeth eclipsed everything.

I heard it hit, heard the raft shatter, heard the grating of teeth on bone. And then the wailing joined in. Countless voices vented anguish in choruses of pain. Howling in the endless darkness. Screaming in the choking, acrid, roasting—

'Coffee?' asked Kirstee, wafting a hand over the freshly filled cafetiere.

I leapt awake, eyes wide.

'Whoa, I only asked. Black, I'll bet.'

'Coffee?' I whispered, trying to find something real to latch on to.

'Made by my own fair hands,' grinned Kirstee.

'Your hands? How did you . . . ?' I looked from her wrists to the handcuffs folded neatly on the bed.

'Practice,' she smiled. 'It's not that hard when you know how.'

'But I thought . . .'

'That I was actually . . . ? Okay, that was a bit of a lie. Sorry. But, hey, nobody's hurt, are they?' She draped herself across me with a creak of leather and placed the coffee cup on my chest.

'Well, no, but you could've told me . . .'

'Hey, if you want an apology, forget it. You aren't wearing that collar any more. And we are consenting adults. At least I am.' Her hand ran down towards my thigh.

How much further it would have gone I haven't a clue. All the way, I imagine. Her exploration was only halted by the door bursting open.

'I've got it. Figured it out,' panted Audrey, standing hunched in the doorway. 'I know why we're here. And I've got news, you can stop calling me Audrey.'

'What?'

'Seems I'm more commonly known as Slippery Slim "The Talons" around the darker corners of Downtown Tumor.'

And alarm bells began to ring inside my head. That sounded familiar. Disturbingly familiar.

'And that's supposed to explain why you're here?'

'Yeah. Witness protection, see?'

My head began to throb.

'It's all part of some cover-up. We're being hidden from someone because we did something or saw something that someone else doesn't want the first someone to know, or something.'

'Well, that's cleared that up,' I groaned and almost wished the shark was back in my head.

'Or it could be that it's the first someone who doesn't want the second someone to know about—'

'Stop babbling,' I snapped. 'What can possibly make you think that we're part of a witness protection programme?'

'Isn't it obvious? St Cedric's Hostel for the Less Than Perfectly Well is just a front. It was established way back in the middle ages on the site of a monastery, one of many throughout the world specifically set up by the Reverend Vex Screed, the then Undertaker-In-Chief of Mortropolis. He knew that there would be plots to discredit him after his landslide election victory and it was this paranoia which led to the establishment of the safe houses.'

'Er, just what is it that gives you that idea?' I asked, not even attempting to hide the sarcasm.

'Oh, this,' said Slim, proudly holding up a glossy brochure. 'It's very helpful.' He looked at Kirstee. 'Seems you were right about them changing the name. They got some management guys in to check on the stress factors involved in keeping us demonic types undercover and decided that naming the place after an ex-Haranguist missionary bent on peddling his truth was a bit much. Especially when he'd been in charge of Mortropolis for the last few thousand years. This gives a whole potted history of Screed on page fifteen.' He waggled the brochure.

'Where did you get that?'

'In the office.'

'You broke in again?'

'Yeah, well, with you two in here doing, er . . . well, I felt a bit left out and . . .'

'But why are you both here?' asked Kirstee.

'This doesn't say,' said Slim, dropping the brochure.

'Hamsters.' I didn't realise I'd actually said it until they turned to stare at me.

'What?'

'It's the only thing we've got in common,' I said. 'Well, that and being here, of course.'

'And you think that's it? The hamster. How?'

'It was valuable and you stole it,' chipped in Kirstee. 'The fabled golden hamster of Mortropolis, its eyes made from obsidian, its teeth ivory, its—'

'Er, Kirstee, they're called golden hamsters because of their colour, not because of what they're made of.'

'I knew that,' she said unconvincingly. 'I did.'

I turned to Slim. 'Look, you seem to know more about yourself than I do. What d'you remember from down there?'

'Wailing and gnashing. All the bloody time. I tell you, it really got on my nerves.'

'But what did you do? Your job?'

His face lit up with pride. 'Supplier,' he grinned. 'Anything you wanted, I was your demon.'

'Anything?'

'Absolutely anything?' asked Kirstee. 'Only I've been thinking, I'd really like a body stocking thing with a kind of scaly finish on it. You know, Michelle Pfeiffer but with attitude, you think you could—?'

'Shipping might be a bit difficult, but leave it with me, I might remember who I used to deal with. What kind of price you looking for?'

'No more than a couple of hundred—'

'Look, I hate to interrupt a deal here but can we get back to the point? What about hamsters? Did you ever supply them?'

Slim stroked his chin thoughtfully. 'Don't think I ever did livestock.'

'You said you did everything.'

'Got to draw the line somewhere. I mean, what if the buyer goes back on his word, eh? Got to feed the damned thing. And that costs . . . What? Why are you looking at me like that? No, don't kiss me!'

I was inches away from him, my heart racing. 'That's it! I remember. Seeds. Black and white seeds. I got them from you.'

'Are you sure?'

An image of acute shadiness flashed across my mind. The darkest of alleys in Downtown Tumor containing a darker shadow holding out a small sack, eyes crimson with expectations. 'Turn your head a bit to the left and scowl. Oh, yes.'

'Did I give you a good price?'

'You think I remember everything?'

Kirstee was looking confused. 'Okay, help me out here. This is all to do with the fact that it's illegal to buy and sell sunflower seeds in hell, right?'

'Er . . . not as such, no,' hedged Slim, shrugging.

'So it's like marijuana, yeah? Not illegal to have but they'll just jump on you when you light up.'

'Er, is that right? I thought just having it in your pocket was enough.'

But Kirstee was off on her customary pleasures-of-the-flesh tangent. 'Hey, does that mean you guys get high on sunflower seed abuse? Cool. So what's the recipe? Roast 'em, smoke 'em? Where's the nearest healthfood shop? This I've got to try.'

I was shaking my head as another snippet of memory settled into the jigsaw. 'It was for the animal.'

'So who was he? The local processor, he roasted it all for you, prepared it all ready for your rollies and—'

'No. A rodent type animal,' I said.

'You bought them for a real hamster?' coughed Slim, suddenly amazed. 'Someone had a pet hamster?'

'And that's the illegal bit, right?' asked Kirstee, furrows of confusion across her fetching little brow.

'Nah, worse,' spluttered Slim.

'What's worse than illegal?'

'Never heard of reputational suicide?'

It was obvious from her deepening furrows that she hadn't.

'No matter how big your teeth . . .' began Slim with relish.

'. . . irrespective of the sharpness of your claws . . .' I added.

'. . . irrelevant to your position of extreme power . . .'

'. . . totally unlinked to how loud you can roar . . .'

'. . . nobody . . .'

'. . . and we really are talking nobody here . . .'

'. . . nobody will take even the mightiest of demons seriously if it becomes common knowledge . . .'

'. . . that they keep small furry animals as pets.'

It was obvious that Kirstee was having trouble getting her head round the concept.

'Just ask yourself this,' I said. 'Would Hitler have got as far as he did if everyone knew he had a thing about parakeets?'

'Or Genghis Khan? What would have happened to his vast Mongol Empire if they found out he liked keeping goldfish?'

'Or Mussolini and his dried flower collection?'

'Yeah, all right. I'm getting the picture,' she said, palms raised.

'There's just one thing, though,' said Slim, tapping a thoughtful talon against the side of his cheek. 'Who could possibly be keeping hamsters in Mortropolis?'

'Haven't a clue,' I shrugged. 'By the way, how does it feel to know you're not a woman?'

'Well, I'll miss the underwear,' confessed Slim.

74

Three heads looked up from their iron bunks as the cell door was unlocked and Rawlings was thrust inside.

'Went well then,' tutted Bernstein the younger, arms crossed in the far corner of the holding cell. 'Bail set for a couple of million?'

'Worse,' groaned Rawlings, picking himself up off the floor.

'What's worse than that?'

'You haven't heard what he's trying to accuse us of.'

'No, wait, don't tell me. Being in league with the devil?' answered Bernstein the younger.

'How did you know?'

'It's Ray's idea. Tell him he's talking crap.'

Rawlings turned to Ray, his jaw dropping. 'You knew?'

'Don't fret, man. It's just a theory. I mean, okay, so it might not hold any water but, hey, it passed the time thinking it up. See, we were bored and I suggested playing poker dice with the runes and they all accused me of cheating.'

'Cheating?'

'I mean, it's bad enough I'm behind bars, but for them to accuse me of that, hey, it dents one's personal pride status, y'know. It was only when the runes came up with the same thing another fifty-five and a half dozen times that they believed I wasn't cheating.'

'The runes,' gasped Rawlings. 'What did they show?'

'Oh, just six circumvolents again.'

'Six! But that's . . .'

'Yeah, yeah, we've been through all this. Six circumvolents is a sign of spirit or spirits of horned appearance from the netherworld. We've discussed that already, man.'

'But don't you see what that means?' coughed Rawlings. 'Fifty-five and a half dozen rolls of the "Sign of Six". Do the maths. Six hundred and sixty-six times. Gentlemen, this is serious.'

'Did they inject you with something when they were interrogating you?' tutted Bernstein the younger. 'He's tripping. I tell you, he's lost it.'

'I don't think so,' whispered Bernstein the elder, standing slowly. 'I saw Matlock's map. All the gemetria he had done pointed to this. He was right. He was actually right.'

'What d'you mean, "right"?' tutted his son. 'You saying

he's actually come up with something? After all these years of searching? After driving God knows how many miles and freezing our balls off in bloody Cornwall?'

Three heads nodded in sync.

'Shit. No kidding?'

Another trio of nods.

'You're not saying that's what killed him?'

Three nods.

'Selfish bastard,' spat Bernstein the younger. 'That's just so typical. I should've known he'd do something like that. He finds a bloody demon and keeps it to himself. He could've told us.That's just greedy.'

'But it killed him.'

'Serves him right.'

'What a way to go,' whispered Ray in amazement. 'It's what he would've wanted, I'm sure. I mean, wow, that's like a real train freak being run over by "Mallard" in full steam on the biggest viaduct I can think of. Er, not that I like trains or anything at all.'

'They've got a CompuFit picture,' said Rawlings.

'What? The cops have got an APB out on Satan? Pull the other one,' tutted Bernstein the younger. 'What's the point of that? They'll never catch him now. He's left the scene of that particular crime . . . unless . . . he's coming back?'

'That's what I've been trying to tell you,' said Ray. 'But you wouldn't listen, would you? Told you the runes had a message, didn't I?'

'And that message is that we've got to get out of here,' whispered Rawlings.

'Geez, I've been saying that ever since we got chucked *in* here,' shouted the younger Bernstein, rolling his eyes. 'You guys are *so* slow. We make a break for it. Split up. Leave the country.'

'What? And miss the greatest sighting of our lives?'

'Eh?'

'It's big, it's horny, it's coming to town. And we ain't going to see it from in here.'

'Wow,' whispered Ray. 'It'll be like seeing Stephenson's "Rocket" pulling "The Flying Scotsman" while being overtaken by a dozen Britannia-class locomotives in their original livery. Er . . . okay, so I like trains. What's wrong with that, eh?'

Rawlings was pounding on the door of the cell. 'Hey, someone. C'mon, we want to talk! Hello? Anybody out there? I want to deal. I only said it was called Audrey because, well, I thought that was its name, all right? Let's start again, hey. We're adults. Bygones?'

On his bunk, Bernstein the younger was frowning. 'Let's just get one thing absolutely straight here, right? When you say that it's big, it's horny and it's coming to town, you aren't talking about the "Miss Sex Kitten Bikini Circus and Big Top", are you?'

'Different kind of horny.'

'Oh. Still, different is good.'

Crossfire

75

Mayor Keswick headed down a set of back stairs deep in the nether regions of Camford's Town Hall. Without warning he stopped, looked warily around him and listened. Except for his heavy breathing and the impatient tapping of feet of three of his staff, all was silent.

'Look,' he said, suddenly turning and looking up at Delia, 'it's not too late to change your mind. You can just turn around, head back up the stairs and I'll pretend none of this happened. All right? Meekins? Haskins?'

Three pairs of eyes stared back at him, unmoving, unblinking.

'I take it that's a "no"?'

'Open the door,' ordered Delia hoarsely.

And Keswick knew there was no refusing her. Somehow he felt that she could have asked him to hurl himself out of the window and he would have obeyed. Defenestration on the whim of a subordinate? Despite himself he was impressed. When this, whatever it was, was over, he vowed to find out what power she was wielding. This went way beyond feminine wiles. After all, somehow it was working for Meekins.

'Look, what's all this about?'

'All in good time,' said Delia. 'Open the door.'

Keswick turned, placed a finger in the small hole behind the banister above the sixteenth step down, and waited a moment. There was the tiny sound of brick grating on brick and a section of the wall vanished. Something vaguely resembling a pair of binoculars appeared in the space.

'Look, if you think I'm expendable after this, then I'm telling you now you're very much—'

'We know. Just get those retinas scanned.'

Keswick inserted his nose in the requisite slot and tried to avoid blinking as a small laser peered into the back of his eye.

'Er, stand back,' said the mayor as red light turned green and the scanner slithered out of sight. With only the slightest growling of subterranean machinery, a large section of the staircase lifted to reveal another steeper set going down.

'Lead on,' commanded Delia.

They descended in close file, spiralling well over fifty feet into the underbelly of the town hall until they finally emerged in a small ante-room. For all the blue neon and brushed aluminium panelling it could have been a trendy coffee emporium.

Keswick typed a six-figure code into a small panel on the wall and another door slid silently open. They stepped through into the extractor-fan hum of Room 101. A galaxy of LEDs dotted the far wall and reeked of far too much computer potential.

'Okay, we're here. What now?'

'Use the machine.'

'What? Use it? That's all? You don't want to destroy it? Or slit my throat and bury me here with my baby?'

'Tempting, but no. We want you to find someone.'

Keswick looked at Delia out of the corner of his eye. 'You do know what this is for, don't you?'

'The Mark Three Community Charge Evader Detection System? Of course.'

'I had hoped this was secret.'

'Secretaries have ears,' smiled Delia.

'As do funding outsourcers,' said Haskins.

Keswick turned to the Staff Improvement Liaison Officer. 'I just heard about it in the pub,' said Meekins with a shrug.

'Are there no secrets?' moaned Keswick. 'Still, the more people who know about it the better. It might get them to cough up their money instead of me having to chase them. And chase them this will,' grinned the mayor.

'Yeah, we know,' tutted Delia.

But Keswick was suddenly gripped by a spasm of civic pride in his baby. 'No one can escape. As soon as the first bill arrives in their houses, I have them.'

'We know.'

'Through the miracle of microencapsulation, the bills are laced with small amounts of readily traceable isotopes of radon which are absorbed through the skin.'

'Yeah,' interrupted Delia, 'and all the reminders have ten times the dose.'

'And,' began Haskins, 'using the specially adapted CCTV cameras, in conjunction with a fleet of dedicated vans, you can spot the non-payers as they glow bright red.'

'So you have heard about it,' sighed Keswick, feeling somewhat cheated out of his speech. 'So who is it you want to find?'

'A non-payer, you'll be pleased to know.'

Keswick's eyes lit up. 'Excellent.' He slammed his palm on to a red mushroom of a button and ten streets away a klaxon sounded.

A group of three people tutted, threw their poker hands on

to a formica table and slid down a greasy pole into the top of a highly equipped white van.

'Alpha watch reporting in,' muttered the one in the driving seat, firing the ignition.

'This is your leader,' grinned Keswick, peering into a TV screen. 'I have a mission for you. Sending the details now.'

Delia handed Keswick a sheet of paper and the mayor held it up to the camera just above the TV.

'Er, Your Worship, is the video link integrity at full strength? Only, see where it says approximate height, it looks like nine foot from here.'

'Height is irrelevant. There are non-payers out there. I want them. Seek and destroy. Out.'

He flicked the video link off, and across town an ex-double-glazing van pulled out of a garage. The only sign there was anything unusual about it was the way the rear was covered with cameras and antennae and a couple of satellite dishes.

Back in Room 101, Delia was frowning. 'This is not a destroy mission.'

'What?' gasped Keswick.

'We want them apprehended.'

'No, you can't. They're cheating me. I must destroy—'

'This is a favour, remember?' cooed Delia gruffly. 'You agreed.'

'Yes, but—'

'No buts. You get your men to apprehend them and we deal with them. Clear?'

'I don't know what has got into you,' sulked Keswick. 'You used to be faithful.'

'I'm just straying a bit right now,' she grinned as the first images came in from the van. Crowds of people-shaped blobs passed across a host of screens, each in a slightly different hue of fuzziness, some green, some orange.

'Some late payers out there,' hissed Keswick. 'Must make notes, send reminders.'

'Later,' tutted Delia. 'They'll keep.'

And way below the streets of Camford, in a small room which went under the name of the Transcendental Travel Company Ltd, a large demon lay back, eyes closed, and silently mouthed the words, 'Later. They'll keep.'

76

With a final heave of effort, Bishop Hutchinson and Brother Lyndsey righted a vast font and settled it back against the wall of the chaos-strewn room.

'Oh God, it's cracked,' whispered the bishop. His finger traced the fracture down past a cavorting cherub, through the cleavage of a particularly pneumatic angel and off down the left-hand side of a large mountain. 'Ruined.'

'Ahh, now, I wouldn't be being quite so hasty,' said Brother Lyndsey. 'Bit of Polyfilla and that'll be right as rain. You'll never know. You could be flinging babies in it before the day's out if I get a bit of time.'

'Have you always been so irritatingly optimistic?' hissed Cardinal Aguilera, scowling across the room.

'Born that way,' smiled Lyndsey. 'That's why I fit in so well here. Spreading the good word. See?'

'I don't see much spreading going on. There aren't exactly thousands of people congregating to be saved.'

'Ahh, well. That's because I'm a practical optimist, see? Once we've actually got this placed cleaned up again and the lighting rig set up with the full sound-scape and stuff, well, then they'll be flooding in. No point just opening the doors and saying "Welcome", nobody'll come then.'

'And if there's an exhibit of a fallen soul, chained to that far wall?'

'Well, that would be nice. Everyone's always interested in the demony bits of religion, aren't they.'

'Yeeeeees,' growled Aguilera. 'Damned seductive basta–'

'You think we can get one?' smiled Lyndsey. 'Have you got something in your bag that'll help us capture one? Hmmmm? Black and big locks, always a good sign that. It looks like the type of bag that'll have something handy in it.'

'More than you'll ever know,' hissed Aguilera.

'Ahhh, now you think that. But I am actually quite intelligent and if I apply myself I bet I could get to know quite a bit of that and–'

There was a sudden squeal and a heavy rumble of falling masonry. Dust erupted out of a side chamber, billowing around the silhouette of a sprinting figure.

'My monastery!' squealed Bishop Hutchinson as Francisco the novice tripped and disappeared under the stormfront of dust. 'He's destroying it!'

'I didn't touch it,' coughed Francisco.

'Well, that's it, we definitely need the builders in.' Hutchinson turned on the cardinal. 'Are you going to authorise that? The expenses? Security clearances?'

'Not until we have victory,' growled Aguilera.

'Victory?' spluttered the bishop, not feeling exactly sure that he liked the sound of that.

But Aguilera was already fiddling with the locks on his black case. 'Here, take this,' he ordered, handing a small wooden object to the bishop, another to Lyndsey and a third to the dust-covered novice.

'It's a cross,' observed the bishop.

'On a piece of string,' added Lyndsey.

'Allowing full rotational movement,' completed Aguilera.

Lyndsey held his out. It hovered horizontally, swinging like a magnet in a field.

'Three of them for triangulation,' said Aguilera, looking at the way they were all facing. 'Follow me.' He headed off towards the exit.

'Hey, this is just like divining rods,' chuckled Lyndsey.

'Of course. We invented them. Never wondered where the name came from?' said the cardinal, ducking into the corridor. The three others followed him out of the rubble-wrecked basement.

77

There were still way too many gaps in my memory. Still far, far too many holes in the colander of my history. Okay, so some of the gaps were filling in, healing over. But for every answer there were more unanswered voids. And they were making me nervous.

'You must remember doing something?' asked Slim. And I was still having trouble remembering to call him that. He'd already almost hit me four times. 'C'mon, you must know what your job was.'

'Well, I . . .' I began and scratched my head.

'Maybe he didn't have a job,' offered Kirstee with a hopeful shrug. 'Like that was his own personal hell. Being bored. I know I get bored if I don't have anything to do, or the telly's broke. An eternity of that would really get up my nose.'

Slim shook his head. 'If there'd been an unemployed demon kicking about, believe me I would have hired him. Deliveries would have been so much easier with an extra pair of claws on my side.'

'Who says you weren't working together?' asked Kirstee. 'No, he definitely bought . . .'

'Working together,' she grinned. 'Like a double act.' And her face lit up. I wasn't sure whether to be delighted by it. Or just even more nervous.

'Look, guys,' she said, slapping her thighs decisively. 'Let's call this delving into the past thing off. Give it a rest, yeah? I mean, it's just making you worry.'

I heard a non-committal grunt.

'Why don't we look to the future?' she smiled. 'Now let's see what we've got, hmmmm? You're here and, listening to what you've been saying, you aren't going back down there in the very near future, right?'

We both shrugged, as neither of us had a clue where she was heading with this.

'And I tell you for one, I ain't going back to Il Diablo's for a while. So . . . what say we do something together, eh?'

More shrugs.

'And I've got the perfect thing in mind. I tell you, it can't fail. What with your bodies and my choreography, well, we'd have hen nights booked up to the end of the century.'

'What have evenings with domesticated poultry got to do with anything?' asked Slim. Fortunately he beat me to it.

'Hen nights. Y'know, girly evenings. No men allowed.'

'Ohhh, why didn't you say?' said Slim. 'And where do we come into this?'

'From the back of the stage. Full spotlights and you can start the first number with full tuxedos. Yeah. And big top hats to hide your horns. And we'll play "Keep Your Hat On", yeah. That'll drive 'em wild when you get the dress shirts off and—'

'What are you on about?'

' "The Full Demonty". Catchy name, huh?'

'You aren't serious,' I coughed. 'You want us to . . . to . . . strip?'

'Why not? Guys, guys, girls'll pay good money to see you two. I mean, get those scales under a glitterball and half the audience'll wet themselves. It's a surefire hit. C'mon, what d'you say?'

'But . . . I can't dance.'

'Who says anything about dancing? You just need to get those pelvic thrusts right and the rest falls into place. C'mon, stand up. Legs apart. Now, thrust. No, slowly. Less of the desperate bowel movement, more imagine you're picking daisies with your butt cheeks. Clench and pluck and clench and . . . Ohh, guys, that's good. That's very, very good.'

78

PC Plain tapped a suspicious finger against his cheek and frowned at the men in the holding cell. 'So just what is it you're trying to tell me here?'

'That we're both right, here,' said Rawlings in his most reasonable tone.

'Meaning?'

'That I do know the face in that picture, but just not as well as you think I might, and that I'm pretty sure I could find her . . . er, it, again if you're interested.'

'Just run it by me one more time,' frowned Plain.

Ranzo Ray stepped back up to the bars again. 'Well, man, like I was looking for a girl to do "Sowing Seeds with . . ."'

'Without the morrisey bits, all right?'

'You're the boss,' shrugged Ray. 'Well, I mean she was just there, y'know. Just like she'd been waitin' for me.'

'And that's where she was wearing nothing but a yellow bed sheet?'

'Yeah.'

'And you didn't think there was anything unusual about this?'

'Hey, if a girl wants to get herself noticed I don't care how she does it, right? And hey, it worked. I noticed her and walked right across to her.'

'Not suspecting, of course, that she was a murderess awaiting her next victim?' said Plain.

'If I'd known that she certainly wouldn't have got a cider out of me. Besides, if anyone's guilty of deceit here it's Matlock. I mean, if he'd told us she was a demon—'

'Look, officer, we've been through this,' said Rawlings. 'Suffice to say that we have told you the truth. As far as we were aware she was called Audrey. The important thing is that she is still here. And, I think she has an accomplice.'

'And just what makes you think that, eh?'

Rawlings took a deep breath. 'Officer, you seem to have a very good grasp of the concept of disbelief.'

'Too right. Part of the job, see? Formula One drivers have a thing about speed. With coppers it's disbelief.'

'And, er . . . you can stop that at any time?'

'Oh yeah. My uniform's made of chocolate, y'know,' he said and raised his sleeve to his mouth. 'Oh no, it's not. See? On, off. Takes skill that does.'

'Okay. Now I want you to take your disbelief and switch it off right now, all right?'

'Can't do that. Not whilst I'm on duty.'

'Ah.'

'Well, not if it's really weird stuff, y'know? Kind of an "open your mind to the possibilities of the universe" kind of thing. I mean, that's just bollocks. But if you're talking about say you thinking that a car was white when it was cream, I can do that.'

'Oh.'

'But I'm off duty in five minutes,' said Plain.

'And that makes a difference?'

'Too right. Me, I'm a professional copper, see?' said Plain with a grin of pride. 'See, believe it or not there are some Formula One racing drivers who are scared of speed, if you get my drift.' He tapped the side of his nose. 'I'll get back to you in five minutes, right?'

Plain closed his eyes and leant against the bars. For the men in the cell it was the longest few minutes of their lives.

Suddenly Plain stood upright, pulled off his hat and peered into the cell. 'You were saying?'

'You're off duty?'

'Sure.'

'Er, "open your mind to the possibilities of the universe",' said Rawlings nervously.

'Cool,' grinned Plain.

'Roll the runes,' shrugged Rawlings and Ray obeyed. A straight line of six circumvolents settled on to the cell floor.

'Wow, six. Neat,' smiled Plain.

'It might take too long to explain. But that's what he's been rolling for hours. Six of them and all in a straight line pointing through that wall. Officer, you've got to get us out of here. And I promise you, you will get your suspect.'

'Well, why didn't you say before? C'mon.' Keys rattled in the lock and PC Plain pulled open the door.

'Er, Ray, lead on,' said Rawlings, sticking a wary foot in the hinge.

79

Four figures strode down the backstreets of Camford, each holding before them a cross on a piece of string. Each seemingly fixed solid in the air. Each showing a tiny variation in angle. In terms of triangulation it wasn't the most effective of placements, but as a united onslaught they were ready. Well, Cardinal Aguilera was at least.

'Can't you feel it?' he said as he strode up the middle of the road. 'Feel the rush of excitement. The adrenaline high that comes from facing the enemy.'

'To tell you the truth I just feel a bit silly,' said Brother Lyndsey, looking at his cross held out above the pavement. 'People keep giving me funny looks. I've even had them try to give me loose change.'

'Ignore them,' said the cardinal. 'Pay them no heed for they cannot comprehend what is afoot. They laughed at me in Alabama when I told them of the evil amongst them. They mocked when I routed wickedness in Dakota. They howled when I suggested it went into the very heart of the White House.'

'Er, that'll be the rabbit-worshipping cult of Coney Island?' said Lyndsey, barely hiding a smirk.

'And had I not nipped that in the bud we would have been making the sign of the carrot before indulging in wild orgiastic rituals of naked nightly indulgence. Twice on every full moon.'

'Remind me, that's bad?'

'Sins of the flesh,' hissed Aguilera. 'Sins of the flesh. But I shall prevent it once again. I shall overcome. Next left.'

'You mean the rabbit cult is here?'

'The evils are the same, only the names have changed.'

'You don't get out much, do you?'

'In some ways I get out too much,' said Aguilera in deeply significant overtones. 'Anywhere that trouble is festering, I go. To each and every dark spot of evil, I attend. Today suburbia, tomorrow the Sahara. Who knows?'

'Sort of Holy Domestos.'

'Second on the right,' hissed the cardinal, somehow making a point of deftly ignoring Lyndsey. He reeled theatrically as he entered the street. 'Can you feel that? We are close.' And, sure enough, the crosses began to show a greater angular variation as they marched on. Aguilera pocketed his cross and checked on his trusty pistol.

'Soon. Soon we shall be joined in yet another chapter of our eternal struggle. We shall fight them on the streets. On the seas and oceans. And we shall never surrender.'

'Yeah, cheers, Winston.'

But Aguilera gestured suddenly, palm flat to the ground. A single index finger pointed towards a ground-floor window three doors down on the right.

'Look at that and tell me it is not as I have said. Is that not the delights of evil? Is that not the very essence of orgy?'

The window was filled with a trio of silhouettes, gleaming against crimson curtains as they gyrated their pelvic regions in gradually deepening thrusts.

'They could just be dancing,' suggested Brother Lyndsey. 'You know, some of that latino stuff can be a bit wearing on the lower back.'

'I see orgy,' hissed Aguilera, heading for the cover of the bushes.

'Whatever you say,' shrugged Lyndsey.

80

If Kirstee had found a whip in the house she would have been wielding it on us, I'm sure.

'No, no. Clench the buttocks, then release. Get that chest out.' She hurled instructions at both of us. It was a constant barrage that only stopped briefly when she came up with a new idea for a name. 'How about "Satan's Little Helpers"?'

I watched her mouth it to herself, rolling the vowels over her tongue. And then, with a flick of an eyebrow, it was discarded. 'Nah, bound to be misspelt come Christmas and, besides, how can either of you two be described as little? No, must find a better name. Ohh, Slim, feel the rhythm. Slower, deeper, longer. Look, imagine you've got a wrecking ball strapped to your middle dangling off fifty foot of rope, okay? Now, wiggling about like a rabbit on heat isn't going to get it swinging, is it? No. Right, we want deep gyrations. Yes, yes, swing those balls. That's it.'

And then her critical gaze fell hard upon me. 'Is that the best you can do with that tail of yours?' she tutted. 'What d'you think it is, a fur stole? Have you never heard of the word seductive?'

I didn't get the chance to answer, which was probably a good thing. I might have asked her to demonstrate and, well, who knows where that would have ended? Instead, all cavorting was stopped in mid-gyration by the sudden explosion of my front door and the appearance of men with crosses.

'Don't even think about running, you are completely surrounded,' announced Cardinal Aguilera as the back window imploded under the Doc Marten's of Francisco the novice.

'The door *was* open,' I observed in the driest tone I could muster. 'One turn of the handle would have been sufficient.'

At least he had the decency to look sheepish.

Unlike the cardinal. 'Sufficient to operate some device of sabotage, no doubt,' he snarled. 'I applaud you on the deft use of the window, Francisco.'

'I hope you're going to pay for that,' I said. 'Glaziers aren't cheap, you know.'

'You should have thought of that before,' sneered the cardinal.

'Before what?'

'Setting foot . . . or should that be hoof, above the territory normally associated with such scum as yourself.'

'I see you're aren't here for a pleasant chat over pie and a snifter of sherry.'

'Your days of sipping sherry are numbered. And that number is one.'

'Look, what is it with you? What have we done to annoy you?'

'You stand there before me and have the nerve to ask that? You, aberrations of nature, twisted freaks of evil—'

'So it's nothing personal, then?' I must admit, I was surprising myself with some of these answers. I guess I was a bit more miffed about being accosted in my own front room than I'd first thought I was. Well, it had been a bit of a weird day.

'—vile blasphemies of—'

'All right, that's enough,' piped up Kirstee. 'Have you ever stopped to think that maybe, just maybe, one man's vile blasphemy is another woman's sex kitten? I mean, face it – just what is wrong with a few scales here and there?'

'If that's all there was to it then it might be a bit different. I could maybe be lenient. But there's the talons and the teeth and those fiery eyes.'

'There you go with that irrational appearance thing again,' tutted Kirstee.

'Yeah,' I grinned. 'Just close your eyes and . . . whey hey, we're innocent.'

'Never,' growled Aguilera.

'That's a little categorical, isn't it?' I asked. 'I mean, aren't you the guys who are big on forgiveness? I seem to re-member something about that.'

The cardinal's eyes burned into mine. 'Some things just cannot be forgiven. Things like the way you abuse every-thing I believe in. A little bit of religion is a dangerous thing.'

And something about the way he was looking at me made me feel like a fourteen-year-old guerrilla with a Kalashnikov facing down a British Army officer. His gaze held the weight of years of training, decades of manoeuvres, centuries of drilled discipline and routine. I fizzed with anarchy.

'And now it's time to die,' he grinned, reaching for his inside pocket.

'Wait. You can't just . . . What about the command-ments?'

'Thou shallt crush the spawn of Satan,' rattled off the cardinal. 'Special Forces Book of Extra Commandments. Not for public use, you understand.' The barrel of his pistol lined up on my forehead. 'And in case you're wondering, this doesn't have a safety catch.'

'Oh,' I whispered as a strange noise floated into my consciousness. The sound of a handbrake ratcheting on.

'Reinforcements?' I asked.

'What?' said the cardinal. It was the moment of hesitation I needed.

'Okay,' called a man, stepping into the room and pulling out a clip-board. 'Hands up anyone who hasn't paid their community charge.'

Fuming, Aguilera hid his pistol.

81

In the clutter of technology that was Room 101, a TV screen crackled into life and was filled with an eager face.

'Target detected and contained,' panted the orderly in the back of the van. 'Co-ordinates transmitting now.'

'Excellent. You will await our arrival,' answered Keswick with not a little pride. 'Ahh, such efficiency makes one happy to be mayor.'

A printer spat a street map into a tray. In the dead centre was a circle of arrows pointing to a single house. Keswick snatched it and dashed across the room. 'Well, if you're coming,' he said and vanished down a fireman's pole.

'After him,' hissed Delia and the others followed.

The dark blue mayoral Rolls-Royce was already revving by the time they landed in the basement garage, the rear door flung wide. 'Do keep up,' shouted Keswick from the leather-trimmed interior.

As Delia, Meekins and Haskins piled into the car, the sound of heavy chains ground underfoot and an entire wall sank into the floor. The uniformed chauffeur floored the accelerator and hit the spiral ramp at a good forty, rubber burning. They hit street level in under ten seconds.

Away across town, things were moving at a pace less hasty.

'This was a joke, wasn't it?' grumbled PC Plain. 'You just said all those things to get out of that cell, didn't you? Face it, you haven't a clue where this so-called demon is going to appear, have you?'

'Not as such, no,' confessed Rawlings.

'Right, back behind bars—'

'When I say I don't know where, that doesn't mean we can't find it. Ray, the runes.'

With a shrug, Ray delved into his pocket, grabbed at them and tossed them on to the pavement.

PC Plain stared at the matching symbols facing in a dead straight line down the street.

'You see?' began Rawlings. 'We go . . .'

His words were temporarily drowned by the sound of a dark blue Rolls-Royce screaming past them.

'. . . that way,' he finished as Ray gathered up the precious chunks of ivory.

'Wish I had a radar gun on me,' tutted Plain. 'That was topping eighty, no problem.'

82

High in a tall strata-scraper, buried safely behind the heat-purpled steel of the front doors of the Transcendental Travel Company Ltd, Seirizzim was pacing the floor.

'What's keeping them? They should have reported in by now.' He glared at the three demons lying on their backs beneath domes of mesh. 'Do they think they're on holiday?'

The hostess-cum-booking-agent shrugged. It was almost impossible to tell what was going on topside if the voyeurs didn't want you to know.

But it seemed in this case that a message was about to be forthcoming. A talon twitched and reached for a pencil.

Seirizzim shoved a sheet of parchment under the tip and hovered expectantly.

Shakily, a set of numbers and symbols were scrawled out. The message ended in a single word. 'Here.'

'Excellent,' grinned Seirizzim. 'Excellent.' He crossed the floor of the travel agent towards a large metal cage. Something moved inside as he approached. Something solid and hungry.

Seirizzim hunched down and grunted in a series of guttural commands, holding up the sheet of parchment as he did so. The cage resonated to the answering howl of the creature cooped up inside.

'Very good, now go,' grinned Seirizzim, drawing back the bolts. His talons were barely clear as the beast burst out in a rattling of exoskeleton. It ran for the nearest wall, scaling it in seconds, and set about the ceiling with its vast mandibles. Dust and rubble rained down as the stalag-mite began chewing towards the surface.

'Excellent,' grinned Seirizzim and began pulling on the first of many thermal layers.

'Hope you're going to pay for that to be fixed,' tutted the bookings clerk, looking at the hole in the ceiling.

Seirizzim fixed her with a powerful glare. 'And why should I do that, hmmm? Don't you know that even the slightest signs of stalag-mite infestation are grounds for fumigation?'

'But you released it.'

'I was never here. And they'll swear by that.' He pointed to his faithful guard on the tables. Eagerly he pulled on a large vest and tucked it in.

83

I was beginning to think that someone had secretly planted a vast hoarding in my front garden inviting all and sundry to a party in my front room. With the speed people were piling in it was the only solution I could think of.

Fortunately, Mayor Keswick was about to put me straight on that one.

'So this is what community charge dodgers look like, is it?' he snarled as he strode into my front room. Two men and a woman fanned out behind him. 'Look at them, spongers, parasites.'

'Er, I hope you're not tarring all of us with that self-same brush,' coughed Brother Lyndsey from behind the sofa. 'I . . . that is, the Bishop and I are just visiting.' The bishop nodded and then looked down at the cross dangling from his piece of string. Slowly, it turned towards the new arrivals. I saw his eyebrow quiver in confusion. And my stomach churned as a distant memory helpfully recalled the purpose of those crosses. My bowels knotted as the conclusion hopped cheerfully to the front of my mind. The Mayor of Camford was in league with the devil.

'Visiting?' grinned Keswick, snatching a small camera-sized device from one of the men from the van. It took a moment for him to bring up an image on the tiny view-finder. 'Visiting from a place which has no community charge, I see?' He turned to his men. 'Ready the secure area, we'll be bringing these in.' There was a flurry of salutes and the population of my front room reduced a little.

'Nobody said we had to pay,' pleaded Brother Lyndsey, his eyes widening nervously. 'It isn't a sin, is it?'

'Oh yes,' hissed Keswick. 'Stealing. Deception. The list goes on.'

'Ignore him,' challenged Cardinal Aguilera. 'We are exempt.'

'What?' coughed the mayor.

'Religious cult, see?' smiled the cardinal.

I must admit I didn't expect Keswick's reaction. He hurled back his head and laughed. 'Pull the other one. You can't tell me you've got priests and demons in the same cult.'

My eyes flicked back to the cardinal. It was a good point. And countered easily.

'*Au contraire.* One needs inmates and guards to make a prison. The victor and the vanquished to make a war.'

'And doctors and patients to make a hospital,' chirped Brother Lyndsey. Everyone stared at him. He looked at his feet.

Keswick's shoulders tensed almost imperceptibly. 'Religious cult,' he whispered, his face reddening. 'How dare God interfere with my municipal ruling?' He glared at everyone in turn. 'I will be back. Mark my words. I will have you all. Come, our business here is over, for the moment.' He made a move towards the door, expecting Delia, Meekins and Haskins to immediately follow.

'Your business may be done,' said Delia huskily. 'Ours has just begun.'

'I don't think I like the sound of that,' whispered Bishop Hutchinson, looking at his cross on a string pointing solidly at the group of town clerks.

'Could be laryngitis,' said Lyndsey, missing the point.

But nobody had the chance to correct him. The noise coming up through the floor saw to that. If earthquakes had teeth, this was the sound of them gnashing – the din of metamorphic rocks exploding under the onslaught of diamond-tipped mandibles. My floorboards and carpet didn't stand a chance.

In a whirlwind of mouthparts, the floor behind the sofa exploded and waves of heat blasted into the room as a four-foot exoskeletonned creature appeared. It was followed moments later by ten foot of bulky silhouette, topped off with a fur-lined hood. Every cross in the room spun to face it.

'So,' growled the apparition, glaring at me with its fiery eyes. 'We meet again.'

'Master,' whispered a trio of town clerks, dropping to their knees.

'What the hell is going on here?' spluttered Keswick. 'Get up off the floor. I'm your boss.'

'Oh, you naive fool,' chuckled the ten-footer, his hood scraping the Artex. 'You are nothing while I am here.'

'Just wh . . . what are you?' spluttered Keswick.

'Bloody cold, actually,' tutted Seirizzim. 'You couldn't just put the fire on, could you?'

And, for some reason, I found myself almost obeying.

84

'Roll them again,' encouraged Rawlings as the morris men and PC Plain stood at a series of junctions.

'Oh yeah, and what's that going to do, hey?' tutted Ray. 'Like these things can really give directions. It's just in the wrist action. You flick like that and you get a straight line every time.'

'You've been doing that?' coughed Rawlings. 'But the six circumvolents . . . ?'

'Oh, I never got the hang of rigging the scores. Geez, I'd have moved to Vegas years back if I could do that.'

'Well, roll them. And no wrist thing.'

Ray frowned and obeyed. The runes rattled to a halt with their usual matching set of characters. But they were far from being in a straight line.

'Told you,' shrugged Ray. 'Looks like a letter "F" if you ask me.'

'No!' spluttered Rawlings. 'It's a sign. A sign. C'mon.'

'Where are you going?'

'It's obvious. Second on the right!'

85

The beast in the arctic hood stared at me, the top of its head scraping the ceiling. 'So, this is where you've been hiding? Don't think much of the decor. Far too many soft furnishings for my liking.' He kicked at the sofa, sending it spinning against the wall. Out of the corner of my eye I saw two blurs of black cassock as Brother Lyndsey and Francisco dived behind it.

'And just who are you to come here and advise me on furniture?' I snarled. Kirstee flashed me a brief admiring glance. It felt good.

'You mean you don't recognise me?' growled the intruder, fiddling awkwardly with the straps of his hood. 'You don't recognise your old boss?' He threw back the fur and glared down at me. I lost count of the number of memories which sprang into my mind. Long obsidian corridors echoed to the sound of my hooves. Lava lamps cast my shadow on the polished walls of power. Flame storms flashed down against the windows of countless strata-scrapers.

'Seirizzim,' whispered Slim in the tones of the genuinely surprised.

'Who else,' grinned the demon. 'And soon, I shall be re-elected as Undertaker-In-Chief of Mortropolis.'

'Wow,' whispered Keswick in the far corner.

'I have the elections totally sewn up, haven't I?' He looked across at the mayoral secretary.

'Absolutely,' nodded Delia. 'Total commitment from all loyal supporters. Amazing what devotion one can command when one has the entire tools of eternal torment at one's talon-tips.'

'Amazing,' whispered Keswick, looking at Delia in a new light.

Meekins and Haskins nodded.

'So, if all that's true,' I asked, 'why this special visit?'

Seirizzim threw his head back and laughed. Two gouges appeared in the Artex as dust fell from his horns. 'Five hundred years in my service and he still doesn't understand me.'

'I understand you enough to know that you hate the cold.'

269

'You . . . you know him?' whispered Kirstee and began looking Seirizzim up and down. 'Think he'd join "Satan's Little Helpers"? It's difficult to tell under all that padding, but if his body is as good as yours then—'

'He can't dance,' I said. 'No sense of rhythm.'

'Tact was something you were often lacking,' growled Seirizzim. 'Something you never got the hang of, which is a shame for a butler.'

I felt the floor move under my feet. It was something I had been trying to deny all day. I had sensed it. Remembered it.

'You were his butler?' coughed Slim.

I nodded.

Kirstee's eyes opened wide with confusion.

'Now it all makes sense,' smiled Slim, calculating. 'Perfect sense.'

Seirizzim glared at him.

'The election. All sorted, is it? Foregone conclusion?' grinned the supplier, licking his fangs. 'Somehow I don't think so. If it was, you wouldn't be here. D'you know, there's a funny thing about things that are sewn up. They are surprisingly easy to unpick. Just one snip and . . .'

'Nonsense,' tutted Seirizzim, with only the slightest twitch of unease. I was the only one to see it. Five hundred years in service taught one these things.

'It would be if I didn't know where to snip,' grinned Slim. He pulled a face which bore a striking resemblance to a small rodent of golden persuasion. 'Amazing how quickly things can unravel when a vote of no confidence is called.'

'You wouldn't,' growled Seirizzim.

'Why not?' smiled Slim in his slipperiest way.

'I could make it worth your while.'

'You cannot have them,' hissed Cardinal Aguilera. 'They are ours now.'

'Yours?' coughed Kirstee. 'You don't want them. I can get the gigs . . .'

'What?'

'Look, I can do you mates' rates for the first couple of religious festivals but after that . . .'

'There will be no public appearances for them,' hissed Aguilera. 'I'm taking them back.'

'I don't think so,' hissed Seirizzim. 'You are outnumbered.'

Aguilera looked around the room. 'Let me see about that. You, bulky clothing, confined space, slow. Three possessed, slow reaction times. Then there's us. Smaller, true. Faster, definitely. Four all. But add in the fact that I have time on my side. You should be feeling rather uncomfortably cold by now. I'd estimate five minutes more before you lose feeling in your talons. That shifts the balance. And then there's the weaponry.' The cardinal waved his pistol.

'Call that a weapon?' spat Seirizzim.

'It's not ideal for battlefield use, I agree,' said Aguilera. 'The effect of hundred per cent proof Holy Water is more for my own pleasure actually. The way demonic flesh dissolves can be so aesthetically pleasing in the right light. And the pleas for mercy gushing from melting throats. Music. Sheer melody.'

'I bet you torment slugs with packets of salt, don't you?' hissed Kirstee.

'Individual grains, my dear. Less is more.'

'So what's to stop me ripping you limb from stinking limb?' snarled Seirizzim. 'You won't kill those two. You'll lose your proof. Without them nobody'll believe that I keep hamsters. The election is mine. And if I get a couple of battle scars disembowelling you, so much the better. It's all good PR.'

'Who's to say you would survive?' smiled Aguilera. 'Er, Francisco, would you mind?'

Reluctantly, the novice scrambled out from behind the sofa, unzipped a large bag and began assembling something. He worked quickly, clicking barrels into catches, snapping range finders on to heavy-duty clips. In seconds the military-spec bazooka was assembled and loaded with an armour-piercing shell.

'Just how long d'you think Mortropolis would survive if they elected twenty stone of mince?' asked the cardinal, lining up the large barrel on Seirizzim's chest.

'Whoa, hold up. Time out,' I called. 'You can't fire that in here.'

'Why not? It's not as if the place isn't already a mess,' tutted Aguilera. 'There's a massive hole in the floor over there for starters.'

'So go ahead, pull the trigger,' sneered Seirizzim. 'You think I'm not wearing the correct protection?'

I saw the cardinal's eye twitch as he considered this. I could tell what was going through his mind. Was it a bluff?

'Before you do,' began Slim, 'I'd like to register the fact that I would be happy to consider any offer which our soon to be re-elected leader would be ready to discuss.'

As the cardinal caressed the trigger, Seirizzim raised an eyebrow.

'For example,' continued Slim, 'I feel certain that a dedicated supplier to the Undertaker-In-Chief would be a valuable and mutually successful business arrangement to—'

'You talk business at a time like this?' squealed Aguilera. The bishop scurried away behind the sofa. 'You dare to? You want him re-elected?'

'Hey, I'm just exploring all options,' said Slim. 'Maximising potential.'

'You! You would sell weapons to the warmongers and first aid to the victims.'

'Hey, good advice. Think I'll take it,' grinned Slim.

It was a mistake.

Cardinal Aguilera screamed as he clenched his fist. And it felt like the whole world exploded. Exhaust gases erupted from the bazooka as the warhead blasted from the barrel. Aguilera recoiled backwards on to the sofa. Seirizzim dived sideways.

But too late. Armour-piercing tip hit scale and ricocheted off on an uncontrollable tangent. In milliseconds it had powered its way through the pink ceramic of my bathroom suite and was heading out through the upstairs window, taking half of the supporting wall with it.

'What are you doing!' squealed Kirstee, shaking her head wildly as adrenaline surged through her body. 'You trying to kill us all? That what you wanted? Well, that's the right way to go about it. Jesus, I cannot believe you just did that. I cannot believe it.' She spun on her heel and kicked the wall. 'You guys are supposed to save souls not . . .'

The sound of brickwork parting company with rafters cut her off in mid-sentence. She looked up as a pink ceramic cistern shattered and gallons of water fell. They were only a few feet ahead of the joist.

I watched in frozen alarm as the water cascaded over her hair, bounced off her shoulders, fountained across her leather-clad body. I tried to scream a warning, tried to move, tried anything. But I was helpless. Trapped in slo-mo as the slab of wood hit her. The sound was sickening.

Too late, I was across the room, wrenching hopelessly at the joist.

'Leave it,' I heard her choke, her voice barely audible above the torrent of water. 'Too late.'

'No, no, it'll be . . .' My throat closed, strangling me.

'Guess that's the tour off,' she whispered. A trickle of blood oozed from her nose.

All I could do was shake my head, attempt denial and stare at her crumpled body. Perfection destroyed in a second. The smell of wet leather filled my nostrils.

'Promise me . . . one . . . thing.'

'Anything,' I mouthed silently, my heart emptying.

'Remem . . . ber . . . clench and pull . . . sexier that . . . way.' Her eyelids flickered once on her final whisper.

How long I stayed there, simply staring at her, I haven't a clue. I wanted to be nowhere else and everywhere else at the same time. Wanted to hit her, hug her, scream at her to wake up. But I knew it wouldn't work. There was something about the colour of her skin.

'It's always the same with the likes of you. Tears before bedtime,' said Aguilera, leaning over my shoulder, hands on his hips, looking at Kirstee. 'Still, there's always some that are expendable. Right, back to the safe house with you.'

I felt my fist clench, anger spreading up my forearm, plunging into my chest. I swung. And hit scales.

I looked up from Slim's palm, fuming, my knuckles millimetres away from the satisfying crack of holy jawbone.

'Sod him,' he said. 'I've got a far better idea. And it's going that way.'

I just caught sight of a pair of horns disappearing through the floor.

85

Keswick's jaw was dangling a good three inches as he watched Delia. Never had he seen her being quite so assertive. In seconds, she had dragged three clergymen out from behind the sofa and was currently frogmarching the cardinal towards the door.

'You're a civilian,' hissed Aguilera. 'This is interfering with priest's business!'

'Just what makes you think I'm a civilian?' she whispered gruffly, her teeth inches from his ear. 'Can civilians do this?' And just for a fraction of a second, the skin on her cheeks turned darker and scalier than anything normally found in the employ of town halls.

Aguilera was out of there in seconds.

And Delia was back, shoving shattered rafters into a certain four-foot hole in the floor.

'In here,' came a voice. 'It's in here, I'm sure.'

Keswick turned, eyes wide, as a troupe of morris men entered the shattered living room.

'And just what makes you think . . . er, Your Worship,' coughed PC Plain, catching sight of the mayor among the debris. 'Er, what are you doing here? What happened?'

'I think you should address any questions through the usual channels,' spluttered Keswick, calling on years of habit of avoiding direct questions. Somehow, he wasn't in the mood for answering such things. Well, not until he had figured out what had actually happened. And then maybe not.

'Delia?' asked Plain.

'She'll tell you, yes. That's right, she'll . . . won't you, Delia?'

'What?' said the mayoral secretary, looking around in confusion. 'Er, where are we?' Her voice was higher pitched than it had been of late. 'Oh my God, what the hell happened?'

'This isn't a bit of overtime?' asked Plain.

'How did we get here?' coughed Meekins, looking around as if awakening from a long sleep.

'Oh, shit,' whispered Keswick. 'Look, this isn't how it looks, honest.'

'I think, Your Worship, that you'd better come down to the station.'

'Am I under arrest?'

'Does she need an ambulance?' He pointed across the room. 'Call Boscombe.'

'Then let's just say, for the sake of politics, that you are an important witness,' said Plain.

'Yeah, and I know what that means too,' whimpered Keswick, holding his hands out at cuff distance.

By the door, the group of morris men were looking distinctly disappointed. 'What's supernatural about this?' tutted Bernstein the younger. 'Another wild-goose chase.'

'I wouldn't be so sure,' grinned Rawlings, bending and picking something up. 'Explain that.' He held out a fragment of talon about the size of a duffle coat toggle. 'A little trophy, I think.'

'And Doctor Boscombe will be delighted to see it,' said Plain, snatching it from the palm of Rawlings's hand. 'And I think you can come back to the station.'

'Hey, you promised.'

'That was before this. Now move.'

87

Queues of damned souls stood bored in the depths of Mortropolis, sweltering in the blistering heat.

'Next,' grunted the demon in the kiosk as he shuffled at a stack of parchments. He liked the feel of it. The importance of it all. The satisfying structure of officialdom.

And once he was in a better mood, well, he'd really begin to feel the power, too. Deciding on the fate of damned souls, sentencing them to eternity in torment. Ahhh, one could be so creative.

'Next,' he hissed again. 'Name,' he said and looked down at the parchment.

'Guess,' came back the answer.

It was a normal answer and ranked up there alongside Elvis and Jesus Christ. He'd already heard them before. It was their one last attempt at defiance.

'Name,' he asked again and peered over the lintel of the kiosk.

A leather-clad woman looked up at him. 'You telling me you've forgotten already? Well, thanks, pal.'

'Ssssh, keep your voice down,' coughed a certain ex-butler, ex-cleaner and ex-priest, his eyes widening with delight. 'You? Is that really you, Kirstee?'

'How many girls d'you know that look like this?' She pointed to the rafter-sized gouge in her side. ''Course it's me.'

'But I'd thought you'd be . . .' He pointed a talon upwards.

'Seems they're more picky about sex before marriage than they tell anyone. I'd have been borderline angel if I wasn't so damned gorgeous.'

'Well, you got your happy ending after all.'

'What? You call getting dead and losing an estimated thirteen million a happy ending?'

The demon grinned and raised his voice slightly. 'Is that right? Your one agonising hatred in all the world is cleaning and cooking and being domesticated?'

'What am I, a cow?'

'Then you've come to the right place,' he grinned, a little too theatrically. 'Your sentence is an eternity of drudgery at this address.' He stamped a sheet of parchment and handed it over to her.

'This anyone's address I know?' she whispered.

He smiled knowingly and nodded. 'Now look pissed off.'

'What?'

'Frown, honey, this is Helian!'

'Oh, I get it. Damn you, you bastard,' she screamed. 'An eternity of that. How dare you. I . . . I hate you! You filthy spawn of . . .' Winking, she was dragged away by a vast monster.

High up on a balcony, way above Reception, a slender creature looked down enviously.

'That's power,' he muttered to himself. 'The way he did that. Shit, what a real bastard.'

'Guys like him make Helian what it is,' came a voice over his shoulder. 'Now, you just looking, or can I interest you in anything else?' Slim, Supplier-In-Chief to the newly elected Undertaker-In-Chief of Mortropolis, grinned.

'Got any sunflower seeds?'

'You're talking to Mr Sunflower, man. How much?'

'Er, how much do I need?'

'This your first time?'

The slender one nodded.

'Look, I'll start you off on a few ounces, right? Good stuff mind, not that dry-roasted stuff. Now, you got the equipment?'

'Equipment?'

'Come into my office and I'll show you the best way to get this stuff buzzing through your system. I tell you, there ain't anything like it.' He slid an overly companionable arm around his shoulder and led off. 'You know,' whispered Slim, 'once upon a time some folk used to feed sunflower seeds to animals. Can you believe that? I mean, what a waste.'